Praise for *Lost at Sea*

"Erica Boyce has crafted a heartfelt, deeply moving novel about identity, friendship, and family. Thought-provoking and propulsive, with a strong sense of place and a set of intriguing, complex characters, *Lost at Sea* is impossible to put down."

—Daniela Petrova, author of *Her Daughter's Mother*

"*Lost at Sea* is a gripping novel about a fishing community and the daily dangers that await them, and the complex relationships surfacing when one of their own disappears. Set in the small New England town of Devil's Purse, Boyce has weaved a spellbinding and atmospheric tale of community, family bonds, love and loss, and the fortitude needed to survive in an unforgiving landscape."

—Kim Michele Richardson, author of
The Book Woman of Troublesome Creek

"With beautiful, tender prose and a captivating web of characters, *Lost at Sea* is a masterful portrait of a fishing village marked by tragedy—and all the secrets therein. Boyce has crafted a poignant and thought-provoking narrative that stuck with me long after I read the final page."

—Andrea Bartz, author of *The Lost Night*

"In *Lost at Sea*, the fear and despair of losing a loved one to the sea is heightened by the helplessness of substance addiction suffered by two young women. This could have been a desperate and sorrowful story, yet in Erica Boyce's skillful hands, it is one of courageous love and the promise of healing through honest connection. The characters lingered in my mind and heart, like dear friends, long after I finished reading."

—Kelli Estes, *USA Today* bestselling author of
The Girl W   *o Home*

D1042786

ALSO BY ERICA BOYCE

The Fifteen Wonders of Daniel Green

ERICA BOYCE

sourcebooks
landmark

Published by Sourcebooks Landmark, an imprint of Sourcebooks
P.O. Box 4410, Naperville, Illinois 60567-4410
(630) 961-3900
sourcebooks.com

Library of Congress Cataloging-in-Publication Data

Names: Boyce, Erica, author.
Title: Lost at sea / Erica Boyce.
Description: Naperville, Illinois : Sourcebooks Landmark, [2020]
Identifiers: LCCN 2019025315 | (trade paperback)
Subjects: LCSH: Missing persons--Fiction. | GSAFD: Mystery fiction. |
    LCGFT: Psychological fiction.
Classification: LCC PS3602.O92494 L67 2020 | DDC 813/.6--dc23
LC record available at https://lccn.loc.gov/2019025315

Printed and bound in the United States of America.
VP 10 9 8 7 6 5 4 3 2 1

To my brother, who taught me everything.

Chapter One

AS A GENERAL RULE, the women of Devil's Purse did not wallow. Loss was a way of life in their small town tucked into northern Massachusetts. They knew how quickly a hungry fire could sprout in the belly of a boat, how a wave could sweep across a deck and brush away their full-grown men. There was a time the town was known as the biggest fishing port on the coast. Nowadays, tourists driving up to Maine wonder why the highway signs all tick down the miles until Devil's Purse. They wonder what could possibly be so important there.

Still, the men fish on, kissing their wives, children, mothers on their sleepy cheeks before dawn and easing out the door. They hold their breaths while hauling in nets and traps and wipe the ocean's spit out of their eyes. And when they fail to return, the women allow themselves one good cry behind closed doors before setting their jaws and searching for job listings. It was rumored that Elise Cunningham found out her husband was missing through a phone call in between clients at her in-home massage parlor. And she hung up the phone, pumped fresh oil into her palms, and pressed her fingers into the next fleshy back. When Evan Bannock was lost at sea, his wife, Shirley, quit her day job and opened a marine supply store selling tackle and rope to her husband's friends. "Someone's gotta make a living off all those years we spent in the industry," she would say to most anyone in earshot, her mouth a bittered twist.

There was no time to wallow. Their families depended on them now.

Chapter Two

Thursday, November 9, 2017

IT WAS LATE AFTERNOON when Lacey's phone buzzed. She stared at the ceiling for a beat, studying the swoops and swirls in the plaster. She pushed her cheek into the cool wall and ground her head into her pillow.

Her phone buzzed again. She rolled over and read the texts.

> Happy belated bday! Dance practice canceled.
> Can u hang out yet? Wanna go 2 library?
> Hello??? I'm waiting outside. :)

She sighed and let her head fall back onto the edge of her bed. Ella. Lacey'd been home a few weeks and still hadn't seen her. No one would want her around Ella anymore. Not now. "Not ever," hissed the beetle that lived inside her. It had been there as long as she could remember, feeding on every last one of her worries and amplifying them. She knew logically that there was no beetle. It was just some defect of her brain that refused to let anything go. But it helped her sometimes to imagine it as something external, small and crushable.

Her phone buzzed a third time, sending tremors up her

arm from her palm. "Fuck it," she muttered and rolled out of bed.

Maureen was waiting at the dining room table. Pretending not to be waiting, chewing on the end of a pencil and staring down at the spreadsheets she always insisted on printing out. Her dirty-blond hair was pulled back into a ponytail that drooped in its elastic. Before, Lacey might've stepped behind her and tightened it for her. Lacey stood in the doorway, tapping her fingertips against the wall. Maureen eyed her.

"I'm going out, Mom," Lacey said. "Do you need anything from the store? Or anything?"

Maureen pushed back from the table. "Where are you going?" She crossed her arms tightly in front of her chest.

"Just to the library."

Maureen studied her face for a moment. "You'll be back within an hour," she said, not a question.

"Yeah."

"Promise."

"I promise."

"And you'll have your phone on you? And answer the minute I call you?"

Lacey promised again and walked out through the kitchen, tripping a little over the upcurled edge of the rainbow-colored rug covering the tile floor. She could feel her mom watching her go.

Once, after a bad day at Devil's Purse High, Lacey had slumped onto the floor, her back against the cabinet door that always stuck a little. She had groaned dramatically and started picking fuzz from the rug. "Why did you ever move us to this godforsaken town? There's, like, nothing to do here, and everybody sucks." She popped the tab on a can of soda, the crack punctuating her point satisfyingly.

Maureen, who had been in the middle of a test run for

the mashed potato bar for the Reynolds wedding, put down her peeler and dropped a half-naked potato in the sink. She turned to her daughter, hands on her hips. The two stared at each other until Lacey's mouth twitched.

That was all Maureen needed. She threw her damp kitchen towel over her head like a kerchief. "Because, dahling," she said and, on her ex-dancer's tiptoe, fluttered across the rug toward Lacey. "Like I've told you before, I wanted to come back to the place where I first held you," she warbled and twirled, "in my arrrms." She finished with a flourish, one leg held behind her in a perfect arc, one arm dangling the towel over Lacey's head. "And also where I signed your adoption papers."

Lacey had rolled her eyes and allowed one giggle before handing her soda up to Maureen. Her mother had sipped it and winked.

Now, Lacey cursed under her breath and kicked at the offending rug edge. It rolled back down placidly as she trudged out the door. Even all these blocks back from the ocean, the wind was blowing in just the right direction, so the air was full of salt, the kind of day where your skin would grow tacky with it if you spent enough time outside. She refused to look back at the house. She knew Maureen would be standing at the window, gripping the sill and biting her lip, watching Lacey until she turned the corner and was gone.

"Finally! It's about time." As promised, Ella was waiting for Lacey in their old usual spot under the huge oak tree at the corner directly between their houses. At nine, her limbs had grown long and knobby in the months since Lacey had seen her, and she no longer fit in the crook of the tree's lowest-lying branch. She leaned awkwardly against the trunk in a pose Ella probably thought was cool and casual. But when Lacey stood before her, Ella could no longer contain herself and threw her arms around Lacey's waist. Was it weird of Lacey to spend her free time with a kid? Maybe. She'd known Ella for years, and sometimes, it seemed like Ella was one of the only people truly happy to see her. Ella was too young and transparent to say anything the beetle could twist around.

"Hey, kidlet," Lacey said, smiling as she gently pried Ella off.

Ella wrinkled her nose, the delicate freckles there folding. "I'm too old for you to call me that!"

"You? Never."

Ella sighed. "Whatever. Are you ready to go to the library or what?"

Lacey hesitated. "Are you sure your mom's okay with this? Did you tell her you'd be with me?"

"I told her you'd be helping me with my homework, and she called the library to make sure Rebecca was going to be there. It makes no sense. We used to hang out all the time. I told her I had to help you celebrate your birthday." Ella pulled a rumpled packet of shortbread cookies out of the backpack slung over her shoulder. They were Ella's favorite, and at some point along the line, Ella had convinced herself they were Lacey's favorite, too. Lacey tore open the packet and passed it back to Ella, who stuffed a cookie in her mouth. "Anyway, who cares what she thinks?" Ella asked, a stray crumb or two escaping with her words.

Lacey did. Lacey cared. One cold fall night the year before, Lacey had come over to babysit or "hang out," as Ella called it. Ella's mom, Mrs. Staybrook, had been fixing her earrings in the front hall mirror and asked absently how Lacey's college applications were going.

Lacey was about to rattle off the list of schools to which she'd already applied when, embarrassingly, the dam broke. Mrs. Staybrook turned expectantly, but Lacey's mouth simply gaped as her eyes filled with tears.

"Lacey? Sweetheart, what's wrong?" She paused for only a moment before dropping her earrings to the floor and stepping to Lacey's side.

"It's just, I don't know, so stressful," Lacey managed. She held her hands to her face to hide her eyes. She couldn't stop the endless swirl of deadlines and essay prompts, and she kept picturing the terse rejection emails she was certain would follow. The beetle had been particularly bad that day, sneering at nearly every word she said. She had tried to ignore it and managed everything with neat, handwritten lists and calendar reminders. But in that moment, with her arms still half in her coat sleeves, ridiculously, it all seemed too much.

Mrs. Staybrook guided her to the small bench in their front hall. It was a decorative bench, and she was constantly asking Ella not to leave her dirty sneakers under it. She smoothed a path between Lacey's shoulder blades with one palm, over and over again. "Tell you what," she said. "Why don't you take the night off and do something fun?"

"But what about your work event?" Lacey snuffed the mucus into her nose and tried to subtly wipe the salty tracks off her cheeks.

"Oh, don't worry about that." She rolled her eyes. "I see those people in the office every day. I don't need to see them at night, too."

Lacey nodded. She pictured her own friends, all of whom would probably be busy studying on a school night like this or out with their boyfriends. Even her mom was getting ready to cater a fall fundraiser. If she left now, she would probably just end up sitting in her room and watching

Netflix. Her and the beetle. She squared her shoulders. "No, really. It's fine. I'm fine. You should go to your thing."

Mrs. Staybrook pursed her lips. "You know, John's been complaining all day about having to go to this," she said. "Hey, honey?"

"Yeah?" Mr. Staybrook replied. He stepped into the hall, still wearing his Carhartts and a sweatshirt.

"What do you say we play hooky and have a movie night with Lacey here? I'm feeling a little tired. And you're dressed for the couch, anyway." She raised one eyebrow at Lacey.

He glanced between Lacey and Mrs. Staybrook. He grinned. "Hallelujah," he said. He turned back toward the living room. "Ella," he bellowed, "Papa Gino's or Smoky's for pizza tonight? We're all eating it, so none of your Hawaiian pineapple crap!"

From somewhere in the house, Ella cheered.

That was the last time Lacey babysat for Ella. "Don't worry about it," Mrs. Staybrook had murmured as she left that night. "Focus on one thing at a time, okay? You'll be fine." She'd brushed a bit of lint off Lacey's coat, and Lacey had believed her. For a few months, Lacey kept meeting Ella after school once a month, treating her to doughnuts and hot chocolate with the money she'd saved from babysitting. She felt it was only fair. But it'd been a while since then.

Ella's voice was accelerating, growing increasingly animated.

Lacey blinked. "Sorry. What were you saying?"

Ella rolled her eyes. "I *said*, it's too bad you were gone last month. They threw a party at the town pool to celebrate the last of the summer people, and they had food trucks and everything!"

Lacey smirked. Fourth grade, and already she'd picked up the exact touch of disdain with which to say "summer people."

"Sorry I missed it. How's school going? Who do you have this year?"

"Ugh, Miss Michaels. She's the worrrst." Ella dragged her feet and slung her arms low as if the mere mention of her name were enough to pull her down to the depths of hell.

Lacey winced. "Oh, yeah, she's a tough one. You know she used to teach sixth grade, right? When I was in her class, she called my mom and told her I cheated on a test. My mom asked what made her think that, and Miss Michaels said my grade was too good. That was the only evidence she had. My mom helped me make a dartboard with her face on it that night." Ella cackled. Lacey tugged on a hank of hair that was stuck under one strap of Ella's backpack. "But you know, maybe if you stopped talking during class and raised your hand every once in a while, she wouldn't be so bad."

"Hey!" Ella grabbed at her hair and scowled at Lacey. "For your information, I'm the top student in her class right now. So maybe she shouldn't complain so much. Race you to the library!" And she was off, her sneakers pounding against the pavement and her backpack swishing from side to side. Lacey ran only a few paces before breathing started to hurt. She slowed to a walk and watched Ella run the rest of the block. When she reached the library, Ella flung her arms out in victory. Only then did she notice how far behind Lacey was. She turned to watch Lacey trudge and folded her arms disapprovingly.

Chapter Three

READY FOR THE AFTER-SCHOOL rush, Becks?"
Addie called from the reference desk.

Rebecca held back a sigh. She shifted out from under the beam of sunlight thrown by the library's '70s-era skylights. No one but Addie called her "Becks," and she called her that no matter how many times Rebecca pointedly fiddled with the nameplate on her desk in Addie's presence. The "after-school rush" consisted of, on average, a few harried stay-at-home moms and one or two lost-looking high schoolers. Addie joked about it nearly every day, and it had ceased being funny months ago.

Rebecca would never say these things out loud. "Sure thing," she said, flashing Addie a thumbs-up. She turned away from the circulation desk to sort through the row of reserved books on the chipped wooden shelves behind her and ran her fingers over their spines. Their jackets shone under the fluorescent lights. Addie notwithstanding, she felt safe here, tucked behind this desk with all these books. She could see the neat rows of new arrival displays stretching out toward the back of the library, where encyclopedias and dictionaries lay forgotten. Behind her, the clacking keyboards of the computer room built a near-constant backbeat to her workdays.

Mack wanted her to quit. "All those kids," he said. "It must be hard for you to spend so much time around them." He eyed her stomach uneasily. He would never mention outright the years they'd spent trying, test after test thrown into the bathroom trash with a dull, plastic *thunk*.

She always shrugged when he said this. "I don't mind it at all," she told him. "Besides, I have to put my degree to good use." In truth, on certain days, the kids were the only things keeping her together. They came to her with bright and sticky faces, asking simple, easily answered questions about where story hour was or who wrote a particular book. They smiled when she helped them. They splayed their chubby hands on the top of the desk while their parents checked them out. They giggled in corners together, and she couldn't bring herself to shush them.

"Excuse me, miss? Could you tell me where your restroom is?"

It was an out-of-towner, that much was certain. Anyone else would've called her by name. She turned, and sure enough, there was a stranger by the desk. A woman. Heavily pregnant. She rubbed her belly with one hand in slow, constant circles, as if she were polishing silver.

"Oh," Rebecca said. "Yes. It's just around that corner." She pointed over her shoulder.

"Thanks," the woman said. She squinted slightly at Rebecca and hitched her pocketbook a little higher on her shoulder. Perhaps Rebecca had been staring at her stomach for too long.

She waited until the woman had waddled out of sight to exhale. No, it wasn't the children she had trouble with. It was the mothers-to-be who brought a strange mix of longing and resentment to the pit at her core. When they smiled peacefully, when they complained sweatily, when they spoke smugly. She knew there was no logic to this hatred. It wasn't as if there were a limited number of babies in the world and they'd run out before she got through the line. And, she often scolded herself, it could always be worse. She and Mack were otherwise perfectly healthy. Her doctor had been perplexed at her last physical, nearly a year ago. "I can't believe you're not pregnant yet!" he'd said.

She tugged at the locket resting at her clavicle, relishing the sting of the little gold chain pinching the back of her neck. It was an old-fashioned thing. Its face was a bit tarnished, darkened by somebody else's fingertips. She liked that about it. Mack had slipped it around her neck while she was still half-asleep in bed before leaving for this latest scalloping trip. He would be gone for two weeks, one of five crewmembers on a massive vessel shucking creamy white scallop meat from shells bigger than his hand. She knew he only did these trips so that he could save up for his own smaller boat and start his own fishing business one day. And she knew that, logically, the big boats were no more dangerous than the small ones.

But still. At least the small boats came back every night. At least if he worked on a small boat, he would be at their kitchen table before supper so she could check him over for broken bones and wounds, set her hands on his shoulders, and think to herself, *Not missing*. Her father and brother were both fishermen in towns nearby. She was familiar with the space below one's breastbone that thumped whenever word spread that someone else had been lost.

Mack knew all this. Hence the necklace, a silent metal kiss of an apology that she almost thought she'd dreamed until she woke up a few hours later and found it still there.

The library doors opened. "—can't believe you'd let me

win like that! You weren't even running. You were barely even walking."

"Ella. Inside voice."

"Whatever." Ella skipped up to the circulation desk. "Hi, Rebecca," she whisper-yelled.

"Hi, Ella." Rebecca tucked a smile back between her lips. "It's okay. Nobody's here right now except Addie over there. You don't have to whisper." She glanced at Lacey, who was leaning against the prehistoric copy machine next to the door.

"Ha! See?" Ella spun around to face Lacey. "Rebecca lets me do whatever I want when we hang out, unlike some people I know."

Rebecca wasn't sure if she should feel flattered or insulted to be used as a pawn in this argument. She decided diversion was probably her best approach. She leaned forward on her elbows. "I heard a rumor that we just got the latest Tamora Pierce book in and no one has checked it out yet."

"Really?" Ella turned back around. Rebecca nodded, and Ella scurried off to the fantasy section, her arms pumping in an exaggerated speed walk. The first time Rebecca babysat for Ella last fall, she had brought a tote bag full of books. It was only after she rang the doorbell that she felt painfully uncool and wondered if she should've brought an iPad or some video games. But when she stacked the books on the Staybrooks' coffee table, Ella had reached for *Alanna: The First Adventure* right away. It had been Rebecca's favorite growing up, too.

"Thanks for that," Lacey said, stepping toward the counter. "You really took the heat off me." She stared after Ella until she disappeared down an aisle.

"No problem." Rebecca reached for a stack of blank check-out cards. She shuffled them once and tapped the edge of the stack against the counter, hoping it looked like she had an official reason for doing so.

"How's the little kidlet doing?" Lacey asked. She said it quietly, as if asking permission.

"She's good," Rebecca said. She ached to brag about Ella's latest drawing and the story they were writing together, to ask how Lacey had ever gotten Ella to go to bed on time. She longed to have those conversations she'd heard from so many mothers' mouths, even though Ella was not her own.

Not twenty minutes before, though, Diane Staybrook had called the library. "It's for you," Addie had said when she transferred it to circulation, her eyebrows raised.

"Rebecca? Diane." Her voice had been so tight, Rebecca almost feared it would snap and twang back through the phone to hit her ear. "Listen, I can't really talk right now, but Ella's heading over with Lacey. I couldn't keep her away from that girl any longer. I need you to watch Ella and make sure she's…make sure she's safe, okay?" Rebecca had barely had time to agree before Diane hung up.

"That's good. I really miss her," Lacey said.

Rebecca looked up from the check-out cards, but Lacey was picking at a dried-up spot of something on the counter. Rebecca took the opportunity to study her face.

She'd heard the rumors, of course. For a week or so there, not a day went by when Mack didn't come home from the docks with a new story about what had happened to Maureen Carson's kid. She'd lived in Devil's Purse long enough to know not to believe anything until she saw it with her own eyes.

In this case, she realized with a sinking sigh, some of those rumors might've actually been right. Lacey was not looking so hot. She'd lost a lot of weight since the last time Rebecca saw her, and there were purplish circles under her eyes. Her hair was greasy, and Lacey seemed to know it—she'd developed a tic of reaching up to cover her part every few minutes. This was not the shining-smiled girl whose photo showed up in the paper every year when the high school gave out their academic achievement awards.

"She misses you, too," Rebecca said and impulsively reached out to touch Lacey's hand where it lay on the counter. Lacey shrank back. Rebecca fiddled with her necklace again, and Lacey's eyes followed her hand to her neck. Lacey's lips pinched in just a hair, just for a moment, and her face grew pale. She gripped the edge of the counter.

"I'm sorry," Lacey said. "I have to go." She glanced behind her at where Ella was now sitting on the floor, leaned back against the dictionary bookcase, her head bowed over a book. A bone-deep sadness flickered across her face. "I really am sorry. I hate to do this to you, but do you, would you be able to—"

"I'll take Ella home after my shift is over."

"Really? Are you sure? It's not too much trouble? It's just that she loves coming here, she loves you, and I don't want to make her leave."

Rebecca's cheeks warmed. "It's completely fine. I was going to head out in an hour anyway, and their house is basically on my way." Neither was true, strictly speaking, but Rebecca was dying to calm the buzz now rising from Lacey's very skin. "Are you okay?"

"Yeah." Lacey shook her head a little. "Yeah. I've gotta go," she repeated and bolted for the doors. They closed behind her with a solid, final click.

"Time for my cigarette break," Addie said, one elbow propped jauntily on the counter. "You okay to hold down the fort for a few minutes?"

"Sure, go ahead."

"You sure? Everything copacetic?"

Rebecca nodded and pretended to type something into the computer. *Copacetic* was probably the latest offering on Addie's word-of-the-day calendar. Addie leaned in closer as if to suck the gossip right out of her. Rebecca knew Addie had watched the whole exchange with Lacey from across the room and was dying for dirt. Rebecca squinted at her screen as though the empty search bar puzzled her. Addie sighed, tapped the desk once, and left.

She and Ella were alone now. Somehow, Ella was so engrossed in her book, she hadn't noticed that Lacey'd been gone for half an hour. Rebecca tucked her hair behind her ears and left her desk.

"Ella?"

She looked up. Rebecca started to kneel before she realized that Ella was probably too old to find it particularly soothing. She stood, knitting her fingers together behind her back. "Lacey had to go. I'll take you home when I get off work at 4:30, okay?"

Ella drooped. The book fell to the floor, and Rebecca resisted the temptation to pick it up and smooth the bent pages. "I knew it," Ella mumbled into her lap. She turned her face up again. "Is she sick? She is, isn't she? Is she dying? Mom said she had to go out of town to see some old family member, like a great-uncle or something, but she never would've missed going to college for that. And she looks so skinny, and she couldn't even run one single block. So she must be sick. Just tell me, is she?" Ella stared up at her.

"I don't know," Rebecca said, grateful it was the truth.

She wouldn't have to step into the tangle of the stories another woman told her daughter.

"She's definitely sick," Ella said, nodding to herself and watching the door. "I'll figure it out. Don't worry, Rebecca." She picked up her book and started reading.

Rebecca managed to turn around before she had to smile.

At 4:30 on the dot, Ella stood in front of the desk. "Ready?" she said, sliding her book across the counter.

"Ready." Rebecca took the book and scanned and stamped it, pleased as always with the firm finality of the stamp under her hand. The past twenty minutes had been a sudden flurry of patrons asking for the Wi-Fi password and demanding books they didn't carry or that were already checked out. Addie was no help whatsoever, responding to even the simplest questions by smiling sweetly and sending the customer directly to Rebecca. When Rebecca looked over at her, exasperated, Addie gazed steadily at her phone. Punishment for failing to spill the details on Lacey, no doubt.

"All right, Rick, I'm off," she called to the evening librarian, who was wolfing down a granola bar in the back office. He raised one hand in a salute. Addie perked up and reached for her pocketbook, even though her shift was nowhere near over. Rebecca turned her back hurriedly and touched Ella's shoulder. "Come on, sweetie. Let's go."

When they were safely out of sight of the library and Addie, Rebecca shoved her fists into the pockets of her coat. Ella picked up a stick and began running it over every chain-link fence they passed. The rattling shot straight up Rebecca's neck.

"When is Mack getting back?" Ella asked, kicking at a pebble on the sidewalk.

"Tomorrow evening." Rebecca took a deep breath. So close.

"Cool! Maybe he can come to the park with us next week."

"Maybe." Her fingers found an old gum wrapper in her pocket and balled it up so tightly, the foil dug into her skin.

Mack didn't know about her babysitting job. She knew he would take it personally, the fact that his wife felt like she had to work two jobs. He would start signing up for more trips, farther and farther away, so he could "provide for his family." She would roll her eyes at him if she weren't so afraid for him.

After her doctor had recommended a specialist, she had come home to tell him on their living room couch. A chill spread over her scalp from the drafty windows, countering the anxious heat on her cheeks. They'd bought the house, a small one, shortly after their wedding. In the years since, they'd discovered the leaky joints hidden behind its skin of white vinyl siding and shiny brass doorknobs. She pulled a blanket over her shoulders.

"Dr. Graham said our best chance for conceiving would be to see a reproductive endocrinologist," she said, carefully enunciating each syllable.

"Okay," he said and reached for her hand.

She almost wanted to shake him in that moment and demand he show some fear or excitement or anything at all. Instead, she dug the remote out from under the cushion and tried to calm the roil in her stomach.

It didn't matter, anyway. That night, she stayed up late, scanning infertility forums and reading through blocks of impenetrable text in the bare-bones health insurance policy they paid for themselves. They wouldn't be able to afford the copays for the required fertility testing, much less any treatments that came after that.

When Diane Staybrook called her two weeks later

looking for a new babysitter, it seemed too good to be true. She decided she would save in secret and surprise Mack when she had enough to cover an appointment, some testing, and maybe an IUI or two. She told herself he would be thrilled then, when getting pregnant seemed like a real possibility again.

It was a little embarrassing, taking a job that had previously been held by a high schooler. But what choice did she have? Jobs were hard to come by here, especially in the off-season. Her only other work experience to speak of was volunteering at the local hospital when she was a student—"candy striping," her mother called it every time she drove her the thirty minutes from their house to her shift. She had worked in the maternity ward, blithely holding back women's hair as they labored, unaware of how long she would have to work to take their place one day. Theoretically, she could reach out to her contacts at the hospital and see if there were any administrative openings, but she shuddered at the thought of being surrounded by pregnant women and blissful new families all day.

No, this was fine, she thought as she followed Ella up the Staybrooks' front steps. Before they'd even reached the door, Diane opened it.

"Hi, Mom," Ella said, squeezing past her through the doorway.

"Hi, Ella-Bella." She ran one hand over the crown of Ella's head as she passed. "Everything go okay?" she murmured, tilting forward over the threshold.

"Yes, everything was fine. She was great." Rebecca had texted Diane to let her know what had happened with Lacey. Diane hadn't responded—Rebecca assumed she was busy on a conference call or something.

"Good. Good." Diane settled back on her heels and

tucked a stray hair into her French twist. "I know I shouldn't worry so much. Ella's such a good girl. And so is Lacey. Or was, anyway." She pulled her hand over her face, dragging her cheeks down ghoulishly. "She's just so…troubled," she said through her fingers.

Rebecca backed up one step. "Well, anyway. She was great," she repeated. "No trouble at all."

"Oh!" Diane's hands flew up. "Here, let me pay you."

"No, no," Rebecca said, but it came out rather weakly. "It really was no trouble. She just read quietly while I worked."

"Don't be silly." She reached into her back pocket. "Never turn down a chance to get paid twice for your time," she said out of the side of her mouth, holding out her hand.

"Thank you," Rebecca said miserably. She took the bill without looking at it and slipped it in with the gum wrapper.

"See you Monday!" Diane wiggled her fingers and closed the door.

Rebecca turned toward home.

Chapter Four

"YOU'RE HOME EARLY," MAUREEN said, peering over her glasses. "Is everything okay?"

"Yup," Lacey said. Her head throbbed. "Be right back. I've really gotta go to the bathroom." She bit her lip and turned before her mom could ask any more questions.

Safe in her room, Lacey eased her bureau away from the wall and knelt down to the hand-sized hole Matt had helped her cut in the drywall there one night while her mom was out. She used to keep her kit under the mattress, but she knew she needed another spot to use for emergencies.

She groped around the stud until she found her diary, then pushed the bureau back into place. Maureen had taken her bedroom door off its hinges, but she hadn't gone so far as to remove the door of the bathroom connected to her room. She wedged a towel under the door and checked twice to be sure it wouldn't open before sitting down on the closed lid of the toilet seat.

The diary was a cheap, plasticky pink thing her grandmother had given her for Christmas when she was around Ella's age. It had a dinky lock on it; she'd lost the key long ago and had to pop it open with an unbent paperclip. She'd written in it exactly once, an imagined conversation between her and the cat who lived next door at the time. Still, she felt a twinge of guilt every time she opened it and saw the pages destroyed, hollowed out into a hiding place.

It was nothing compared to how she felt when she saw the pictures lying there. Two tiny, carefully cut faces—Maureen and Lacey—bent a little at the edges from being held in the locket. Her mom hadn't asked yet where her high school graduation gift had gone. "It's not that Tiffany's stuff some of your friends wear," Maureen had said almost shyly as Lacey unwrapped it. "But my mom gave it to me when I graduated, and I figured it was time to pass it down." Lacey had hugged her tightly around the neck, and for just a second, she forgot about the beetle and all her secrets.

Maureen was bound to notice soon, and Lacey didn't know what she'd tell her. She was so tired of lying, but she couldn't possibly say she'd sold it. That it was now hanging around that librarian's neck. It would shatter both of them.

She gritted her teeth and pushed the photos aside. There, in a ragged plastic baggie, was what she'd bought with the money.

Matt had warned her that it might be too much for her. "Fentanyl is on a whole other level from Oxy or Percs. It'll knock you straight on your ass." She'd reached for the baggie mutely, but he'd held it out of reach and grabbed her wrist with his other hand, ducking his head to meet her eye. "I'm serious, Lace. Be careful with this, okay?"

"I will," she had said, palm still outstretched. He'd laid the baggie in it, folded her fingers around it, and kissed the knuckles swiftly.

She kept it separate from the rest, hidden away to be used only when she really needed it. Her room was so neat when she got back from rehab, folds crisp and corners tucked, that she knew her mom had torn it apart and found her kit. But she hadn't pulled the bureau back from the wall.

She held the baggie up to the overhead light. The pills were starting to break down into dust, as if they were shedding their skin, waiting for her. Her arm trembled slightly. She clamped her fingers around her wrist.

The beetle unfurled its wings and started to dance. "Everyone saw you at the library," it whispered gleefully. "They saw you for what you are. Worthless addict. Ella hates you now. This whole town hates you."

"No," she whispered. She squeezed her eyes shut. She had never told her caseworker, Ms. Bray, about the beetle. She knew it wasn't real, that it was some freakish fold in her brain, some character flaw. In Ms. Bray's bland office with the plastic-fronded fern, she was too embarrassed to mention it. Now, she almost reached for her phone to call Ms. Bray. She'd given Lacey her card with her cell phone number on it and looked straight into Lacey's eyes, so intensely it made Lacey squirm a little, and told her to call her whenever she needed someone to talk to. But Lacey knew Ms. Bray would probably just hum thoughtfully and recommend some deep-breathing exercises to manage it.

Lacey knew the truth, though. There was only one thing that had ever worked to shut the beetle up. She shook the baggie, and the pills shifted to the other corner.

"Good idea," the beetle said. "Prove them right."

"No," she said again, even quieter this time. She was stronger than that. That was why she couldn't throw them out. She needed to keep them, these pills that only she knew about, that she would never take. She needed to keep them, untouched, so that she could remind herself that she was strong. She slipped the baggie back behind the photos and slapped the book shut.

"You still in there?" Maureen's voice passed, muffled, through the bathroom door.

"Almost finished," Lacey yelled. She hid the diary in the vanity, tucked behind the sink piping. She flushed the toilet and turned on the faucet, wetting her fingers for good measure and wiping them on her jeans. Maureen always teased her for doing that when there was a perfectly good hand towel hanging right there.

Her mom was waiting for her in the bathroom doorway. "That was a quick trip," she said. "What happened? Are you okay?" She grasped Lacey's chin. "You look a little pale."

"I'm fine, Mom." Lacey held herself very, very still.

"Are you sure?" Maureen tilted Lacey's face toward the light. Her jaw tightened, ratcheting a single degree. "You weren't with Matt, were you?"

"No." Lacey wrenched away. "I was with Ella, like I said. I started to feel a little sick is all," she said, knowing if she mentioned the symptoms, Maureen would tuck her into bed and pretend this was something familiar that she could fix with clear fluids and canned chicken soup. Lacey wished so badly that it were.

Something like fear flashed behind Maureen's eyes. "Ella? Are you sure that's such a good idea? Is she… Did you take her home afterward? Did Diane see you?"

"Rebecca said she would take her. The librarian." She chewed at her bottom lip.

"Okay. Okay, good." Maureen rested her hand at the base of her rib cage and breathed deep. "You have to be careful with her, you know? She's just a kid. I don't want Diane to think…"

"Yeah, I'm aware." Lacey crossed her arms, holding back all the meaner, angrier words she could say. As much as Lacey cared about what Mrs. Staybrook thought, her mom cared even more. Her mom was always worrying about Mrs. Staybrook's opinion.

Maureen nodded briskly. "Well. Don't forget we're working the benefit tonight. We need to leave here in an hour."

"Fine." Lacey turned her back and fiddled with the dusty pile of books on her bureau until she heard her mother's steps on the staircase.

"She doesn't love you anymore," the beetle whispered. "You are losing her."

She picked up the stack of books and slammed them down on the bureau's surface. The mirror above it rattled so that she barely recognized herself in it.

Chapter Five

MAUREEN AND LACEY WERE both silent in the van as they drove to the benefit. Maureen tried, with every minute that passed, to come up with a story or joke that would pull and tease her daughter back out of herself. But each minute, as in all the minutes since Lacey had returned home, her mind was empty save for this: Why?

And she knew, from all the books and articles she'd read, all the meetings she'd attended where the grief loomed so huge and black it was hard to breathe, that she could not ask this. The addict, so they said, would feel out the grain of blame at the center of that pearl and would shut down. A piece of Maureen wondered, every time she'd heard this: if Lacey wasn't to blame for her surrender to the pills, then who was?

She could never ask. So they spent the twenty-minute drive with nothing but the clanking of the industrial-sized pots and chafing dishes in the back of the van. Every time Maureen glanced over, Lacey was curling the edge of her seat belt. When she was a toddler, she used to squirm at the restraint and the rubbing at her neck.

It was a relief when they got to the town hall. Lacey sprung her door open as soon as Maureen put the van in park and grabbed a stack of pans. She paused next to Jude, their server, who was smoking a cigarette under the blue-and-gold banner that yelled, "Welcome to the 2017 Friends of the Devil's Purse Library Dinner!" Lacey laughed into the crook of her arm at something Jude said before continuing on into the building.

No sooner was Lacey out of sight than Ophelia Walsh appeared at Maureen's elbow, dressed in an impeccable sheath dress with a thin silver chain around her neck. "Oh, good, you're here," Ophelia said. "I was beginning to worry."

Maureen glanced at her watch and willed her left eyebrow not to raise. She was precisely three minutes late. "Yup. Here I am," she said, hoisting a case of chardonnay (New Zealand, not California, per Ophelia's instructions) onto her hip.

"And everything's in order? Remember, you can only use the kitchen for an hour before the cleaners I hired have to come in and tidy up." Ophelia followed her into the building empty-handed and watched as Maureen found a folding table not cluttered with brochures and silent auction items, put the wine on the table, and began to drag it toward the side of the room. Every year, she told Ophelia the bar should be there so the line wouldn't block the entrance. Every year, Ophelia apparently forgot.

"Yes, everything's good." Maureen stood straight, brushing the dust from the underside of the table off onto her slacks. Ophelia eyed the gray streaks it left behind on the black fabric. "Shrimp cocktail and tuna tartare are ready to go. I just have to sear the crab cakes and bake the vegetable flatbreads."

As if on cue, Lacey and Jude pushed through the doors carrying plastic fillet tubs glowing pinkly with cooked, peeled, tail-on jumbo shrimp. She'd gently suggested to

Ophelia that since she was raising money to support a coastal community, perhaps she should consider serving seafood that could actually be caught off the shores of Devil's Purse. She'd allowed herself to get carried away and drew up a mock menu of spiny dogfish croquettes, skate wing sliders, and razor clam ceviche. Ophelia had held the menu up a moment before looking at Maureen. "But," she had said, "our donors really love your shrimp cocktail sauce. They rave about it every year."

"Okay, that's fine. We can stick with the standards." She'd tucked the menu back into her bag, and Ophelia's slightly wrinkled forehead had smoothed out again. Nate at the fish market had smirked when she asked him for yet another order of frozen shellfish.

"Excellent," Ophelia said now, fluffing up her hair. "Oh, dear, I specifically asked Margaret to put the massage gift certificates on the same table as the Nantucket gift basket. Excuse me, Maureen." She flitted off.

Maureen took bar duty that night, leaving Lacey to pass the apps and Jude to plate. She hated working the bar and would've preferred to stay in the kitchen out of sight and plating crab cakes, dusty pants and all, but she needed to keep an eye on Lacey, and she wasn't sure what her daughter would do behind the bar, surrounded by sweating bottles of alcohol. Besides, Lacey was oddly suited for the role of server, with her calm smile and one hand at the small of her back while she waited for guests to finish sucking the meat off toothpicks. When they tucked their dirty napkins onto her tray, she slipped them into her pocket before moving on to the next group. She even knew how to skirt past the cluster of women who gathered near the kitchen doors to descend on each tray as it emerged.

Maureen scanned the room again. She didn't recognize

anyone. They were all from neighboring beach towns. None of them would've heard about Lacey. There would be no roundabout questions about how she was doing or backs turned at the last minute when Lacey approached with her tray.

When Lacey came home from rehab and Maureen told her she would be working as a server for the foreseeable future, all Maureen had been thinking was that she had to keep Lacey safe and in sight, and she could not afford to give up her business. She hadn't considered she'd be throwing Lacey to the gossip wolves every time they worked a community event. Lacey always handled the jobs well, making little jokes with the guests and spinning on her toes to serve the next one. The few times Maureen brought it up, Lacey either brushed off her halting apologies or said, "I don't want to talk about it." But Maureen could tell it wore on her. There was a new flush in her cheeks tonight when she leaned in, smiling, to tell Jude something on her way out of the kitchen. She was alive among strangers. Among people who knew no better.

The only person who did seem to know something was Rebecca, one of the librarians who got trotted around to these events as the face of the library. She set her hands on the tabletop while Maureen poured her a glass of sparkling water and asked, "Is Lacey okay?"

Maureen overpoured the cup, and the seltzer fizzled across her hand. She wiped her palm on a corner of the tablecloth and passed the drink to Rebecca. "Sure," she said. "She's fine."

Rebecca looked like she was about to say more when Ophelia appeared and grasped her elbow. "Rebecca, dear, a new potential donor just arrived, and I'd love to introduce you to him."

Rebecca glanced at Maureen and pulled at the collar of her turtleneck, revealing a flash of gold, the chain of a necklace tastefully concealed beneath its fabric.

Maureen smiled quickly, releasing Rebecca from their conversation before it could get any more awkward, and turned to the man standing in line behind her.

"Just a splash of the cab," he said, winking. He tugged at the knot in his tie as she poured. When she handed it back to him, he said, "You can fill it more than that, honey."

She took the half-full glass from him, murmuring an apology, and tipped the bottle back into it.

Chapter Six

WHEN JESS CONNELLY APPEARED on Diane and John's front porch that evening, her eyes fixed on the welcome mat and her feet in a puddle, Diane knew just what she was going to say.

"I'm not sure what happened," Jess said. "To tell the truth, he took another boat out tonight and had me running his. One minute, he was there on the radio, talking to me, and the next—" She scrubbed at her forehead to hide her tears from her captain's wife. Later, the men who had been at the docks that night would say when she returned on the *Diane & Ella* alone and white-faced, they'd never seen her look so shaken.

Diane, for her part, leaned heavily against the doorway, fingers to her mouth. She heard Jess apologizing in one choked tangle. "It's all right," Diane said, though of course it wasn't. She wanted so desperately for this part to be over. She touched Jess's trembling shoulder, which seemed to break the spell. Jess met her eyes, nodded once, and left, her boots leaving wet footprints on the stairs that vanished within minutes.

Diane closed the door. She walked, unseeing, toward their well-worn couch. She pushed aside a pile of Ella's paperback fantasies and sat. Rested her head in her hands, her elbows on her knees. She would wait until morning to tell Ella, she decided. Let her daughter sleep these last few hours in peace, her yellow hair flung across the pillow, her mouth wide open, her breath milky.

She went to the microwave and heated up a mug of tea, watching the numbers tick down. When it beeped, it took her a minute to remember to open the door and retrieve her cup. The sides scalded her hands. She sat at the counter. She allowed herself exactly one hour to stare into the cup while its heat dulled to room temperature. And then, she hurled the cup against the wall. She wasn't strong enough—only the handle broke off. She could see the tea dripping down the wall in a sad, pathetic trickle through the scrim of her tears. How could he be gone? How could he possibly be gone? Her eyes and throat burned.

She forced herself to think. She wondered if she could crawl into bed with Ella unnoticed. The girl had developed a habit recently of pushing Diane away—sometimes physically—embarrassed of her mother. She was far too young for that, Diane thought. She was only nine. She was far too young for any of this.

She wondered if this was finally her chance to escape Devil's Purse and get out of this town that had claimed her husband so fully, right up to the very end. God knew, she did not want their daughter falling in love with a fisherman—or worse, becoming one herself.

And she wondered, in a small, sure voice that slithered up her spine in the dark house, if Jess was lying. Jess, tagging along with John all those years. Maybe she knew he'd written her into his will. Maybe she knew what would happen if John disappeared. There was an irrational bitterness to this thought, Diane realized. But how else to explain it all? John never would've left them like this.

"Never," she whispered to herself and knelt to the floor to collect the mug and its handle.

Something was wrong with Lacey. It was the end of the night. The guests had picked up the auction items they'd won and left empty glasses and plastic plates in their places, crowing at each other on their way out the door. Ophelia, having waved off the last of them, sat in the corner in a folding chair and pecked at her phone. Normally, Lacey would be scooting around collecting napkins and wiping tables by now.

Instead, she stood in the kitchen doorway, bowing her head toward Jude. He held her elbow and whispered something in her ear. Her hand swept up to cover her mouth, then her eyes. Even from the other side of the room, Maureen could tell she was close to tears.

A dark and vicious part of Maureen that she preferred not to look at head-on hoped it was about Matt. He was just a kid, though, she reminded herself as she crossed the room. A kid whose parents would now be told the worst imaginable news.

"Lacey," she said, touching her daughter's hair when she didn't look up. "Honey, what is it?"

Jude slipped away to pack up more pots. He picked up a pair of their big metal tongs and stood still, staring at it with more concentration than was strictly necessary.

Lacey scrubbed at her eyes and wiped her nose with the back of her wrist. "It's John Staybrook," she said. "Ella's dad."

Maureen's muscles went rigid.

"Jude just got a text from his cousin. He's lost at sea."

"No," Maureen said. She braced herself against the doorway. "Oh, shit."

Their silence on the way home was a different one, more echoey and watery. Maureen drove more deliberately than usual, her foot pressing the brake a full half block before the red lights. Lacey's hands were still. Maureen wondered if she, too, was remembering the last time she'd talked to John.

Maureen had been drawing herself a bath to reward her aching muscles for pulling off another wedding season. She only allowed herself these moments when Lacey wasn't home. She worried a little about what Lacey would say if she found out her mother took bubble baths, like the overworked mom in a scented candle commercial. How odd that she worried about what her daughter thought. After all, she'd cradled Lacey's tiny, naked body in the kitchen sink in the weeks after she was born and had coached Lacey through her first tampon from the other side of the bathroom door. In less than a week's time, Lacey would be off to college, and Maureen would be able to sit in the bath until all her fingers pruned. Maureen tried to look forward to it.

The phone rang. Maureen left the water running to pick it up.

"Hey, Maureen. It's John. John Staybrook."

"Oh, hi, John! How's it going?" She perched on the edge of the closed toilet seat and studied her cuticles. She hadn't seen John in months, not since the last time she picked Lacey up on her way to somewhere else. He was probably calling to ask about Maureen's plans with Diane. They were meeting up that night to watch a movie.

"It's good, it's good." He paused. "Um, listen," he said.

"I was just walking across the parking lot at Dunkie's, and I saw Lacey. She didn't look so good."

Maureen's spine straightened. "What do you mean? Is she sick?"

John took the longest breath she'd ever heard. It echoed down the tunnel of the phone line. "I don't know. She was passed out in someone's car. I don't want to accuse her or anything, but it really looked like she was high."

She almost laughed. Impossible. She'd just seen Lacey that morning. Her eyes had twinkled the way they always did over the rim of her coffee mug. She'd joked with Maureen about one of the regulars at Dunkin' Donuts, the man who sat at the counter every morning and read just the obituaries in the *Boston Globe*. Hadn't she?

John cleared his throat. "I would stay put and wait for the ambulance, but"—he lowered his voice to a dull rumble— "I've got Ella here with me. She's the one who spotted Lacey on our way out the door from the store. I had to tell her she was just sleeping, you know?"

"Yes," Maureen said, or thought she said.

She stared at the water still gushing into the tub. Droplets flew off the surface and clung to the walls. Lacey had helped her paint them. "Let's do a more muted shade in here, Mom," she'd said. "You want it to be nice and calming, right?"

John was still talking, something about recognizing the signs from one of his former crew. Also an addict. Maureen could only nod. Her hand dropped into her lap with the phone in it. His voice was manageable from a distance. Eventually, it was replaced with the tinny whine of the dial tone and the whoosh of the faucet. She sat until the water lapped up over the lip of the tub. Until it crept across the floor and reached, tentatively, for her bare toes.

They didn't speak until Maureen had pulled into their driveway. "We have to go see them," Lacey said as Maureen tugged the keys out of the ignition.

Maureen was tempted to ask who, but she knew who. To ask might snap this thin thread of conversation in two. "I'm sure they've got plenty of friends to help them," she said into the ticking of the engine.

"I need to make sure Ella's okay."

Maureen sighed and pressed the edge of her forehead. "Fine. We can head over tomorrow. Just for a few minutes, okay?"

Lacey nodded, her ponytail a dark furl against the streetlight outside. She opened the door and dropped out into the night.

Maureen watched her walk up the front path. "Dammit," she said under her breath.

Chapter Seven

THE DOOR OF THE Breakwater opened at 5:00 p.m. All the guys called it "the Break," as in, "I need a Break from all this shit." The owner shoved a wooden wedge under the door and nodded at the men gathered there.

"Jimmy."

"How's it going tonight, fellas?"

"That depends. You know what to tell my wife when she calls, right?"

"That I'm about to send you on your way back home." He winked, and the men roared with laughter that echoed across the damp parking lot.

"Rough day today?" he said as they filed past him.

"Winds at 35 knots and fog you can't see shit through? Nah, never better. Makes you stronger," Will Feeney said.

Gus March coughed up a laugh behind him and ground his cigarette under his work boot before following Will into the bar.

Soon enough, the place caught its nightly rhythm, Jimmy pulling pints of Bud while neon lights flickered above his head. Occasionally, a tourist would wander in, having heard that the Breakwater served the best cup of clam chowder in town. Their eyes would widen, taking in the tiny, dark room filled to the brim with fishermen, leaning up against the bar and standing by the windows in clusters, their paint-swabbed jeans and old sweatshirts, their faces beaten to a certain kind of red-tanned sameness by the sun and the salt, swearing and laughing and wiping at their watery eyes. The tourists tended to turn tail at the sight, ushering their children back out the door with hands on their shoulders.

At around ten, somebody got a phone call, and the news began to eddy through the room.

"Staybrook? Fuck. You sure?"

"I told that son of a bitch *Diane & Ella* wasn't seaworthy, least not in weather like this."

"Was he even on *Diane & Ella*? You notice that new tuna boat was gone today, too?"

"Shit. No way he'd've taken that job. Not today. Jess say if he went out separate or fell off his own boat?"

"Don't think she has. All she told Rick was he's missing, then she went off to the harbor master."

"Jesus. John always had balls. Remember Alaska?"

"Think he's still out there?"

"Could be, could be."

"We gonna pay our respects tomorrow?"

"I better tell my wife."

Jimmy poured a round on the house. Glasses passed from hand to quiet hand. Beer sloshed out of them along the way so the guys in the back only got half-full pints. They drank together, glancing up at the ceiling as they swallowed. A small miracle, they knew, that it wasn't them this time.

"I saw Jess," Ben O'Malley said from his spot near the doorway. He'd just gotten there, but his glass was already empty. His shoulders were wet, the fabric of his T-shirt glued to his skin. None of them had noticed it started raining. "When she came back on the *Diane & Ella*. By herself. Looked like she'd seen a ghost or something."

"Maybe she did," Sammy Mitchell said and barked with laughter. The guys around him chuckled warily. Sammy was a little crazy. One of them would have to drive him back to his daughter's at the end of the night.

"Shit, I don't blame her. Wonder what she knows?"

"Even if he wasn't on the boat with her. Taking the boss's boat out without him? She's up to something."

"Aw, come on, Ralphie. She's a good kid. Knows what she's doing."

"Something weird about it, though. Johnny hardly trusted that boat to anyone. Recommended ten welders to him before he finally picked one."

"Yeah, and one from all the way down the Cape, too."

"Sorry. Tried to get him to hire your brother. You know how he is. Was."

"A real idiot, apparently. Who the hell goes tuna fishing in weather like this?"

"You'd have gone, too, if you'd had the chance. I've heard you talking about buying a tuna rig for years."

The screen door slapped sharply against its frame. Jess stood in the entrance, eyes haggard. She needed a drink and some other faces. Still, she'd hoped against hope it wouldn't be a packed night.

"Evening, Jess."

"Boys."

"See anything spooky tonight?"

"Shut up, Sammy. Leave her be."

"Here, have a seat. Butt's fallen asleep."

"Thanks, Frank."

"You doing okay? We heard some fu—Sorry. Some screwed-up shi…stories."

Jess shrugged and took the glass Jimmy held out. "I don't even know what happened. He was talking to me on the radio, backseat driving the damn boat from clear across the bay, and then—" She shook her head slowly and coughed back tears. She should've gone straight home and blasted *Jeopardy* reruns until the corduroy surface of her couch imprinted itself on her arms.

Whispers moved through the crowd. "You mean he wasn't with you on his boat?"

She shook her head. "He was running that tuna boat. Didn't want anyone to know before he left in case Diane found out and tried to stop him."

"What was he even thinking, going out tuna fishing on a day like this?"

"Yeah, even I didn't bother making a trip when I saw the forecast this morning," Danny Colbert said.

A few exchanged sidelong glances. "Danny, you look for any excuse you can get not to go out! I've seen your boat tied up at the pier damn near every day this month," Sammy shouted. Some real laughter this time. Danny glowered at his beer.

"Seriously, though. You know why he went out today?" *Why it was him and not us.* "Seems like a downright dumb decision."

Jess felt her shoulders tense up. Johnny was always teasing her about that, the habit she had of hunching up into herself. She took a long sip of beer and closed her eyes against the expectant silence. "He wasn't dumb. He was one of the best fishermen in this town, and you know it." She looked around and pressed the tip of her forefinger into the table as if its grimy surface contained the whole of Devil's Purse and she was catching it by the tail. "If anyone could've pulled it off, it was Johnny. But he couldn't."

Everyone nodded solemnly at that, even Sammy. If there were any doubts remaining, they wouldn't be spoken tonight. Not in front of her.

"Hi, honey." Abby, a waitress at the Break, slipped up behind her husband, Frank, and kissed him on the cheek while she tied an apron around her waist. "Oh, Jess," she said, "I'm real sorry to hear about poor Johnny." She put one hand on Jess's shoulder. "You let me know if there's anything I can do, all right? Anything at all."

Jess nodded and shifted out from under her touch.

Abby turned to the rest of the room. "Now, I know you boys aren't done for the night yet. Who's ready for another round?" Hands raised in all directions, and she grinned, plunging into the crowd with her order pad ready. Every male eye in the house watched her blue-jeaned hips swish back and forth, and Jess watched them watch her.

She'd never figured out how women like that managed to command a room and shape the mood and desires of everyone in it. She'd missed that day in school, apparently. She drained the rest of her beer and slipped, unnoticed, back into the damp and unforgiving night.

Chapter Eight

Friday, November 10, 2017

DIANE WAS WATCHING WHEN Ella woke up. She sat on the edge of her daughter's bed, mussing the duvet and studying the flush of Ella's cheeks. Diane's vision blurred from lack of sleep, but she knew exactly how Ella's eyelashes fringed her cheekbones and her forehead wrinkled when she dreamed.

"Morning, Mom." Ella rubbed one fist across her face. "What's for breakfast?"

"Hi, Ella-Bella." She slid her hand over Ella's shin, a mountain range under the covers. She held the bones of her ankle. She wanted to tell her there was a stack of steaming pancakes waiting for her on the kitchen counter.

Ella flinched and tugged her leg away, out of the grip that'd suddenly become viselike.

"I have some bad news. Your dad, he's—" Diane looked away to hide what was collecting in her face. She needed to be stronger than this.

Ella's eyes widened as she sat up straight, pulling farther away. She hugged her knees to her chest like an anchor. It was almost as if she knew already. *How quickly we all learn in this damn town*, Diane thought.

She tried again. "Jess came by last night. Your dad is missing, baby."

Ella always hated when she called her that, but this time, she didn't notice. She shook her head hard, her skull knocking against the wall. "That doesn't make any sense. Jess wouldn't have come home without him. She wouldn't do that."

"I know." Diane sighed, shaky. "I know. But he wasn't on the boat with Jess. I guess he took a tuna boat out by himself." She pulled the threads of doubt out of her voice. Her daughter needed certainty.

Ella's face turned red. Tears crept from her eyes. "He wouldn't do that," she whimpered. "He would never."

Diane shifted closer on the bed and pulled Ella in. At first, Ella resisted, her muscles stiff, but finally, she collapsed into her mom's lap. Diane drew her fingers through Ella's hair. She could remember, in that moment, every time she'd done it before, soothing every fear and pain, every nightmare and canceled playdate. It all seemed so manageable in retrospect. John would stand in the doorway and offer to beat up the offending friend, or he'd crouch on the floor and shine a flashlight under the bed and into closets until Ella giggled. Diane realized with a start that she was waiting for him to appear now, to make everything better. Easier.

With a great sniff, something in Ella hardened. She sat up and stared at her mother. "You're lying," she said.

Diane froze. "What?"

"I heard you guys fighting the other night. Dad probably left you, and you want me to think he's dead. But you're lying, I know it." She was screaming now, her mouth bleeding hate.

Diane paused, bewildered. "Oh, baby, no." How could she possibly imagine this? She reached again for Ella's shoulder.

Her daughter scuttled to the far corner of the bed. "Get out. Get out!" she screeched.

And Diane, not knowing what else to do, stood on shaky knees and tottered to the door. She glanced back at Ella, who was already lying on her side, her trembling back facing Diane. Diane eased the door shut behind her, thinking it might help to let Ella process her grief in private. Last night, after she stared at the wedding portrait gone dusty on the mantle, she turned to her computer. She needed something to do and a place to put her anguish. She started reading the message boards. Terrible, inconceivable posts about how to help your child through the loss of your spouse, their parent. They all said new widows should first let their child "process their grief," as if the loss were a fruit that could be whirred into an easily digestible puree. She wished she could still call up Maureen and describe the image to her. She would've laughed at that.

Not ten seconds after she'd closed Ella's door, Diane heard her bare feet patter across the floor. Diane allowed her heart to lift a little, imagining Ella would throw herself back into Diane's arms, processing be damned. Instead, there was the angry tick of the button lock in the doorknob. Diane had asked John a thousand times to remove that lock, imagining their daughter trapped in there. She made an irritated mental note to ask him once again when he got home before she remembered with a sucking swoosh that she wouldn't be able to. She slid to the floor, her back against the door, and hid her face in her hands.

All her life, Ella had been around boats. Her dad used to let her run around the deck of the *Diane & Ella* while he cleaned and made repairs. He would grin and tell her to watch out for the puddles she'd obviously already seen. Sometimes, he even took her on short trips around the bay. He let her steer the heavy wheel and showed her how to cast for striped bass with the rod he'd given her for Christmas. His arms smelled like low tide when they closed around her, but she didn't mind. She would crane her neck back and stare at the frame of the boat arching high above her, all steel and rust and winches and chains. It was like a skeleton, like armor, and she wasn't afraid.

Then, one and a half years ago, Bobby Cunningham's dad got hit by the dredge frame as it was lifted out of the water, and he was knocked overboard and never seen again. Ella and her classmates signed cards for Bobby, whispering about him before the bell every morning when he missed yet another day of school. When he finally came back a few weeks later, he hardly said anything, and he never smiled, even when the teacher complimented him for getting a question right. By the next fall, he was gone. Everyone said he and his mom had moved away to a dry, dusty state far away from any coastline.

After that, Ella started to pay more attention to her dad's boat. She stared at the dredge, noticing how it hung so high, swinging a little as her dad moved under it. He caught her picking up a piece of chain and testing its cold, wet weight in her hand and dropping it to the deck with a deadly clang. He knelt next to her, his knees right in a blotch of tar. It was going to stain his favorite lucky Carhartts. Before she could say anything, he put one hand on her shoulder. It felt even heavier than the chain.

"It's scary what happened to Bobby's dad, huh?"

Ella nodded, picking at a chip of paint on the boat railing.

"Yeah, it's got us all pretty freaked out," he said.

45

Ella looked at him, surprised. She couldn't imagine her dad being afraid. He laughed too hard, and he knew everything. But he scratched his stubble and sighed. "There's a lot to be scared of in this world, whether you're fishing or not. I promise you this, though"—and his voice dropped so low, she knew it was serious—"I will always play it safe out there, and I'll always come back to you and Mom."

"Pinky swear?" she whispered.

He held up his hand, pinky extended, and she linked it with hers, and they shook on it, the calluses on his finger a little scratchy against her skin.

From that day on, for every trip he took, he leaned over her in the wee hours before leaving and whispered, "See you tonight, First Mate." And she poked her pinky sleepily out from under the covers so he could wrap it in his own before she rolled her face back into her pillow.

Not yesterday morning. Yesterday morning, through the pea soup fog of a dream, she heard her door creak open and his feet shuffle across the floor. She didn't hear his whisper, and she didn't make him pinky swear.

As she stared out the window at the street below, she told herself that was not why he'd disappeared. Probably, it had more to do with the fight he'd had with her mom the night before he left.

A month or two ago, they'd started arguing after sending her up to bed in hissing whispers that carried up the stairs and made her back stiffen against the headboard where she sat. She mostly couldn't make out any words, but a couple of nights ago, they'd forgotten themselves and were practically yelling.

"It's not like I wear it anyway. It's too dangerous with all the gear. I could lose a finger. You know that, Di."

"So now you want to sell it." It was her lawyer voice, the

one she used on the phone with work when she was talking to the other side.

"So what? Everyone knows I'm married. They know I'm spoken for." His voice softened. "You want me to get a tattoo? Get something more permanent on my finger to show 'em all?"

"No, I don't!" Her mom would not be distracted. "I want you to keep the ring I put on your finger when we said our vows, just like I kept mine."

"We need the money, Di," he said even more gently. "If they'd offered more than fifty bucks, I would've sold it."

"No, we don't. We fucking don't!" She was screaming then. It echoed around his silence, which stretched out to a whole minute, maybe longer. And then, the front door swished open and thudded shut.

Ella had lain there in the dark, counting her breaths. Had she eaten too much at dinner? Did she ask for too much for her birthday? She knew they weren't rich—all the rich kids in town went to the private school ten miles away. Haley Buford, whose dad owned half the grocery stores in the state, had transferred there that fall, and she wouldn't shut up about it before she left. Apparently, they had horseback riding lessons instead of gym.

She thought they were doing okay, though. Everyone said her dad was the best fisherman in town, and her mom had a good job working for the state that required her parents to go to lots of fancy parties and dinners. They'd even gone to Disney World the year before over Christmas break.

Something must've changed. Her dad must be in some kind of trouble, selling his wedding ring like that. He kept it on a chain around his neck, and he always touched that spot under his shirt collar absentmindedly when he stood at the wheel of the boat. She knew he wouldn't sell it unless he really needed to. He was in trouble, and her mom refused to help.

Or maybe her mom's screaming was too much for him, the final straw in something Ella hadn't even noticed. Maybe he'd left her, both of them. According to Becca Larson, that was what happened to Max Dercelli's dad. Max would never admit it, though. He just acted really angry all the time.

Either way, she knew she had to find him. Her dad was out there somewhere, and she had to get him to come home.

Chapter Nine

MAUREEN HELD HER BREATH as she rang the Staybrooks' doorbell. She could tell from the hard set of Lacey's shoulders that she was holding hers, too. The fog and rain clouds had cleared overnight, and every corner of Diane's porch shone in the aching sunlight. Maureen wondered for perhaps the thousandth time that fall how the weather could be so beautiful when everything else was going to shit.

When the door finally opened, Diane looked lost, her eyes glossy and distant. Her hair was tangled and pushed up on one side.

"Oh. Hello," she said.

"Di, we heard about John last night. We're so sorry." Maureen resisted the urge to gather her into a hug. Perhaps it wouldn't be welcome. "We just wanted to stop by and see if there was anything we could do." She turned to Lacey, who wouldn't look up from her feet. They should've brought a casserole or something. Wasn't that what you were supposed to do for the bereaved? Wasn't that her job, to cook for the people who needed it?

Diane opened the door wider and stepped back. The two of them crowded into the entryway, shoulders jostling.

Diane stared at Lacey for a moment before her eyes flicked to her pocketbook, hanging on a hook behind Lacey's head. Maureen felt the shame grow in her chest. She kept her own wallet in a locked drawer of the table in their front hall now. A woman in her support group had advised it, "for her own good."

Diane rubbed her forehead, and it looked so oddly child-like. "Ella's shut herself in her room and won't come out. She's refusing to talk to me. She…she thinks it's my fault somehow. Could you maybe see if she'll let you in?" She looked up at Lacey.

Lacey turned to Maureen, who shrugged just the tiniest bit. "Sure," she said and slipped up the stairs to Ella's room.

Maureen tugged on the zipper pull of her jacket, the metal teeth buzzing loudly in the silence.

"Would you like some coffee?" Diane asked. "I was just about to make a cup."

Maureen nodded and followed her into the kitchen. They had one of those single-serving coffee machines, so there wasn't even anything she could offer to help with as Diane moved around the kitchen. Maureen sat at the counter and braced her hands against it, counting the spots in the granite between her fingers. This was not what she'd planned. She wanted to swoop in and help her friend when she most wanted it, not sit here and let Diane serve her. Diane slid a mug toward her as she perched on a stool with her own. Maureen took a sip. Diane had used one of the strong pods and left it black, just like she liked it. She smiled a little, but Diane busied herself with folding a napkin into her lap.

"You know it's not your fault, right?" Maureen almost whispered. "Ella's upset, and kids say some pretty crazy things when they're upset." She could've come up with any number of examples of frenzied, hurtful things Lacey had said over the years—that they'd said to each other—and later apologized for. She bit her lip.

"I guess you're right," Diane said. She dropped the napkin and didn't seem to notice when it fell on the floor. "John and I had a fight." She gripped her mug and glanced at the door. "The night before he...left. I think Ella heard us."

"Oh." Maureen faltered. "Well. All couples argue every once in a while, right?" she said, but really, what did she know about it? "I'm sure Ella understands that," she added uncertainly.

Diane shook her head. "I was angry with him. So angry. I think I may have even yelled at him. He walked out to get some air," she continued, trancelike. "He didn't come back until I was asleep. I can't stop thinking about it, how it was the last—" She pressed her fingertips to her mouth as if to pinch the words back.

"Oh, honey." Maureen hopped off her stool and pulled Diane into a hug. Diane did not cry—she never did—but she did lay her head on Maureen's shoulder. They stayed that way for a moment, Diane's sharp chin digging into her neck. And then Diane moved away, bending to retrieve her napkin.

"If you ever need any help with Ella," Maureen said to the back of her head, "I'm your girl. It's tough to raise a kid on your own, and God knows, I've learned some lessons along the way," she continued, realizing too late that she'd lost any claims to authority on how to bring your child into functioning adulthood. For a second, she wanted to cry.

The faint smile vanished from Diane's face. "Thanks," she said. She took the handles of the two nearly full mugs into one hand. "I hate to be rude, but you might want to get on your way. Folks will probably be coming in and out of here all day to check on us, and I really don't want to overwhelm Ella with too many people in the house at once." She dumped the coffee into the sink. The drain gurgled.

"Sure. Okay." Maureen pulled a stray thread from her T-shirt, stalling. "You'll let me know if there's anything I can do? Maybe I'll drop by later this week with some food. We've always got leftovers after events."

"Whatever you want." Diane began to yank clean dishes out of the drying rack next to the sink and wash them again, her elbow jerking in and out while she scrubbed. She glanced over her shoulder at Maureen.

Maureen opened her mouth, then closed it. There was nothing more she could say. Their friendship had already faded. This wasn't going to revive it. Maureen walked to the door. She paused at the base of the steps and listened to the quiet murmur of her daughter's voice through Ella's door, interrupted by the younger girl's laughter. She shot Lacey a text saying she was heading home and to let her know as soon as she left the Staybrooks', and then she was out the door and gone again.

She'd met John first. This was eight years ago. At the time, Maureen and Lacey had been in Devil's Purse for only a year, and Lacey had already accumulated a pool of bubbly, shrieking friends. She'd recently decided she wanted to volunteer at the local animal shelter after school—"All those dogs and cats without a home, Mom," she said, her eyes shining dangerously. "Can you even imagine?" So every Wednesday, Maureen dropped her off at the dank, gray building before parking in a deserted beach parking lot to plan her menus with only the restless green waves and the piping plovers to distract her.

One day, she had walked into the shelter at the end of Lacey's shift and heard her daughter's rapid-fire chatter coming from the cat room. She assumed one of Lacey's friends had stopped by until she peeked in the window on the door. There her daughter crouched, holding a very disgruntled-looking tabby up to a pink-and-purple stroller. One pale, chubby forearm extended past the lip of the stroller to poke the cat, which eyed the arm warily. Lacey smiled and demonstrated the proper petting technique. "See? Nice and gentle," she said.

Maureen opened the door.

"Oh, hi, Mom." Lacey barely glanced up.

"You ready to go, honey?"

"In a minute. Just gotta finish helping Ella convince her dad she needs a pet."

The baby burbled.

"Sorry about that. They've been shootin' the shit for almost twenty minutes now."

She turned to see a man standing up against the wall of cages, idly poking a finger through the bars at a rangy calico that was in no way interested in being touched.

"John Staybrook."

"Maureen Carson." She shook the hand he offered. It felt oddly formal in a room that smelled like kitty litter. "Looks like you've already met my daughter, Lacey."

"Oh yeah." He smiled down at them. Lacey had taken Ella's wrist between two fingers and was running her tiny palm slowly over the cat's back. Ella's mouth had fallen open, and she was breathing loudly in concentration.

"She's great with the little ones," he said.

Maureen nodded knowingly, though it was news to her. As far as she knew, Lacey still *was* a little one.

"You got another one at home or something?" he asked.

"Nope, just us two."

She waited for him to say, "That's too bad," or to ask about her husband. But he said, "She ever think about babysitting?"

She could practically see Lacey's ears perk up—she'd been begging Maureen for a bigger allowance—but Lacey kept her head bowed and pretended to stay focused on the baby.

"My wife, she's looking to go back to work in the summer," he continued. "Part-time from home for starters, but she could use some help with this one while she does. Like a mother's helper type thing, you know? Is that what they call it?" He chucked his chin toward Ella, who was now thrusting her cat-petting fingers directly into her mouth. "If I'm honest, I think she kinda wishes she could just stay home with the baby," he muttered, eyes glinting a little bit. "But no way can my boat support this one's hungry little mouth, eh?" He chuckled.

"Um," Maureen said. She wondered how his wife would feel about him sharing all this information with a near stranger. He raised his eyebrows expectantly. She wanted to demur. Lacey was too young. There was something about his eyes, though. They were so bright and familiar somehow. She was struck with the feeling that she could trust him completely. And Maureen had always been one to listen to her gut. Besides, it wasn't like Lacey would be left alone in the house with a baby. Hadn't he said his wife would just be working in another room?

When she said she'd think about it, she saw Lacey do a quick little golf clap out of the corner of her eye. The relief on John's face was profound. It occurred to her, too late, that his wife might be a difficult employer who'd already turned down a procession of mother's helpers. As she gave him her number, part of her hoped he'd forget who she was by the time summer rolled around.

He didn't. That June, she stood on the Staybrooks' porch for the first time, Lacey at her side. She was going to meet with John's wife that day while their daughters played for a bit, just to make sure everything went okay.

"Maybe I'll even make enough to buy a 32-gig," Lacey was saying. "Sarah told me she can fit thousands of songs on hers. Thousands!"

"You know you're actually going to have to work before this family gives you any money, right?" Maureen said as she rang the doorbell.

"Psh, I'm not worried about that." Lacey waved her hand. "Ella and I are simpatico."

Before Maureen could ask her where the hell she'd learned that word, the door opened, and she had to bite the inside of her cheek, hard. In a flash, she knew why she'd recognized John. He'd been a guest at one of the weddings Maureen had worked at. She'd seen him swaying a woman on the dance floor that night, her lips at his ear, her face unpinched. The woman was a little uptight and had asked Maureen if the crabmeat in the sushi rolls was real or imitation. The woman was, obviously, his wife. Standing before Maureen now in leggings and an oversized pullover.

"You must be Maureen and Lacey." She scanned Lacey from top to bottom. Maureen held on to her daughter's shoulder. "I'm Diane. Come on in. I told John I didn't really need help and would just work while Ella napped," she said as she led them through the house and into the living room, "but he insisted. He wanted to be here to say hi to you both, but the weather was so good today, he had to go catch some scallops. Didn't he?" she said to Ella, sitting on the floor amid the wreckage of a block tower city.

Ella held her arms up toward Diane, and Diane obliged, hoisting her onto one hip. Ella pressed her palms to her mother's cheeks, and Diane tilted her head so their foreheads touched, puckering her lips into an exaggerated, fishy pout.

Lacey shifted from one foot to the other. Ella saw her and squealed, smacking her hands together. Diane put her down, and she toddled unsteadily over to Lacey, planting her face between Lacey's knees.

"Wow. Your daughter must've made quite an impression on her at the animal shelter." Diane smiled through closed lips as Lacey crouched down and began clapping along with Ella. "We decided not to get a cat after all. Too much work," she explained to Lacey, who nodded without looking up. "Shall we go drink some tea while they play?"

"Sure," Maureen said, glancing at Lacey and following Diane into the kitchen.

"So are you guys new in town? I don't think I've seen you around before," Diane said. She filled a mug with the kettle standing ready on the stove and handed it to Maureen.

Maureen took a sip and held back a grimace. Instant tea. And lukewarm, no less. Maybe Diane didn't have her shit quite as together as it looked.

"Sort of." She pushed the mug to the edge of her placemat. She preferred coffee anyway. "I work at a catering company, so that keeps me pretty busy. We've seen our next-door neighbors I think once or twice? I don't think they were too psyched to have a single mom and a preteen move in next door. They give me the stink eye through their curtains every time I come home late from an event, like I missed my curfew."

Diane put down her mug and laughed, one hand on her chest. "Oh, that's just Devil's Purse," she said. She sat down at the counter. "It takes them a while to warm up to outsiders. When I married John, I swear I caught the mother of his ex-girlfriend stalling outside our front gate at least three times.

She thought he'd made a terrible mistake. Mind you, he hasn't seen the girl since high school, and she got out of town and is living her own life God knows where." She laughed again, and damned if it didn't sound a bit like a whinny.

Maureen couldn't help but laugh along, letting loose a full-on snort. Soon, there were tears in both their eyes.

Diane sighed and sipped her tea. "Well, don't worry. They'll warm up soon enough."

When John came home that night, Maureen was still there, making a sauce out of butter, an onion, and a dented can of tomatoes she'd found in the back of their cupboards. "Ladies," he said as he sat down to drag his boots off, smiling like he was trying to catch up with whatever they were giggling at.

"Hi, honey." Diane leaned down to peck him on the cheek. "Maureen and Lacey are having dinner with us."

It went on like that for years. Even after Lacey stopped babysitting, the two of them still met up for drinks every week in a bar twenty minutes away so they could safely gripe about Devil's Purse natives. When Diane's mother died, Maureen made the food for the wake and called her every month on the date of her passing. When Maureen decided to open her own catering company, Diane put a stack of Maureen's business cards in her purse in case anyone in earshot mentioned planning a party.

And when Lacey got sick, Diane was there for her, too. At least at first. She held Maureen's hand in the hospital while they waited for Lacey to wake up. Maureen could picture it so clearly, the glossy pink ovals of Diane's nails against the pale, ragged burn scars crossing the backs of Maureen's hands. Diane was the one who found the rehab facility, the only residential teen program within a fifty-mile radius, and she haggled on the phone with Maureen's insurance provider over medical necessity.

Lacey's caseworker had referred Maureen to a support network for parents of addicts, and once, one of the mothers invited her to their home. Maureen sat in an armchair in their living room, the leather sticking to her thighs, while the mother and her husband sipped coffee and shared pained glances. The mother started leaking tears when she talked about the nasty voicemail a neighbor had left accusing her son of stealing a package from their front steps. The woman had compressed the tissue in her hand into a tight pellet, and it left little white flakes on her face when she rubbed her nose. Her husband squeezed her knee and said, "In this part of the world, you can't twist an ankle without everyone calling you to see how you're doing." He glared defiantly at Maureen; she couldn't tell if he was looking for someone to take the blame for the injustice or if he was trying to commiserate. "But addiction is a whole other story." His voice hiccupped a little. "They've decided it's one of our faults, and we should be ashamed. Or get over it. Or give up on him."

Maureen had nodded along, but really, she felt a little smug about it. She may have dealt with the whispers at the grocery store, and her bookings may have gone down a bit lately. And when Lacey asked after various people around town during Maureen's visits, she may not have known how to answer. But at least she had Diane. Diane would always stick by her and support her, no matter what anyone else said.

And then gradually, over the course of the month, Diane grew more distant. She stopped calling to ask how Lacey was doing. When Maureen rehashed something her caseworker had said or fretted about a new medical study she'd read online, Diane no longer answered in full sentences. When Maureen told her about all the things she was doing to prepare for Lacey's return, to "ease the transition," Diane looked up from her phone and snapped, "She's going to have to face the consequences of her decisions sooner or later, no matter what you do."

After that, Maureen stopped calling Diane and started texting excuses to get out of their standing coffee dates. Deep down, she knew Diane was right: Lacey was the victim of her own bad choices, and Maureen should not have let her make them. She couldn't bear seeing the truth of it reflected in Diane's disapproving eyes anymore. They'd barely spoken since Lacey got home.

And Diane made no effort to reach out to Maureen, either. Whenever the guilt was replaced with an anger in Maureen's stomach that simmered into a full boil, she told herself it probably wasn't easy for Diane, either, watching a girl who was once so close to her own daughter spiral out of control like that. Maybe she was worried it would happen to Ella one day.

Ella opened her door for Lacey right away and scampered back to her desk so that by the time Lacey entered the room, her face was lit bright white by her computer. It was a hand-me-down desktop from when her mom used to work from home, and a growl rose from her while she waited for her search results to load.

"Hey, kidlet," Lacey said, her fingers still on the door-knob. "I heard about your dad."

"He's not gone, if that's what you think." Ella shook the mouse one more time before meeting Lacey's eyes, her chin jutting out. "He's not."

Lacey sighed and finally walked over. "Ella, I know it's tough. Your mom's really worried about you—"

"She should be. I know what she did."

"What? What did she do?" Lacey gripped the back of Ella's chair.

"She made my dad leave us, and now I'm going to find him."

Silence. Lacey inhaled, but before she could say anything, Ella groaned and spun around to face her. "Will you help me with this, please?"

Lacey bent down to her eye level and lowered her voice so it was all soft. "Sweetie, Jess heard it all on the VHF radio. I think he's really gone."

Ella grimaced at the pet name. "Please?" Ella clasped her hands below her chin. "I really need you. I've missed you."

Lacey stood up and paused. Her shoulders fell. "Okay. Fine." It had been so long since someone had asked for her help rather than insisting that she needed theirs. And when Ella finished her search and finally accepted the truth—well, Lacey would be there for her.

"Yes!" Ella clapped and turned back to her computer. "I heard my mom yelling at my dad the night before he left. He tried to sell his wedding ring, so I wanna find out where he went to sell it. Maybe he went back there, or maybe he told them something when he was there. But when I googled places to buy rings around here, it came up with, like, a million results."

"The pawn shop on Columbus gives the best prices in town. It was probably that." Lacey sat on the edge of the bed and pulled the keyboard toward her. She took a deep breath before typing anything.

"Hey, don't worry," Ella said. "We'll find him. I know it."

Lacey smiled a little. "Here. That's the address." She pointed at the screen.

"Wow. You're really good at this." Ella stared at the address for a minute. It was less than a mile away. She glanced sideways at Lacey. "Did you ever try to look for your real mom?"

"My real mom is downstairs." Lacey pushed the keyboard back into place.

"No, no." Ella rolled her eyes. "Your real mom. You know, the one who gave birth to you?"

Lacey bent her head down between her knees and gathered her hair into a ponytail. When she came back up, her face was flushed. "No," she said, but she avoided Ella's gaze. She didn't want her to see the lie.

Chapter Ten

IT WAS NO SECRET that Lacey was adopted. It never had been. She and Maureen almost could've passed as biological, though; they were both thin and pale with a little bit of grace in their limbs. Sometimes, Lacey wished Maureen had pretended they were biological so that she could live in a fantasy bubble where it was just the two of them with nobody else out there to tug on them.

Maureen thought it was important for Lacey to "know her past" and to know that Maureen loved that part of her, too. When Lacey was small, Maureen bought her a picture book, *On the Day You Were Adopted*. It was cheaply made, with softly focused illustrations. Maureen had read it to Lacey over and over again until the binding admitted defeat. Maureen's sister once asked her at a family Thanksgiving if she was sad she couldn't have her own children. Maureen had stared at her and circled one arm around Lacey's little shoulders. "What do you mean? Lacey is my own." They didn't see her sister very often after that.

Adoption was such a part of her that for a while, she even bragged about it. On her first day of kindergarten, she asked the boy who shared her desk if he'd been adopted, too.

"Adopted?" he said, his face all screwed up. "What's that?"

"It's when your real parents go to the hospital and get you from your first parents," she explained patiently. "I was adopted on my birthday. October 9, 1998," she said, chest puffed out.

The boy still looked confused. "I only have real parents."

"You're not adopted, then." She shook her head until the tip of her ponytail whipped at her face. "You're not special, like I am."

Apparently, this was more information than the boy could take. He burst into tears. The teacher hurried over and knelt by his side to ask what was the matter. The story came out between his hitching breaths while Lacey drew a dog on her brand-new notepad.

"Don't worry, Brian," the teacher said. "You're right! You only have one mommy and one daddy. Most people do." Lacey glanced up. The teacher looked over at her, and her eyes widened a little. "Which makes you extra special, Lacey!"

Brian scowled. Lacey beamed.

When she grew older, once a month, she allowed herself to google her birth date and hospital along with all the flecks of information she knew: Maureen's name, her birth mother's approximate age. It always came up cluttered with useless search results. She knew it would.

One time, in fourth grade, her mom had caught her. "Whatcha looking at?"

Her mom's hand on her shoulder startled her. She didn't have time to close the window. "We Can Help You Find Your Birth Parents!" it promised. She knew the words would hurt Maureen's feelings. The company required you to be at least eighteen before they'd search for you anyway. They all did.

Maureen sighed. "I wish it'd been an open adoption so we could've met her," she said.

"I know, Mom," Lacey said. She leaned back into her

mom's arms. Closed adoptions were increasingly rare. More and more, adoptees were telling stories on the forums about birthdays spent with both sets of parents and update letters sent to the birth mom complete with photos. Lacey was one of the chosen few with a closed adoption.

Maureen didn't believe in God—"I'm an agnostic, not an atheist," she said, whatever that meant—so her options had been limited. Most of the domestic adoption agencies mentioned Christ in every brochure and on every page of their website. Many of them had told Maureen under no uncertain terms that they preferred their children to go to good, Christian homes with two parents. "We believe a child flourishes with both a mother and a father," they'd told her primly during her screening interviews. By the time Lacey was born, Maureen had been on the agency's list for three years and no longer felt she had any say over whether the adoption was open or closed.

"I've got an idea," her mom said, squeezing her close.

Lacey smiled a little, waiting for her to suggest funfetti pancakes or her famous mint brownie sundae.

Maureen said, "What if we take a trip back to Devil's Purse, where you were born?"

"Really?" Lacey turned to face her.

"Definitely. One weekend this summer, okay? I want you to see where you came from," Maureen said, and her smile wiggled almost imperceptibly.

It took two flights and an hour-long car ride for them to get there from Minnesota. By the time Maureen pulled the car into the town beach parking lot, it was dark, and Lacey was hopped up on Twizzlers and the Cokes she'd ordered from the stewardesses while her mom slept.

"Let's get some air before we check into the hotel," Maureen said as she parked.

They left their shoes and socks by the asphalt path to the beach. Lacey watched the still-warm sand sift between her toes. There were only a couple of people left, everyone else gone back to their houses for dinner. They walked all the way down to the water. Lacey shivered, surprised, as the ocean coiled around her ankles—it was almost as cold as a Duluth winter, and her skin reddened instantly at its touch. She thought it would feel more natural to her. Even though she was born here, her body didn't seem to know the ocean.

Maureen wound her sweater tighter around her middle. "I came here while I was waiting for you to be born."

Lacey stared. She thought she'd heard every possible story about her birth, every moment, but this one was new.

Maureen pushed a tangle of hair back from Lacey's forehead, blown there by a damp wind. "When the agency called, I rushed straight to the hospital. There's a lot of hurry up and wait involved with giving birth. The waiting room was making me nervous, all those balloons and the vending machine coffee. So I drove here for a break. I stood in this exact spot."

The water stretched darkly toward the horizon. The stars were a perfect, pure white. Maureen said, "I know it sounds crazy, but I felt like the waves were whispering something to me that night. They were telling me it was okay, that you were going to be fine. I felt so at home in that moment. So at peace."

Lacey listened hard, but the waves wouldn't tell her anything. Just a quiet, constant hush.

"And then my beeper buzzed," her mom said, "and you were here." She leaned over and tucked one arm behind Lacey's knees and swept her, giggling, up to her chest, swinging her around while the water sloshed noisily at her feet. Lacey gripped her mom's neck tightly, at first so she wouldn't fall and then because she knew Maureen needed her to.

When Maureen finally put her down, her smile went all the way to her eyes. "Maybe it's time for us to move back here," she said. "What do you think?"

So they did. Before the school year even started, her mom had found a small house and a job, and everywhere they went, Lacey watched women closely. Was she the checkout girl who winked and snuck her a stick of gum? Was she the real estate agent whose face was posted on half the for-sale signs around town? Before, her fantasies about finding her birth parents were just that: fantasies. Now, though, her biological mom might actually be nearby—never mind that she didn't know if the woman had been from Devil's Purse or simply passing through or if she still lived in Massachusetts at all. She could be here.

Maureen posted a countdown of the number of months until Lacey turned eighteen and the state would allow them to request information about her biological parents. There were ninety-seven months. During her study periods at school, she sometimes went to the library and paged through yearbooks from before she was born to see if she recognized anyone.

And then, in eighth grade, they had their first sex ed unit. It was hard to learn much of anything useful with the giant, mysterious diagrams of private parts projected on the white board. The teacher did her best to stay blasé, but her class was, by turns, horrified and hilarious. Finally, she literally threw up her hands and said, "Just keep it in your pants for now, okay?" The students roared with laughter, and she shouted, "But know that you do have options if you end up with something…unwanted."

For some reason, Lacey's stomach clenched at that. The

beetle, by now a familiar presence, started to move, which she thought was silly, since she was hardly in danger of doing any of the disgusting things the teacher had told them about. The beetle never really listened to reason, though.

The teacher began to hand stacks of brochures down the rows of desks. Most of the students stuck the pamphlets under their binders, to be left behind at the end of the class. A few slipped them into their backpacks when they thought no one was looking. Lacey fanned them out on her desk and stared. There were three of them, pink, with stock photos of thirtysomething models meant to look like distraught teenagers. They were titled "STDs and You," "So You're Pregnant. Now What?" and "Putting Your Baby Up for Adoption."

The teacher had given up entirely and was sitting at her desk, flipping through her planner. While the classroom descended into mayhem around her, Lacey slowly opened the third brochure.

There were more photos inside: one of a very pregnant woman holding one hand to her belly and the other to her forehead, evidently in pain or confusion, and another of that same woman standing in front of a middle-aged couple in khakis and polos. The man's hair was copious and swept back, and the woman wore pearls. Lacey forced herself to focus on the text.

"A child is a blessing," it read, "but for you, it may not be a wanted one. Rest assured, there are plenty of hopeful couples ready and willing for you to put your baby up for adoption."

So that was it, then. That word: *unwanted*. That was her. She knew in an instant that was why she felt so ill. She knew the beetle would never let her forget that word and who she was. She folded the brochure up small until it was a pudgy little square she couldn't fold anymore and tossed it on the floor. She ground the heel of her shoe against it until she could feel it through the sole, a sharp, dusty pebble.

She hardly said anything at dinner that night. She shrugged when her mom asked her how her day was. When Maureen scooped three different types of pureed squash onto her plate—she was testing out recipes—Lacey drew the tines of her fork through them all so they were indistinguishable. Maureen took the hint and let her eat in silence, but after she'd loaded the dishes into the dishwasher, she pulled a chair up close to Lacey's.

"All right," she said. "What's the deal?" She leaned forward, elbows on thighs, hands clasped, ready to problem solve.

Lacey stared down at her napkin. "Nothing," she muttered.

Maureen raised one eyebrow and waited.

When the silence grew too full, Lacey burst. "Why did you want me?" she said.

Surprise fluttered across Maureen's face. She coughed. "I could lie to you and tell you I always knew I was going to adopt. That I was charity-minded and worried about the state of the world or whatever." She reached for the salt-and-pepper shakers and pushed them together so their shoulders clicked, two little soldiers in the middle of the table. "But the truth is, I wanted a kid. More than anything in the world, I wanted one. And the minute they put you in my arms, I knew it was you. You were the one I'd waited for." Maureen pulled Lacey's chin up until they were staring at each other. It was cheesy, but Lacey nodded.

"And besides," her mom continued, wiggling Lacey's chin back and forth, "my body was all busted up from all those years of dancing. I didn't want to spend all that money on treatments just so I could have a bio kid. You know you can lose your period if you exercise too much, right? It's true. Your old mom can't menstruate."

Lacey groaned. "Gross. TMI." But she'd looked it up on one of the school computers. Adoption was just as expensive as a round of IVF. Maybe some part of her mom really had known she was meant for Lacey.

She stopped looking for her biological mom after that. She decided she didn't care. She lived in fear, in fact, of looks of recognition passing over strangers' faces and out-of-the-blue questions about where and when she was born. She didn't want to learn who had given her up.

Her mom never let it go, though. She kept the count-down on the fridge faithfully. Once, Lacey overheard her on the phone, saying, "It's not fair, you know? A kid deserves to know she's loved, from every angle. I don't want her grow-ing up and feeling like she's missing anything."

Part of Lacey wondered if it was all an act and her mom was only doing what she thought she should do. Lacey'd read so many stories online about adoptive parents who feared the biological ones would want to take their child back and burst into tears when their kids announced they were searching for their biological parents. One woman wrote an entire post titled "Am I Not Enough?" Lacey could only read it for five minutes before she closed it in disgust.

On the morning of her eighteenth birthday, her mom was sitting at the kitchen table, grinning expectantly. There was a sheet of paper laid out next to her cereal bowl. "Happy birthday, baby," Maureen said as Lacey squinted at it. It was an application to the adoption agency requesting non-identifiable information—the nameless, faceless facts that were the first step in any search for biological parents.

One month later, in November, there was an envelope

waiting for her by the front door when she came home from school. "Open it! Open it!" Her mom danced around her before she'd even taken off her backpack.

The results were less than inspiring. A single page, typed out in the same font she used to write her school reports. Her birth mother had been seventeen, brown hair, blue eyes, 5'6". No information available on the father. "Hmm. That's less than I thought it would be," her mom said, reading over her shoulder. "Don't worry. I already printed out the identifiable information follow-up form. Did you know we can submit that now, as long as you've got my signature on it?"

Lacey did know. So one month later, it was the same deal. An envelope waiting by the door, her mother standing behind it with her hands clasped. "You'd better not be this annoying when my college decisions start coming in," Lacey said, but her hands shook slightly as she ripped the envelope and pulled out one impossibly small sheet of paper.

"What does it say?" Maureen said, tears in her eyes.

"It says she doesn't want to be found."

"What?" Her mom snatched the paper out of her hands and scanned it. "No, that can't be true. There's got to be some mistake. This never happens."

"It's rare, but it does happen sometimes." Lacey dropped her backpack and started hunting through it for a book, hiding her face. "It's fine, Mom. She just doesn't want to be contacted."

"No, it's not. It's not fine." Maureen tossed the letter onto the couch. "We'll go down to the agency this weekend and sort it all out, okay?"

Lacey nodded weakly.

The beetle got louder over the days that followed. "Don't you think it's a little suspicious she's so eager to find you another mom?" it hissed. "Seems she doesn't really want to know you anymore, either." Ridiculous things it said. She gripped her hair close to the scalp when no one was looking, trying to dislodge the words. By the time Saturday morning rolled around and she hoisted herself into Maureen's van, she was exhausted.

"Don't worry," her mom said as she put the car into gear. "We can fix this."

Lacey said nothing and stared through her reflection in the rearview mirror.

The adoption agency was twenty miles away, a low, brick building surrounded by a shell of colorful tulips and lilacs and daffodils blooming incongruously in the brisk December air. When they got closer, Lacey saw that they were fake, their cheap fabric petals fraying at their edges. Next to the door, there was a single potted poinsettia, garishly red. Someone must take it inside every night and put it out every morning.

Maureen put one hand at the small of Lacey's back and steered her toward the door. Lacey fought the urge to shrink away and run. Inside, they had to take a number, like at the deli or the DMV, even though Maureen had called ahead to make an appointment. They sat in the waiting room on vinyl chairs that creaked when they moved. The room was filled with bored-looking pregnant women—some of them girls, but a lot of them older, mom-aged—and a few couples holding hands, their knuckles whitened with the effort. There was nobody in there who looked like Lacey and her mom. Maureen's toes tapped across the linoleum.

After an hour, it was their turn. They were ushered into a cubicle where a woman sat staring at her computer. Her nameplate read "Elizabeth Clancy," and someone had stuck glittery star stickers along its edges in a neat row. Maureen motioned for Lacey to sit in the only chair and glanced around nervously until Elizabeth Clancy reached around her desk and retrieved a folding chair.

"What can I help you with?" Elizabeth said as Maureen settled into the chair.

"It's this letter you guys sent my daughter." Maureen pulled it from her coat pocket and held it out. "She—we requested identifiable information, and it says her biological mother doesn't want to be contacted."

"Hmm." Elizabeth flicked the letter open with one hand and glanced at it. "And are you the sole adoptive parent?" She lowered her chin to glare at Maureen from over her glasses.

"Yes." Maureen folded her hands in her lap.

"Hmm." Elizabeth began to type something into her computer. There was a plaque hanging on her cubicle wall. In jaunty Comic Sans, it said, "Well-behaved women seldom make history." Lacey stared at it until the letters ceased to make sense.

Elizabeth pushed her glasses up the bridge of her nose and squinted at the screen. "Yes, the letter is correct." She slid the sheet across her desk. "The biological mother did not sign the identifiable information release." She looked straight at Lacey. "Means she does not wish to be contacted," she added unhelpfully.

"But that can't be right," Maureen said. She placed her hand on the paper and didn't pick it up. "It's very rare that birth mothers don't want to get in touch with their children. Everybody says so."

"It's rare, but it does happen." Elizabeth shrugged. "At the end of the day, we need to respect her wishes."

"Respect her wishes? What kind of person wouldn't want to know this girl?"

Lacey looked up, startled.

Maureen's hands flew to her face, and she wiped briskly at her tears. "I just don't understand."

Elizabeth glanced between Maureen and Lacey and sighed. "Look, I know it's hard to hear, but adoption can be a very difficult process for the biological parents. Sometimes, it's simply too painful for them to open that door again." She took off her glasses and folded them into her palm. "I wish I had better news for you, but I'm afraid my hands are tied. Now, is there anything else I can help you with today?"

"No." Maureen sniffed. "No, that was it." She didn't look up as she took the letter and stuffed it into her pocketbook.

Lacey knew Maureen was embarrassed. She tried to smile goodbye on her mom's behalf as they left the cubicle, but Elizabeth was already frowning intently at her computer and typing something new.

By the time they got back to the car, her mom had recovered. As she slung her arm over Lacey's headrest to back out of the parking spot, her hand brushed gently over the crown of Lacey's head. It sent warmth all the way down into her toes.

"Well, that was a bust," Maureen said with a halfhearted chuckle. "Last night, I was reading online about these investigators. They call themselves 'search angels.' Apparently, with just a few details, they can help you find your—"

"That's okay," Lacey said. "I really don't need to."

"Are you sure? I don't want you to grow up regretting anything."

"The only thing I regret is not tearing out all those stupid fake flowers. Who were they kidding with that shit?"

Maureen threw her head back and laughed. "They were pretty terrible, weren't they?"

"The worst." Lacey hoisted one foot up and fiddled

with her shoelace, though it didn't need retying. "Seriously, Mom. I'm fine. I kinda wish you would drop it."

Maureen grew quiet until they reached a stoplight. She patted Lacey's knee and said, "Consider it dropped."

"You'll meet me after school so we can go to this pawn shop, right?"

"Yeah," Lacey said, opening Ella's bedroom door. "You sure your mom won't mind?"

Ella shrugged as she thumped down the stairs, one hand skimming the bannister. "She probably won't even notice. She'll be busy with other stuff." She paused, and as if on cue, Diane's voice echoed up the stairwell from the kitchen.

"Yes, I heard you, dammit," she was saying. "I was there when John drafted it for Christ's sake. I'm just having a hard time understanding why he amended it to this particular arrangement. He knows how I feel about—"

In the silence that followed, Ella turned and raised her eyebrows at Lacey. "See?" she stage-whispered. "She said he *knows*, not he *knew*. He's still alive." She skipped down the remaining steps and out the front door.

Lacey swallowed her response and followed her.

They barely made it to the sidewalk before the door opened behind them again. "Ella, wait!" Diane said, phone clutched to her chest. She hesitated only a moment before running down to the sidewalk in her stocking feet.

Ella stopped, staring out at the street.

"Are you sure you want to go to school today?" Diane said when she'd reached them. "You could stay home with me and watch TV. I could make you grilled cheese and soup." She tugged lightly on the handle at the top of Ella's backpack.

Ella jerked away. "No." She gripped her backpack straps with both hands. "I'm going," she said and walked away without a single glance back.

Diane turned to Lacey, waiting for something. Her eyes roamed Lacey's face.

Lacey tried not to look away and said, "I'm sorry."

Diane's mouth pursed. There was a particular shade of lipstick she always wore, a sort of coral pink. Lacey used to wonder how she got the lines so precise. Now, her lips were bare, cracked. There was a tiny spot of blood in one corner where she'd chewed it too much. Diane nodded once, folded her arms across her chest, and walked back to the house. "Be careful with my daughter," she said with her back turned. "You fucking addict," she said, or maybe it was just the beetle who added that part.

Chapter Eleven

February 27, 1998

ANNIE FITZPATRICK WAS SEVENTEEN when she took the pregnancy test. She locked the door of the basement powder room and wedged a chair from her father's workbench up under the doorknob, even though hardly anyone came down there. The bathroom wasn't even finished, the floor still concrete, and she could feel the dirt and dust through her socks while she tried to aim her pee into the tiny plastic cup.

The cup was warm when she finished, almost disturbingly so. She tried not to dwell on it too much as she placed it on the tissue she'd laid out on the sink counter. She leaned over and read the instructions she'd tossed on the floor and tore open the packaging on the test itself. She dipped the test into the pee.

Now, she was supposed to wait. For ten minutes, according to the instructions. Which seemed like an awfully long time, considering. She stood up and studied her face in the mirror. She'd forgotten to line her eyes that morning, and she looked so much younger that way. Innocent, even.

She wasn't, though. She brushed her bangs to one side. Her boyfriend had just left for Alaska, along with his brother and a passel of other Devil's Purse boys. Her ex-boyfriend.

They made a mutual decision to break up the night before his flight. He'd be fishing out of a village with only two phones, and she wasn't about to keep up a relationship via letter. They'd had one last night in the bed of his Dodge Ram, and it was reckless in the way that goodbye sex sometimes was. She'd loved the fact that he'd had his own car, a nice used one that he paid for with his own summer earnings and only a little help from his parents.

And now she'd gotten maybe pregnant, literally in the back of a truck.

It had to have been ten minutes by now. She held her breath and leaned in to look. She'd heard these things could have false positives with faint second lines.

Hers wasn't faint. It was there. Two harsh lines. Definitely pregnant. Her stomach turned all the way over. She gasped for air around it. "Shit," she whispered and sat down on the floor. It was the first time she'd sworn under her parents' roof, and a little thrill frizzed between her shoulders in spite of everything. She thunked her head back against the unpainted drywall and closed her eyes. They burned with tears. She took a deep breath and tried to slow her heartbeat, thrumming in her throat. How could this happen?

She couldn't tell her ex. He'd probably left on a fishing trip by now and wouldn't even be back on land to read a letter until God knew when. Besides, she wasn't sure he'd be much help. They'd met during one of her shifts at the local movie theater when he was on a date with another girl. He seemed to intuit that his white, cockeyed grin was irresistible enough that she would overlook his date. He seemed not to recognize Annie, even though they'd both gone to DP High.

In other words, they were a fling, something with which to fill the time, although she supposed they'd been exclusive.

Her parents didn't even know about him. He would have no clue what to do with this accusatory plastic stick.

And her friends? She didn't have very many, or at least none who she could trust not to spill the news elsewhere. In a town like this, it would spread in a second, and then she wouldn't be able to walk down the halls without the whispers sticking to her skin like cobwebs.

Which pretty much just left her parents. Annie almost laughed at the thought of telling them. Talk about a meltdown of epic proportions. She dipped her head down between her legs, pushing her knees into her temples. From there, she studied her stomach. She poked at the tiny bulge of flesh that always appeared there when she bent like this. It dimpled around her finger. She felt her face start to compress with a sob, but she swallowed it down. No time for that.

She poured her urine into the toilet and flushed. She rinsed out the cup and wrapped it in a wad of toilet paper along with the test. She stuck it all up under her shirt to throw out later, at work maybe. At least she'd worn a sweatshirt that day. You could barely tell she was hiding something under there. She gathered a handful of nails and screws from her dad's dusty toolbox on her way up the stairs.

"There you are," her mom said when she emerged from the basement. She stood up from the oven, where she'd been checking on her Tuesday night tuna noodle casserole. "Dinner's almost ready. What were you doing down there?"

"Grabbing some stuff I need for a shop project." She held out her hand.

Her mother shook her head. They'd had a long, drawn-out fight when Annie'd told her she wanted to take shop instead of presentation skills, like a proper future member of corporate society. Apparently, the fact that Annie had found working with her hands fun and interesting was not reason enough for her mom.

"I'll be right back," Annie said and headed up the stairs to her room.

"Okay, but remember, dinner is in five minutes!" her mom called up after her.

Annie suppressed a sigh. They had had dinner at the exact same time every single night since she was a kid.

She dumped the nails and screws onto her desk. One or two rolled onto her carpet, a pink monstrosity she'd picked out when she was six. The toilet paper bundle went into her backpack, buried under her astronomy textbook and some old, crumpled homework assignments. She hoped it wouldn't smell too much like pee. That would be a hard one to explain.

At six o'clock exactly, she sat down at the table with her parents. Her mom served them from the casserole dish: two scoops for her father, one and a half for Annie, and one for herself. Iceberg lettuce with ranch dressing and garlic bread all around. Annie picked at her plate, peeling individual egg noodles out of the congealed mass, and watched her parents.

They were so painfully polite with each other. She asked him how his day was as she unfolded her napkin. He regaled them all with stories from his fascinating life as an accountant. He, in turn, asked her mom about the PTO meeting. Annie had heard they were making a movie starring Robin Williams where he played a robot servant. Her parents were something like that.

Then again, she seemed to be having no trouble keeping this secret from them, the biggest secret possible. She told them about pop quizzes and the upcoming winter formal with the exact same noncommittal tone she always used with them. She was feeling kind of numb about it all, actually.

Only the slightest sting in her eyes when she considered shielding them from this for the rest of her life. Maybe she was a sociopath.

In bed that night, she drew the covers up to her chin and tried to keep her thoughts straight for long enough to figure out what the hell she should do. She'd always assumed she'd have kids, in a vague, far-off kind of way. Being a mom wasn't her number-one goal in life right now, though. Not even close. She wasn't sure what her number-one goal was yet, but it definitely wasn't that. Plus, she was pretty sure she'd make an awful mom at this point. Minimum wage at the movie theater probably wouldn't cover diapers, and between that and school, she'd barely be around for the kid.

The thought of ending the pregnancy was not something she could study straight on. At seventeen in Massachusetts, she would need her parents' signatures to have the procedure done. Her churchgoing, tuna casserole–eating parents. In theory, she could forge their signatures, but just over three years before, a man had shot five people in a Planned Parenthood clinic in Brookline, less than an hour away from Devil's Purse. She learned all the details in school when they came back from Christmas break. Two receptionists had died. The president had called it terrorism. The gunman had asked if it was the preterm clinic before taking out his gun and saying something religious about God or Jesus. The FBI had hunted for two days before they found him. The clinics didn't seem safe to her.

There was adoption. She thought she liked the idea of giving another family a chance to raise a baby, maybe a couple who really wanted one but couldn't have their own. She couldn't picture such a couple, what they looked like or what she wanted them to say. But there were plenty of them out there, she was sure.

Adoption meant carrying the baby to term, which meant telling her parents. The thought made her feel sick. She would tell them at some point. Soon, she promised herself as she settled back into her pillows. She would find a way.

And she meant to, she did. But every time she opened her mouth, over breakfast while her dad sipped his coffee or in the afternoons when she did her homework and her mom cooked dinner, she would picture their faces. Her dad would be furious, no doubt, in that scary-quiet way he had whenever she missed curfew. And her mom would probably cry.

At first, it was fairly easy to hide the pregnancy. It was winter in New England, so she layered old flannel shirts and her puffy jacket over her slowly growing belly. Every once in a while, she had to rush to the bathroom to puke, peering under the other stalls afterward to make sure no one had heard, but that was the only symptom she had. Sometimes, she would look down in class to make sure it was still there, that hard, round mound. It felt like something entirely separate from her body. Doctor's appointments were out of the question, and she couldn't even think about using the family computer to look up adoption agencies or anything for fear of her parents somehow finding evidence.

And then, one morning, she couldn't button her jeans. She couldn't even see the fly around the fleshy swell of her. She turned sideways in the mirror and scrutinized herself. She took a deep breath. She knew what she had to do.

She spent the rest of the week making her plan. She dug the newspaper out of a recycling bin on the way to school one day and paged through the classifieds in a corner behind the cafeteria, running her finger over the column of people seeking roommates before she found a place she could afford a few towns over. It was perfect: no one would recognize her there, but it wasn't so far away she'd have to spend half her savings on a bus ticket. She would lie low for a while, have the baby, give it to the right family, and then. And then? Well, then, she supposed she'd come back home.

She wrote a letter to her parents. It took her three nights to get it right. She tore up all her drafts and threw them out in the trash can at the theater before her shift, scattering the bits of paper over popcorn buckets and ticket stubs. Ultimately, she decided to tell them the truth. She knew it was cowardly to tell them in a letter like that, but she still couldn't bear to tell them to their faces. She didn't want them thinking she'd been kidnapped or she'd run away because she didn't love them or some stupid reason like that. She needed them to be embarrassed so they would leave her alone. She promised she would call them once a week, though in all honesty, she wasn't sure if she could afford to contribute to her roommates' phone bill.

On the night she left, she watched her parents more closely than usual, noticing the hairs on the back of her father's hands and the way her mother wiped at the corners of her mouth after every third bite of dinner. "What is it?" her mom said when she saw Annie staring. "Do I have a new wrinkle or something?" Her hand flew to her forehead, and Annie almost cried. It must've been the hormones.

She set an alarm for very early the following morning, though she didn't need it. She stayed awake all night, lying on her back, one hand to her abdomen. *We're getting out of here today*, she thought to herself and was surprised to note that she thought of herself as two now, her and the baby.

At four in the morning, she turned off her alarm clock and pulled her suitcase out from under her bed. It was heavier than she expected, and it took a lot of effort not to bang it against the walls as she carried it down the stairs. She circled the kitchen for a moment. She wanted to find the right place to leave the letter, somewhere mundane enough that it might not break their hearts quite as much, like taped to the milk jug in the fridge. In the end, she just put it in the middle of the table. And she called a taxi, murmuring her address into the phone, and left.

Her new roommates were surprised to see her there so early. She had to ring the doorbell three times before one of them let her in. The apartment was above a bakery, and the scent of muffins and cinnamon rolls made her stomach rumble. When the door opened, her gut growled so loudly, it sounded like an earthquake.

Her roommates were two girls who went to the nearby college. One of them stood before her now in an oversized T-shirt and a pair of long johns that sagged at the knees.

"I'm Annie," she apologized.

"Oh, hey," the girl said, rubbing at the side of her forehead. "Sophia. We weren't expecting you till later."

"Yeah," Annie said and could think of nothing more to add. *My parents don't know I'm gone, and I had to leave before they woke up* seemed a bit much for an introduction.

Sophia shrugged and opened the door. "Nobody's up yet, but you can hang out in your room, I guess." She led Annie through a queasy-green-colored kitchen and a cluttered living room to a small, square bedroom with a scuffed wood floor and a mattress on top of a metal bed frame. "Our old roommate left her bed behind. You can use it if you want," Sophia explained before stretching her arms overhead. "I'm going back to sleep. See you in a couple hours."

She closed the door behind her, and Annie was alone again. She opened her suitcase and organized her clothes into stacks on the floor. She thought about making pancakes for the others—maybe they'd like her if they woke up to the smell of maple syrup. But she wasn't sure if they had any

Bisquick or even where they kept the pans. So she curled up on the mattress and tried to fall asleep. *This is our home now*, she told herself as her face grew damp with tears.

After what felt like an entire day had passed, she heard high-pitched laughter and the groan of a coffee grinder coming from the kitchen. She shuffled in to see Sophia and the other roommate sitting at the table with mugs.

"Hey, I'm Eve," the roommate said. "You want a cup of coffee?"

She very much wanted to have one so she could seem older than she was. She pulled at the hem of her shirt. "Actually, well, I can't. I'm pregnant?" Annie had read about the restriction in a pregnancy book she'd found in the back corner of the library at home. She shoved the book back onto the shelf as soon as she heard someone else approaching but not before she realized that most fun and delicious things were off-limits for her now.

Sophia's eyes widened. Eve froze midsip.

"It's okay, though," Annie rushed to explain. "I'm giving it up for adoption, so it's not like the baby will be staying here or anything."

Sophia nodded. "You've got first and last month's rent, though, right?"

Eve put down her mug. "Oh, you poor thing. Did you run away from home? Here, come sit down."

At noon, she went to the movie theater down the block to get a job application. Sophia worked there and told Annie she'd vouch for her. Annie filled out the form in the lobby, using one of the big glass doors as a writing surface. When she handed the form back to the manager, he glanced at it and slipped it into a drawer. "Can you start tomorrow?" he said. No vouching necessary.

Triumphant, she marched back out into the day. Eve had let her use her computer to look up nearby adoption agencies, and she'd written the addresses down on a Post-it that she kept in her pocket. She needed to figure out what she was doing with this baby. Today.

She walked to the bus stop on the corner. She sat there for ten minutes, the cold from the metal bench seeping up into her hips, but when the bus trundled to a stop in front of her, she stood up and walked away.

She used the phone in the apartment's kitchen to call her mom.

"Annie! Oh, thank goodness. We've been worried sick. How could you do such a thing to us?" She continued on for a minute, maybe two, variations on the theme. Not once did she tell Annie to come home.

"I'm sorry, Mom. I had to. Should I call back tonight so I can talk to Dad, too?"

The silence hissed. "I think you'd better not," her mother said. "Your father is… Well, he's still getting used to it all. You understand."

Annie said she did.

Chapter Twelve

Friday, November 10, 2017

JESS WAS MAKING LUNCH. It was scallops from the freezer that John had sent her home with on their last trip together, and she wanted to be extra careful not to burn this batch. "Your tip," he'd said, tossing the bag into the bed of her truck. "For services rendered."

She'd reached into the truck and snatched it up, then thrown it onto the passenger's seat. "Don't think for a minute you're taking this outta my share of the revenues." She flexed her fingers, out and in. They still ached. It'd been a good trip, and she'd shucked all the way home while John handled the boat.

John laughed. "Wouldn't dream of it." He vaulted gracefully into his own truck and slammed the door. Leaning out the window, arm dangling down, he said, "Looks like it's gonna blow pretty hard next couple days. Plan on Thursday?"

"You got it," Jess said. She scrambled into her truck. It still wasn't really second nature. She knew her ass poked out awkwardly while she tried to arrange her arms in the right spots. John smiled a little and touched the brim of his baseball cap before driving away.

Hot oil leapt up from the pan, spattering her collarbone,

and she flinched. She grabbed a spatula and turned the scallops with a flick of her wrist. The cooked sides were golden brown and crusty. Perfect. She sighed.

She didn't know what she was going to do now that John was gone. All the other captains bitched and moaned night after night in the Break about how tough it was to find clean crewmembers, about the relapses at sea that turned the boat around, the day wasted. And still, they didn't trust her enough to hire her.

The way she saw it, she had two things working against her.

One was that though she was born and raised in Devil's Purse, she didn't come from a fishing family. Her father worked at a bank two towns over, and her mother was a second-grade teacher. She'd only started fishing when she was eighteen—her parents barely tolerant of the idea—and in this town, that was late. No matter how many years she'd been working (seventeen), the guys would always be a little worried that fishing was a whim she'd give up on midway through the season.

Two, of course, was that she was a woman. Not that women weren't involved in the fishing business; behind almost every fishing boat was a wife or a mother crunching the numbers and meeting with the tax accountant. Hell, they earned the right to have those boats named after them, *Donna* and *Cheryl* and *Elaine* painted in white, always in white, on the blue or red or green hulls. But it was rare for a grown woman's body and not just her name to be on a boat—and rarer still for her to be working for someone else. All the fisherwomen around these parts were captains and vessel owners running the businesses they'd inherited or bought with the income from other jobs.

Oh, the men were nice enough to her at the docks; it

wasn't like that. That was the problem, though. Whenever they saw her hauling an unruly mass of net or bags of scallops to or from John's boat, they hurried over to her, jamming their arms and hands under her own no matter how much she protested.

Jess liked working for John. Always had. When she graduated high school, he'd just gotten back from Alaska. He was flush with crabbing cash, but he'd lost his brother out there, and no one really knew what to say to him about it. That summer, she went down to the docks every morning when the air was still cool and misty, the scent of seaweed suspended in it. She went to see if anyone needed an extra man. The answer was always no, with a polite smile and a glance at her still-squeaky Xtratuf boots.

So she watched. She watched as they smiled at John and shouted boisterous greetings while he worked on his new boat, then muttered among themselves and stared at his back. They were worse than the moms at the school playground. There were rumors that John had been steering the boat and that he'd had too much to drink when his brother went over. That he'd rigged the gear wrong or that he'd ignored the captain's orders. Every one of the rumors was born on those docks, and he didn't say a word to refute them.

One morning, he brought a step stool and a small can of paint and began to put the finishing touches on the name. *Diane*. A risky move, naming your boat after a girlfriend who wasn't yet a wife—and one whom Devil's Purse hadn't seen hide nor hair of yet. The old men were having a field day that morning. None of them made a move as John struggled to balance the can in one hand, the brush in another, and steady himself against the hull at the same time.

Finally, Jess sighed and heaved herself up off the park bench she'd been sitting on. She walked down through the parking lot and onto the dock. By now, her knees no longer swayed when a strong wave pushed up on the underside of the pier. "Need a hand?" she said, nearly the same exact words she'd asked every other man there that morning. She held one out to him.

"Oh. Yeah, that'd be great. Thanks." John handed the can to her and dipped his brush in it. They worked like that for at least thirty minutes, her holding the can out and him leaning down periodically to refill his brush. Though the can was a little heavy, her arms did not shake. She hoped the others were watching.

He jumped down from the ladder and pulled a rag from his back pocket, started wiping his fingers without meeting her eye.

"Real sorry to hear about your brother, by the way," she said, watching the greasy fabric smear the paint further into his skin.

He looked up at her then. "Thank you." He squinted. "You're Jess, right?"

"That's me." Her stomach fluttered. Even in high school, he'd been a bit of a legend. Fishing since he was ten, running his dad's boat in the summer since he was fifteen. It was sort of like getting recognized by the star quarterback, only she didn't give a shit about football.

He looked her up and down. "You killing time watching us old farts work or something?"

She raised an eyebrow. Yeah, killing time in rubber over-alls and an old bait shop T-shirt. "Or something. Looking for work, actually. Crew."

He stared her straight in the face as if waiting for her to crack. When she didn't, he said, "That's interesting. I'm looking for help myself. And having a hard time of it, too, with all the gossip these guys are churning out." He jerked his thumb over her shoulder where a cluster of men were standing and, sure enough, staring outright at the two of them. "You interested?"

"Sure." She shrugged. "Why not."

"Cool. We start in a couple weeks, I think. Give me your number, and I'll call you."

"Cool," she echoed. She read out her digits, pausing after each one as he fumbled to figure out how to program them into his phone. And when she turned to cross the parking lot toward home, she bit her lip, hard, so that she wouldn't grin.

It took six months for him to talk about his brother. They were out at sea, and he'd just let the gear out to trawl the faraway bottom for scallops. They'd had a bad run of luck, days where the dredge came back full of rocks and starfish with only a scattering of scallops. Jess stood to one side of the boat, staring out at the horizon and sending a quick prayer to Saint Andrew.

"Should've listened to Simon," he said. Jess turned to him. He pushed his baseball cap up on his head and scratched his forehead with one grubby hand, squinting at the winch. "He always told me these grounds were all dried up and we'd have to get rich elsewhere."

"Like in Alaska?" she said.

"Yeah. Alaska was supposed to be it. But then he had to go and get himself killed." He stopped and stepped into the wheelhouse to check their bearings. He stayed that way, back to her, one hand on the wheel.

She edged closer and said, "What happened?" She had to shout over the grinding whirr of the engine.

"You probably heard he went down in a blaze of glory,

doing what he loved on some huge vessel, right?" he called over his shoulder. He shook his head. "Load of bullshit. It was a bar fight, plain and simple."

He turned, one arm still resting on the wheel. "We all went out drinking at the only bar in town, like we did most every night. His buddy started hitting on the wrong girl, got a local dude all pissed. You know how it goes."

Jess didn't, not really.

"Anyway, Simon tried to step in, calm things down. Guy brings a full beer bottle down on his head. Must've hit just the right spot, 'cause he went down. I ran over to help him back up, but it was too late. He was gone before he even hit the floor."

He stared back out the window. Jess realized she'd never seen him drink. When they went to the Break after a long day of fishing, he always ordered a water with lemon, waving off any teasing from the others. Which was odd, now that Jess thought about it, because there used to be stories about him outdrinking even the most weathered of old dudes at the Break. People used to say he kept Coronas in the pockets of his foul weather gear and would crack one every morning on deck while they steamed out to the fishing grounds, no matter what time it was. They used to say he had the beginnings of a problem growing there.

"But you let them believe he died fishing, making some huge mistake."

"And who's to say it wasn't a huge mistake?" he spat. "Besides, it's what he would've wanted. No one in this town thought he'd make a serious fisherman. Three years older than me and he still hadn't really tried. But now, they all think he died sacrificing himself to this job."

"The guy who killed him is still walking around out there in Alaska?"

He shrugged again. "Probably having a hard go of it. I saw his face when we were trying to bring Simon back. He ran out the door before anyone could call the cops. They've got one patrol car covering ten, twelve towns out there, so they probably wouldn't have caught him anyway. Di thinks I should press charges. She wants to go to law school, and to a hammer, everything looks like a nail, you know?" He laughed, and Jess smiled a little. "She thinks it'd give me closure. It's as closed as it's ever gonna get, though. He's gone, and I'm still here."

He nudged past her and threw the switch to haul the gear up. They held their breaths as the chain reeled in and the trawl inched into view until the chain-linked bag finally hung, dripping, over the deck.

It was heavy with scallops. They shone red-brown in the light, some of them still clapping open and shut like so many hungry mouths. It took Jess's breath away. Her best haul yet.

John bounced up and down on his toes. "Son of a bitch," he murmured. Then, "Suck on that, Simon!" he yelled to the sky with affection. He pounded Jess once, twice, between the shoulder blades, and they got to work.

The phone rang just as she was sliding the scallops onto her plate. She wedged the receiver between her ear and her shoulder and scanned her fridge for something to eat them with. Nothing but a weeks-old bag of spinach, the leaves gone dark and slimy.

"Jess? It's Larry. Larry Mayfield, attorney." He sounded harried.

"I know who you are, Larry. We were in the same class

at DP High." She closed the door on the spinach. She'd deal with that later.

"Right. Right." He paused. "Listen, it's about John Staybrook's will."

Her hand flew to her stomach. "But the Coast Guard's still looking for him," she said feebly, though she knew better than anyone they weren't going to find anything good.

"I know." He sighed heavily. "And it's highly unethical for me to tell you anything until he's been declared deceased. But my useless intern called John's wife up prematurely and divulged some things he shouldn't have. You hear that, Charlie?" he yelled, not bothering to cover the receiver. "If you weren't already unpaid, I would dock your check for this!"

She didn't laugh.

"In any event," he continued, "there are some details I should tell you about before his wife comes after you with a pitchfork."

"Okay," she said. On autopilot, she picked up her plate and sat down at the card table where she ate all her meals. It had been her mother's. She'd insisted Jess take it when they moved down to Florida.

Larry waited for more. When it was clear there was nothing coming, he started again. "Well. Okay. So. His boat. The *Diane* and, uh…"

"*Diane & Ella*."

"Right. That. He left it to you."

She swallowed, hard. "No, he didn't."

"I assure you, he did. Highly unusual in my practice," he mused as if it were a logic puzzle for him to solve. "Ordinarily, the boat goes to the widow."

It always went to the widow. She was to sell it and put the

proceeds toward their kids' college funds or toward getting the hell out of town. Fear rose in Jess's gullet.

"He came in a few months back asking to change it, though. Said you'd earned it, fair and square, working for him for so long. And also, he left the fishing permits to Diane."

Jess closed her eyes. Without a permit, the boat was useless, nothing more than a pleasure craft. She couldn't so much as cast for a single striped bass from its deck.

"That's everything, then," he said. "That's all I can tell you. And actually"—he lowered his voice—"I could get disbarred for even telling you that much, so keep it to yourself, would you?"

"Sure," she said, then, "Yup."

"Excellent. Much obliged," he said, suddenly chipper. "Just thought I'd give you a heads-up. I respect you and what you're doing, really. You know how Diane can be. I didn't want to see you get blindsided by it all. Have a great day now!"

Her hand fell to the table with the phone in it. She stared at it for a second. She forced herself to eat a scallop, but it had cooled to room temperature, and she couldn't taste anything.

She dropped her fork. "Dammit, John," she muttered.

For years and years, there'd been a sort of uneasy acceptance between Jess and Diane. Every December, the Staybrooks invited her to their Christmas party. "We've gotta include Jess," she imagined John telling his wife. "She doesn't have anybody else in town anymore." And every year, she went, because she didn't have anybody else. She hugged Diane hello (really, the only physical contact they ever had) and usually wound up in the playroom with Ella and Lacey, sitting on the floor in her only skirt while Ella constructed elaborate games and fairy tales for Lacey to act out. Without fail, Diane would appear in the doorway at some point in the night.

"Everything okay in here?" she would say. She held a wineglass in her hand, its rim clouded with lipstick.

"Yeahhh," Ella intoned while Lacey smiled up at Diane and nodded.

"Well. That's good." Diane lingered in the doorway for a few more seconds. Inevitably, this was when Jess looked down and realized she'd missed a spot when shaving her legs.

"I'll just be upstairs if you need me. Okay, Ella?" Diane said. Ella didn't respond, and Diane tapped her fingers on the doorway and turned to leave.

It was always that way between them, every time a wary kind of circling that left Jess wondering if she'd even been walking in the right direction. And always John in the middle, amiable John, trying to pull these two women closer together.

Even after his death, still trying. Diane could conceivably lease the permit to someone else in town and sever ties with Jess completely. But at one of those Christmas parties—toward the end, when she'd had a few glasses of wine—she had pulled Jess aside and murmured, "Thanks for helping John out with his taxes this year. I know I should be managing it, like all the other fishing wives, but I don't want anything to do with it, to be honest." She burped delicately.

Jess had stuttered. She wasn't sure what to do with this secret, which, after all, wasn't much of a secret; everyone in town had already discussed the fact that Diane hardly ever put in an appearance on the docks. She wasn't sure what

Diane wanted her to do with it. She forced a smile and said, "No problem. Happy to help."

No, Diane wouldn't want to get involved in the business of leasing or selling the permit to someone else. Jess jammed a few scallops in her mouth and tossed the rest in the trash. The simplest thing would be for her to lease it to the person who'd already been fishing it: Jess. Of course, the right thing to do would be to give the boat back to Diane. For just a moment, Jess tried to think of where she could get two hundred, three hundred grand to buy another one. Impossible. This might be her only chance.

So they were tied together, Diane with the permit and Jess with the boat. Somewhere, John was mighty pleased with himself. Jess chuckled at the thought, then sighed, and then, for the first time since she'd returned to shore the night before, she allowed herself to cry.

Diane was doing nothing in particular when the doorbell rang. There were so many things she should be doing, she knew. Calling the Coast Guard to make sure they knew how important it was to find her husband. Speaking to the principal at Ella's school to discuss how they were going to handle her sorrow. Getting in touch with her office to explain the cursory email she'd sent late last night saying she wouldn't be in this week. She was almost grateful for the doorbell, for the small, contained task it afforded her: open door, accept casserole, smile. Say something brief and profound about John and the kind of life he'd chosen.

When she opened the door, Jess was standing there, red-eyed and disheveled. And was it her imagination, or was the woman swaying a little bit on her feet?

"Diane," she said. "Can we talk?"

Diane glanced back, looking for evidence of the many other things she had to spend her time on today. There was nothing. She stepped back to let Jess in. Yes, she definitely stumbled a little as she walked toward the kitchen. When Jess pulled out one of the stools, its feet skidded across the floor. Diane winced.

"I just wanted to say again how sorry I am," Jess began. "He was such a good man, and I can't imagine—" She folded her arms and tucked her chin to her chest.

Diane realized she was still standing in the kitchen doorway, and she walked to the counter calmly, deliberately, giving herself a moment to rearrange her features. How dare this woman come into her home and spill her grief onto the kitchen floor? How dare she express herself so freely? How dare she lay claim to John in this way?

When Jess looked up, Diane had balled her hands into fists. "I got a call from Larry Mayfield," Jess said. That incompetent lawyer. "I was gonna wait for you to bring it up. But, well, I'm really sorry, Diane. John shouldn't have done that."

Diane walked over to the other side of the counter and steadied herself against it. Jess watched her like she was a shark. "Sorry?" Diane said. "Why are you sorry? You got what you wanted, didn't you?" She immediately regretted it. The words felt hot and unruly as they left her mouth.

Jess bowed her head again. Her short, cropped hair fell over her forehead.

Anger gripped Diane by the shoulders anew. Jess's relationship with John was always so uncomplicated. He asked her to do things, and she did them, and then John would admire her work ethic, her drive. And all the while, Diane was onshore, sitting at her computer or making meatballs with macaroni just the way their daughter liked, wondering when John would be coming home that night. Wondering how many hours of shitty TV reruns she'd have to watch until the door opened and she could finally fall asleep.

It was all so lucky for Jess. Once again, it crossed Diane's mind that it wasn't a mistake. Perhaps John had been on that boat with Jess, and she'd—what? Pushed him over? It seemed absurd, but Ella was right. Going out on your own in a tuna boat was a reckless thing to do. Her husband was not a reckless man.

She went on. "Must be nice for you, having a business fall in your lap like this. Must've been waiting for that, all those years of working away for him." She knew that was why Jess had come: to talk about the permit. She stepped the heel of one foot onto the toes of the other and ground down until the pain shot up her leg, clean and gratifying. "But if you think I'm going to lease you that permit to go with it, you're sorely mistaken."

Jess finally met her eye. "I understand," Jess said.

Diane wanted to scream. She shouldn't understand. She should fight back and yell and throw their nice pepper grinder at the wall.

Instead, Jess stood up and said, "Let me know if there's anything I can do to help." And she walked out the door.

Diane watched her from the kitchen window as she headed down the sidewalk, her hands tucked up into her sweatshirt sleeves. Diane noticed for the first time that there were slippers on Jess's feet.

She reached for her phone and pulled up Maureen's number. She needed someone to tell her that her anger was justified and she'd done the right thing. Maureen was good at that. She let Diane say even what was unspeakable and convinced her that there was at least one person who understood. She was on Diane's side. By the end of their conversations, Diane was always laughing.

The phone rang only once before Diane came to her senses and hung up. She couldn't lean on Maureen. Not now. Not ever. Diane had burned that bridge—and with good reason, she told herself.

If John were here, he would touch her shoulder in that way he had whenever she said something he knew she'd regret, too bitter or mean. Sometimes, she hated it and would walk away to do the dishes or check her email, playing the conversation over and over in her head, imagining all the ways it could have gone differently. But sometimes, she turned into his arms, and he'd rest his chin on her head and say, "It's okay. You just care so much you get carried away sometimes." And she would nod into his chest, yes, yes, wanting so badly to believe him.

That wasn't right, though. She'd crossed a line with Jess, and he would've wiped his mouth and left the room without looking at her. This was Jess, after all. He reminded her year after year that Jess was family and deserved to be invited to parties and dinners on top of the hours the woman already spent with John every day.

"Remember," he'd said to her the year before, "you have her to thank for every night I come home safe."

Diane had looked up from the Christmas card list she'd been annotating. "Don't I know it," she said flatly. He shrugged and continued on to the living room, knocking his fist against the lintel as he went. There was a graying spot in the paint where his hand always hit that no amount of scrubbing would remove.

He would never forgive her for this.

Chapter Thirteen

LACEY CHECKED THE CLOCK on her mom's van for the twelfth time. Ella got out of school in two hours. It was thirty minutes to the clinic, thirty minutes back. Kind of like a math problem. *Exactly how screwed is Lacey?*

"You take your Suboxone this morning?" Maureen asked, even though Lacey knew she'd been watching from the dining room table when she did.

"Yup." Those individually wrapped orange strips that she had to stick inside her cheek every morning coated her tongue with a cough-syrupy taste. It was supposed to curb her cravings by binding to the same receptors in her brain that were built just for the pills. Maureen stored them in a drawer in the kitchen, next to a tin of Altoids. Her mom had read peppermint helped fight the flavor, so when the Suboxone was all dissolved, Lacey followed it, dutifully, with a mint chaser. It made her mouth ache.

"Is that all working for you?" Maureen motioned vaguely at the windshield.

"Sure. I guess." Lacey leaned toward the window and closed her eyes. Lately, she'd been waking up in the middle of the night. She'd been dreaming of pills, of a flame under foil.

"Great! Maybe you could talk to Ms. Bray about lowering your dose?"

"Yeah, maybe." She wanted to say more and make Maureen laugh the way she once would've. The beetle told her she had to. But after the morning with Ella, she didn't have the energy.

Lacey had just dozed off when they got to the clinic. "We're here," Maureen said, one uncertain hand on her shoulder. "I'll be waiting for you when you get out," she said while Lacey squinted out at the sky.

"Okay. Thanks, Mom," she said.

When the D.A.R.E. program came to her sixth grade classroom, a wave of snickers passed around her as the cop stood at the front of the room with his arms crossed and started talking about good decision-making. It was Officer MacArthur, and everyone knew he had just been busted for public urination in the next town over. The boys in the back of the class made a *psst* noise meant to approximate the sound of pee hitting the side of the building. Officer MacArthur reddened and ran his forefinger and thumb over his mustache.

He decided to pull out the big guns. He reached into the cardboard box behind him and, one by one, laid baggie after baggie on the table in precise, right-angled lines. When he was finished, he pressed his fists into the table and glared out at the class.

"These were all confiscated in drug busts this year. I want you to know what to look out for and avoid"—he narrowed his stare at the back row—"now that you're in middle school. Come on. Get a closer look."

Chairs squealed across linoleum as everyone wandered to the table. They watched, awestruck, as Officer MacArthur pointed one meaty finger at each bag and identified it. Cocaine. Oxy. Heroin. Meth. When he pointed to a bag of blunts, one boy crowed, "Hey, Skinner, you know what those are!" This time, all Officer MacArthur had to do was glance up, and the giggles ground to a halt.

Dread burned quietly in Lacey's stomach. She had heard about drugs before, of course; she'd taken fervent notes during the D.A.R.E. classes in the two prior years. When her mom came home from a parent presentation at the beginning of the school year, she sat Lacey down and solemnly asked her to promise that, if she needed a ride home from a party, she would call her. "I won't ask any questions, I swear," Maureen had said. "I just want you to be safe. And not get a DUI."

Lacey stared at her, bewildered. She wouldn't even have a learners' permit for another four years.

This was the first time she'd actually seen drugs herself, in person. Her fingers twitched, and she crossed her arms tightly, jamming her hands between her ribs and her biceps as if they might otherwise reach out and grab something. The beetle's wings clicked. They looked so innocent and boring, the white powders and pills.

Officer MacArthur scanned the crowd of transfixed twelve-year-olds and cleared his throat uneasily. "Well, you get the point," he said and started gathering the baggies up again. "That's enough for today."

She saw the substances only a handful of times after that. There were Solo cups and dubious bowls of punch at every house party, of course, and she drank it wincingly once or twice, but for the most part, she clutched her water bottle and tried to ignore the beetle telling her everybody thought she was a loser. Other than that, there was a pack of kids who hung out at the end of the school driveway every day, just outside the school property line. "Druggies," her friend Amanda would mutter as they passed, coughing delicately at the cloud of pot smoke. Not once did the kids even acknowledge their presence, much less leap out into their path and offer them free smokes, as Officer MacArthur had implied they would.

Her senior spring, she was up at bat during softball practice. She relished her turns at bat and the way the rubber grip felt between her palms, how it turned her hands raw and red after a particularly long session. She liked to imagine the ball as the beetle, and when she got a clean hit to the sweet spot, it went soaring high and away, and she felt so clear.

This time, though, when she twisted with the bat and grinned as the ball flew toward the woods, she heard a small and quiet *pop*. And her knee seemed to forget how to hold up her body. She laughed along with her teammates and pushed herself back up from the dirt, but the minute she tried to take a step, she fell again.

Coach Johnson was there in an instant. "You okay, Carson?" The whistle around her neck dangled in Lacey's face.

"It's my knee," Lacey said, cradling the kneecap between her hands.

"Shit." Coach Johnson stood. "Can one of you girls call her mom?"

The doctor said she'd torn her ACL. By that time, her knee had swollen to the size of a grapefruit. "I'm recommending a couple days of Percocet for the pain and six weeks of physical therapy," he said, pointing to the X-ray.

"Um," Lacey said. "Sorry. Is there any way I could do something other than Percocet?"

The doctor glanced between her and her mom.

"It's just, you hear all these stories," she faltered. The beetle took that as its cue and started rattling off all the things that could go wrong and probably would one day. Lacey pushed her fingers into her closed eyes and wished for the bat.

The doctor shrugged. "Suit yourself. You can try something over-the-counter, but you should let us know if that's not working for you. These things can be pretty painful. Don't suffer in silence, okay?"

A week later, she was suffering all right. But it wasn't entirely her knee's fault. She sat on the couch in Amanda's basement, her crutches propped up against the coffee table. She was wedged between Amanda and her other best friend, Chloe. Their boyfriends, Derek and Mike, bookended the couch. There was some sort of superhero movie on TV. Though the volume was cranked all the way up, the crashing cars and tumbling buildings did little to drown out the sucking of Amanda's and Derek's mouths and Chloe's laughter as Mike reached one arm over her shoulders and whispered something in her ear.

Amanda's elbow jabbed into her arm like Lacey wasn't even there, and Lacey bit back tears. What had happened to the days when they would share bags of gummy bears and potato chips and walk to the playground after midnight? In a few short months, they'd be off to different colleges and might never hang out anymore. Even after everything they'd been through together. The people who loved her by choice and not because they had to, gone. Hell, they were gone already. The beetle told her so. She suddenly felt impossibly old.

The crutches didn't help. She stood gingerly, finding places to push off against the couch that weren't already occupied by various limbs and hands. She picked up the crutches and stuck them in her armpits where they dug into the bruises that had bloomed there over the past week. She turned to say she was going to get a soda, but nobody looked up.

By the time she'd climbed the stairs, putting more weight on the bannister than it was ever intended to bear, she was out of breath and her knee was twinging. The Advil she'd taken that morning had worn off. Soda excuse forgotten, she collapsed into the living room couch. Spikes of pain drove their way up her thigh. She was about to prop her foot on a side table when Amanda's mom appeared.

"Lacey!" she said. "How's it going down there? Does my daughter still have all her clothes on?" She cackled and sat down in an armchair.

Lacey felt her cheeks warm, and she lowered her foot back down and slid forward to the edge of the cushion.

"Hi, Mrs. Warner," she said. "I was just going to grab a drink."

"Oh, no, sit, honey. And please, for the millionth time, it's Nicole." Mrs. Warner stood, grunting, and walked toward the kitchen. "You getting excited for graduation? I hear you got into Brown, Miss Smarty-Pants."

Lacey picked at a hangnail until it stung. "Yeah, thanks. Not sure how I snuck under their radar." She wanted it to sound casual and jokey, but it came out pathetic.

"Don't be silly," Mrs. Warner said, handing her a can of Coke.

Lacey hated Coke, but the can was a relief, cool against her sweaty palms.

"With your grades, I'm sure they couldn't send the acceptance fast enough."

Lacey pressed the can to her knee and held back a wince. Ice packs worked better, but this would do.

Mrs. Warner glanced down at it and frowned. "How's that injury doing? ACL, right?"

"Right." She took the can away. "It hurts," she said, too tired to lie. "Four weeks of PT left. Hopefully I'll be able to walk without crutches soon."

Mrs. Warner tapped her chin, a pantomime of thought. "I might have something that could help you with that." She reached for the overstuffed pocketbook on the table behind her, her sweater lifting to reveal a band of flesh. "Yup, here we go. Strong stuff right here." She shook a prescription bottle and handed it over.

Lacey eyed the pills.

"Don't worry. It's perfectly safe," Mrs. Warner said. "Brian got them for his wisdom tooth removal, and I took them from him so he wouldn't try to sell 'em. But I know I can trust you. Just don't take them all at once." She cackled again.

Lacey held the bottle between her fingertips. She thought of Officer MacArthur and of her mother's face, more serious than she'd ever seen it. Downstairs, Amanda and Chloe shrieked with laughter. She didn't need the beetle to tell her they hadn't noticed she was gone. She shifted in her seat just a little, and it was like someone had taken her leg above and below her knee and wrung it out.

Fuck it. She wrenched the bottle open, shook a single pill into her palm, and flung it into her mouth.

"You can keep the whole bottle," Mrs. Warner said. She stood and dropped her pocketbook back on the table. "Have fun down there." She grinned and walked toward the kitchen, tapping Lacey's shoulder as she passed.

Lacey did her best not to shrink away.

She walked down to the basement, hoisting herself against the bannister again, and sat in the exact same spot as before.

"Hey, why didn't you tell me you were getting that? I'm so fuckin' thirsty," Derek said, grinning mischievously at Amanda, who giggled and buried her head in his neck.

"Oh. Sorry." Lacey pulled the Coke can out of her sweat-shirt pocket, where it'd been poking out. She'd completely forgotten about it. "Here." She handed it to Derek.

"Thanks. You're the best." He cracked the can and gulped it down, his Adam's apple sliding up and down beneath the raw, stubbled skin of his throat.

Lacey looked away and heaved her foot up onto the coffee table.

Within an hour, the superhero on the TV had saved the world and her knee no longer hurt. She felt she could get up and dance on it when she realized the beetle was silent. In fact, when she prodded at the back of her mind, she realized it was gone. She no longer cared what the others thought or did or what they thought of her. It no longer mattered to her that Amanda and Chloe were being assholes, that she hadn't started studying for finals yet, or that who-knows-what chemicals were being pumped through her body that very minute. It wasn't like she always thought it would be: a sharp hit to her system and she was somebody else. Her body slipped into it easily, naturally, like this was how she was always supposed to be. She felt curiously warm and safer than she'd ever been. She felt gloriously, sparklingly fine.

Later that night, after Chloe had dropped her back home, she had looked it up online and learned the drug she had taken was specifically built to match up with a receptor in her brain and cook up euphoria. The website was written in an ominous tone, but for once in her life, Lacey was not afraid. She saw it so clearly. This was the puzzle piece she'd been missing. This was the manhole cover she could slide neatly into place and keep the beetle out forever.

A few weeks later, she left class to go to the bathroom and instead found herself shoving through the big doors to the back of the building. She leaned against the sun-warmed brick and closed her eyes, pulling in the cool, clean air. Seagulls wheeled and screeched overhead.

Her knee was throbbing. She'd gone without her pill that morning to show herself she could. She'd tucked the bottle into her backpack, just in case.

She pulled the bottle from her pocket and unscrewed the lid. She could see the bottom of the bottle now—only a few pills left. Her hands rattled like she was starving. She tried not to worry about it, shaking one out into her palm.

"You know you're doing that wrong." The voice came from her right, in the shadow cast by a basketball hoop.

She swallowed hard around the pill, a dry lump in her throat, and shoved the bottle back into her pocket, coughing. "Doing what—I mean—what?" It was impossible to tell who it was or what he'd seen until he finally stepped into the light.

Matt Duvry. He held a cigarette pinched between his thumb and his middle finger, casually, as though it'd always been there. Lacey knew better. She remembered digging holes on the beach with him when they were kids, the sand achingly cold beneath their fingers. When they were in fifth grade, their teacher had set up big sheets of paper around the room, each one labeled with a classmate's name, and told them all to go around and write a compliment for each person. "I like your laugh," he had written on Lacey's in his small, distinctive handwriting. For weeks afterward, she would study each giggle, muffling it in the dip of her palm until it no longer sounded like her own.

"You're supposed to smoke it," he said. His light-blond hair fell over his forehead as he nodded at the bottle that wasn't there anymore. "That'll give you a better high. Or you could shoot it up if you're really hardcore." One side of his mouth hitched up a little.

"I'm not. It's not. No." Lacey frowned, frustrated, and focused on stringing a sentence together. Stupid Matt. Since when did he leave her tongue-tied? And who did he think he was? Hadn't he heard about her injury? "They're for my knee," she managed and pointed at the offending joint. She'd been holding it out at an unwieldy angle to avoid putting any weight on it.

"Suit yourself." He shrugged and flicked his cigarette away.

Was he trying to look cool? It was hard to tell, but she held her breath as he walked back to the building.

If her life had been a movie, he would've met her eye every time she and Amanda walked by after that. He would've smiled slightly from over his friends' shoulders, and she would look away quickly, a little thrilled and a little terrified by what she'd seen there. Maybe she would've tossed her hair over her shoulder, and Amanda would've asked her what she was grinning about. Maybe he would've called her by a nickname, like "Hardcore" or "Knee," something unoriginal and exciting.

But what really happened was Matt more or less went back to ignoring her. He was busy with his buddies when she walked by after school.

"Come on. Hurry up. I want to finish my homework before Derek comes over," Amanda whined, and Lacey ducked her head down until they reached Amanda's car.

What really happened was she ran out of pills.

And she was fine, she was. But by the following morning, she could barely hear her mom's coffee-fueled chatter over the buzzing in her bones. In her English class, she stared down at a question about *Macbeth* on the AP practice exam until the letters swirled together. She asked to go to the bathroom, where she locked the door behind her and vomited in the toilet until her face was covered in clammy sweat. By the time she got home, every part of her ached. And the beetle was back and bigger than before.

She dropped her backpack at the base of the stairs. "Mom, I forgot one of my books in my locker. I'm gonna go get it."

"Okay, sweetie," her mom called from the dining room. "Want me to drive you? I don't want you to mess up your knee again. It's doing so well." Her voice grew closer as she walked toward Lacey.

"No, it's fine." Lacey spun back toward the door. "It's a short walk, and I need the fresh air." Her chest twinged with the lie, but she could barely feel it over everything else.

As she expected, Matt and his friends were still in their spot near the school. The others were sprawled out over boulders and laughing noisily. He was perched on a log, scowling as he scrolled through his phone. He didn't look up when she stood over him.

"Hi, Matt," she whispered. She kicked the log next to his leg, dislodging chunks of bark. "Hey," she said again, louder.

He glanced up, then scrambled to his feet in a way that almost made her smile. "Oh, hi, Lacey." He put his phone away.

She braced herself for the taunts from his friends, asking what he was doing talking to the nerd, but they were largely oblivious.

"Um, listen," she said, her gaze sliding away from him. "Do you have any…any painkillers?"

He didn't pretend not to know what she was talking about, and she was grateful for that. He peered into her face. "Are you sure about this?"

"Please," she whispered. As if on cue, her arms began to shake a little bit.

He reached out to grab her shoulder. The bald intimacy of it made her shake harder. "Hey, hey, okay," he said. "Follow me."

And she did.

It happened quickly after that. He taught her how to break the pills into chunks on the center console of his car, cradle the chunks with small pieces of foil, and brush the flame of a lighter under it. He kept a stash of McDonald's straws in his car to inhale the smoke. She hesitated, and he touched her back lightly, gently. "It'll help you feel better," he said.

He was right. After the initial coughing pain, the medicine swept through her brain and cleared it out, filling the holes like it always did, but in seconds, not hours, and her muscles finally unclenched and her bones felt whole again and her head fell back against the headrest.

She knew, vaguely, that there were places she could get the pills for herself. She heard rumors over the years about this parent or that senior-year dropout. But she was afraid to do it alone, afraid of the swiftness with which it took her. This was no slow slide. This was a quicker mercy. So the next morning, she woke before her alarm and left a note for her mom on the kitchen table saying she had to go work on a group project. And she walked to school and waited for Matt. This time, she slipped a couple of curled-up bills she still had left from her babysitting across the center console. He pocketed them without a word.

She spent the rest of the day drifting above it all. At lunchtime, when she saw Derek and Mike sitting with

Amanda and Chloe, she kept walking, straight through the doors and outside. She ate on the curb of the parking lot with her plastic tray balanced on her knees and fingers of sunlight combing through her hair. When she and Amanda walked by Matt's group on their way to Amanda's car, Lacey stopped and told Amanda she'd see her later.

"Wait, what?" Amanda said to her back. "What are you doing with them? The fuck?"

It had been a few hours, and the beetle was starting to break through. Lacey quickened her steps.

He was waiting for her this time, spinning the tie of his hoodie between his fingers.

On the fifth day, after he'd taken the money but before he'd brought out the pills, she leaned over and kissed him. It was a quick, dry kiss, almost in passing. She wasn't even sure why she'd done it. The beetle, which had been silent for days, woke up as Matt's eyes widened.

But then he smiled. "Let's try that again," he said and took her face in his hands, and they did.

She spent as much time with him as she could. Even when he was with his friends, she was there, too, high or not. Unlike Chloe and Amanda, they never asked her questions she couldn't answer that made the beetle's legs twitch. They just let her be. They might've even thought of her as one of their own. At the senior bonfire, they cheered when she found them lounging at the outskirts of the party. One of them, Nick, lent her his jacket when she shivered. His whole head blushed when she thanked him. She tried not to stare at the ugly, knobby sores in the soft creases of his elbows that showed when he pulled the jacket off. He hurried to roll down the sleeves of his T-shirt. He shot heroin sometimes. *No needles*, she thought to herself. *Never needles.*

Her mom took her prom dress shopping at the local thrift

store. "Diane told me there are deals here you wouldn't believe," Maureen said as she held the store door open for her. "Girls buy the most beautiful dresses and wear them once, then sell them for college spending money."

Lacey nodded. Her mom's face fell. She was starting to worry, Lacey could tell. Lacey had been losing weight, and it was getting too warm to hide it under baggy clothes. She tried to start conversations over dinner and breakfast, scrambling for warm, innocuous topics to assure her mom that everything was fine. But her mind was empty, a hollow *whoosh*.

Her mom pulled her over to the dresses and began pulling length after length of jewel-toned fabric from the racks. Her smile was so hopeful that Lacey's chest hurt, and all she could do was smile in return. This was where her mom belonged: in colors and laughter.

The dressing room was dusty and empty. The harsh yellow light hurt Lacey's head. The first dress she tried on was a red halter top in shiny, garish fabric. It bagged around her hips and breasts, but her mom's eyes lit up when she walked out in it.

"Oh, I can't believe you're trying on prom dresses. It seems like yesterday I was elbow-deep in poopy diapers."

Lacey mustered an eye roll.

Her mom stepped toward the mirror with her and laid one hand on the triangle of her shoulder blade. "Lacey," she said, and Lacey felt herself squirm. "Are you okay? You seem so sad lately. Do you want to see a doctor or something?"

Lacey took a half step away and adjusted the strap of her dress. "I'm fine. I've been thinking about getting a job, actually. At Dunkin Donuts. Just to distract me from the stress of college starting soon, you know?" She met her mom's eye in the mirror. She needed more money and an excuse to get out of the house, especially once she graduated and summer started. A few months ago, the beetle would've screeched at her ingratitude for lying to the one person who always loved her. Now, the beetle was silent. The pills kept it muffled. Lacey raised her chin.

"I'm so proud of you," her mom whispered, and Lacey felt it like a punch.

They ended up picking a deep-green, glitter-dusted number that ended at her knees. "It looks so lovely with your skin tone," her mom said.

Before the pills, Lacey would've followed up with something like "Yeah, it's hard to find colors that go well with a shade shy of marshmallow," but now, she just nodded.

She had to admit her mom was right, though, as she studied herself in the rearview mirror of the limo Chloe had rented. The color made her alive. Chloe and Amanda pulled their boyfriends to the dance floor as soon as they got to the gym. Lacey poured herself a cup of punch from a table half-assedly decorated with purple streamers and sat at their assigned dinner table.

It took a half hour for him to appear in the doorway and nod at her. By then, Chloe and Amanda were sitting down with her and gossiping about who would be prom queen. When Lacey stood, Chloe followed her gaze toward Matt and sighed loudly.

"Seriously?" Amanda said. "Why are you even with that guy?" She heard their voices dip into a whisper as she walked away, but she didn't care. This time, she really didn't.

As soon as they'd closed the car doors, the words slipped out of her. "I think I bombed the AP exams."

He raised his eyebrows. He'd raked the hair off his forehead with some hair gel, even though they both knew they weren't going to be doing any dancing. It was cute. "Really?" he said.

She nodded down into her lap. The exams had all been held the week before, day after day of bubble sheets. She wound up staring at the test booklets for too long. When she finally opened them, instead of formulas and explanations slotting neatly into place, she found nothing at all. She could barely bring herself to pick up the pencil and guess the answers.

"It doesn't matter, anyway," she said. "Not like they can stop me from graduating just because I got all ones."

He brushed his knuckles over his mouth. "Come here," he said, holding his arms open. She climbed over his lap, a stitch in her dress snapping as she angled her legs to avoid the steering wheel. Perched on top of him, her head grazed the car roof, and she wished she were so much smaller.

"I'm sure you did fine," he said into her collarbone. "You're so smart, Lace. It's one of the things I love about you."

She turned her face toward the window and rested her cheek on the top of his head. Felt the stiffened locks of hair scratch against her chin and tucked the words into a pocket of her memory for later, when she would surely need them.

They stayed like that for what felt like hours with the stereo on low while a weak rain began to fall. Amanda and Chloe would be furious when they came out—the drizzle would ruin their hair and their shoes. Maybe, if she were lucky, it would make them forget she'd disappeared.

An old song came on the radio for '90s week. In it, the singer kept listing off all the things she'd gotten wrong about the man she loved. It was maybe the saddest song Lacey had ever heard. She reached over to the stereo and flicked it off during the second chorus before tumbling back into the passenger's seat. "All right," she said, gathering her hair into a ponytail at the nape of her neck. "You got it?"

One day that summer, when they met in the beach parking lot, all the color had leached out of Matt's face. For a second, she wondered if he'd started without her. But when he turned to face her, his eyes were bloodshot. He'd been crying.

"Nick died," he said before she could ask.

Everything felt too hot and bright, the pavement radiating through her thin rubber flip-flops, the sunlight bouncing off the cars around them and right onto her face.

"They found him in his room," Matt continued. "His mom found him. This morning."

Lacey crouched down. Her bad knee sang with it. He sat down next to her, straight on the asphalt. The heat became too much to bear, and then they sat a few minutes more. Penance. He dropped his head into his hands.

"We have to quit," he said to the ground. And then, finally, he looked at her. "It's too much. We have to."

She nodded, yes. Of course they did. Of course they would. Even though she could already hear the beetle skittering back. It was too much.

It only took one day for it to get bad. Really bad, much worse than the first time she ran out of pills. As soon as she got back from the beach, she told her mom she wasn't feeling well and went up to her room. She knew it'd be better if whatever was coming happened behind the closed door of her bedroom. Her mom came in and out with Gatorade and cool compresses. Lacey tried to smile at her each time, but the truth was, she wasn't sure when her mom was actually there and when she was just imagining it.

Dawn took forever to come the next morning, breaking through the knots of pain massed at the end of her every nerve. She stumbled into the bathroom. She lay on the floor and silently begged the tiles to be colder, colder. She wanted nothing more than to get out of her skin, to get the hell out of it, and "You did this to yourself," the beetle sneered. She thought she might be sobbing. She couldn't tell.

Her mom opened the door. Whatever she saw made her sink to her knees. She laid her palm on Lacey's forehead and flinched.

"Have you been puking?" her mom said. She glanced into the toilet. Then, before Lacey could answer, "That's it. I'm calling the doctor."

No. No no no no. No doctor. He would know. He would know everything. "Go away," Lacey growled, not knowing if she meant it for her mom or for the things churning through her body. She didn't think it mattered much.

Maureen sat back on her heels and pursed her lips. The beetle screamed at Lacey to look at the hurt she'd put into her mom's eyes. "Fine," Maureen said, "but only so I can call the hospital."

Lacey stared at the grout edging the base of the tub. It was gray with dirt and dust. She knew what she had to do.

She pulled herself to standing and staggered to her bedroom window. The garage roof formed a ledge under it—she used to climb out onto it at night sometimes for the sheer terror of imagining what her mom would do if she found her there. From there, it was only a drop of six feet or so to the ground. She launched herself out the window and rolled. The gutter was a brief wet squelch of old leaves against her back before she fell. The ground was harder than she expected. Her knee wailed. "Good for nothing, good for nothing, good for nothing," the beetle said. She paused for a second to see if her mom had heard the fall. No signs of life from the house. Her mom must still be on the phone with the doctor.

Matt's house was a few blocks away, but it might've been miles. She made it to the nearest corner before it all brought her down. The sun was heavy on her head. She pulled her phone out of her pocket and texted Matt and told him where she was. Help.

By the time she saw him coming, gray-skinned and dripping with sweat, she was curled on her side on the edge of someone's lawn. She panted unevenly and squeezed her knee. She hoped no one would walk by and see her there, but mostly, she didn't care. She needed this to end. Her skin felt stretched beyond all capacity. The grass itched and scraped against her cheek. Matt bent down close, and she could breathe again.

"What happened? Are you okay?" he said.

"Not…really."

He pulled her to her feet with a heave and held her by the elbow as she steadied herself. His eyes were bloodshot, and his hands twitched. He reached his arms out, and she buried her face in his neck. They felt each other shake.

"Please," she wanted to whisper, like she did that first time.

She didn't have to.

"Fuck this," he murmured as her knees buckled again. He hoisted her up against his shoulder, and they told each other they would try again. Later. When they were ready for it.

―――――――――――――

The sliding doors of the clinic sucked shut behind Lacey, sealing her in with the sickly scent of industrial cleaner. The bulletin board in the front hall was labelled "Client Success Stories"—they were called clients, not patients. As if that was supposed to empower them. As if that were the issue. The same exact postcards had been tacked to the cork since her first day here. They hadn't added a single one.

They had, however, changed the poster by the check-in window. It used to have a girl with a toothy smile and a high ponytail, with "HOPE" written above her face in big yellow letters and "is my drug of choice" written below it. One day, during free time, when the receptionist was on her bathroom break, she and Tammy Grey had snuck over to the poster with a thick Sharpie. And Tammy, with her dark, empty eyes, had laughed as she'd crossed out "HOPE" and replaced it with "METH."

Tammy'd only lasted a couple of weeks before her insurance wouldn't pay anymore. Lacey heard a rumor that she'd relapsed and died. Now, there was a photo of a nondescript field hanging where the poster once was. The receptionist didn't look up when she signed in and slid her driver's license through the slot in the window, and Lacey wondered if she somehow knew what she and Tammy had done. A vandal as well as an addict.

Lacey smiled brightly at the top of the receptionist's head. The door next to the window buzzed as the woman pressed a button to unlock it. Lacey straightened her shoulders and opened it.

The halls were lined with construction paper posters covered with pictures and letters cut out of magazines. Visioning exercises. They'd done them in group once. Lacey's had a picture of a man who looked just like Matt, only more filled out and a few years older. Already, though, this was a new batch. She didn't know where they'd put the ones her group made. Probably threw them out.

At this time of day, everyone would be in group. Lacey's footsteps echoed down the hallway. The first day she came here, it felt like going to a new school. She held a sheet of paper with a schedule packed with group sessions and individual sessions, each meal typed out: blueberry pancakes, chicken nuggets, taco night. The schedule soothed her.

That was before she found out that "groups" meant sitting in a circle with a bunch of other scraggly teenagers who didn't want to say much of anything, and "individuals" meant sitting in Mr. Cole's office while he stared tiredly at her and sighed, waiting for her to talk. One day, after her fifth shrug, he'd tossed his pen onto his desk and said, "You're lucky to be here in a nice, clean facility like this. Lucky your insurance covers what it does."

She'd picked at the sleeve of her sweatshirt while her cheeks burned. How many times had she heard about how lucky she was? Usually, it was after people learned she'd been adopted. They raised their eyebrows and smiled at Maureen, who was always just out of earshot for these conversations. They all loved Maureen. "Well, lucky you!" they said. She wondered what alternatives they were picturing for her. An orphanage? A life ferried from one foster home to another? They'd all heard the stories. The beetle always added the afterthought, "Ungrateful. Undeserving. Too much to lose."

Eventually, the clinic had transferred her to Ms. Bray, who didn't mind doing most of the talking. She came to the door marked "Ms. Bray" and knocked.

"Come on in, Lacey-Girl," Ms. Bray sang. She had nicknames for all the clients, "Sweetheart" and "Bud" and "Bruiser," like she worked at a day care and not a rehab. All the other kids made fun of her behind her back, but Lacey kind of liked it. She was the only one whose nickname actually included her real name, and it made her feel sort of special.

She sat in the chair while Ms. Bray spun around from the computer and pushed her glasses up onto her forehead. She had the beginnings of wrinkles around her eyes that deepened when she smiled, like she did now as she nudged a chocolate cruller on a paper plate toward Lacey. The other thing Ms. Bray was known for was asking each of her clients what their favorite snack was and then having one on hand for every outpatient session. "I'm not saying I'm bribing you to come back to your next appointment," she said the first time she had a doughnut ready for Lacey, "but I'm kind of doing that."

Lacey breathed in the smell of cocoa and sugar as she bit into the cruller. Its coat of icing crackled under her teeth. It wasn't quite as good as her mom's homemade jelly-filled, but then, nothing would be.

"So. How are we doing this week?" Ms. Bray finally asked.

"All right."

Ms. Bray tilted her head to one side. Her bangs broke free from her glasses. "Having trouble sleeping?"

Lacey knotted her fingers together and hitched one shoulder up. It wasn't quite a shrug, she told herself. She took another bite of the doughnut so she wouldn't have to answer out loud.

"I figured you would." Ms. Bray leaned forward, elbows on her knees. "It's called post-acute withdrawal syndrome. PAWS, they say. Like on a dog. Cute, right?" She raised an eyebrow to let Lacey in on the joke.

"PAWS," Lacey repeated, because she knew Ms. Bray was waiting for it.

"It's a real bitch for a while, let me tell you. Think you're all recovered and then the cravings come back, even worse than before, like that." She snapped her fingers. "Happens in ninety percent of opiate addiction cases. As long as you don't start using again, you should make it out the other side just fine, okay?"

Lacey nodded, though it was unclear how she was supposed to get to the other side of this sucking black pool. Her hands twitched.

A knock came at the door, and one of the other counselors poked his head around it. "Hey, Patty," he said over Lacey's head. "We're heading out to grab some pizza. You want anything?"

"Uh, no," Ms. Bray said. The irritation was plain on her face. "All set."

The counselor nodded at Lacey and was gone.

"Sorry about that," Ms. Bray said. "Usually, we don't interrupt each other's sessions, but, you know. Pizza." She widened her eyes, and Lacey smirked. Ms. Bray propped her chin on one hand. "How's things with your mom?"

"The same," Lacey said, biting at a hangnail. "She doesn't really trust me anymore. Keeps her wallet locked up. Not that I blame her."

It was embarrassing—her biggest problem was a mom who worried too much. At mealtimes when she was a resident, the kids at her table would crumple paper napkins in their fists and talk about parents who shot up right alongside them. Lacey was the only one who had someone there at every visiting hour. She knew the others noticed; they watched her carefully in group.

At their first family session with Ms. Bray, her mom sat in the folding chair and ran the strap of her purse back and forth between her fingers. "I don't get it," Maureen said. "I did everything I could. I gave her everything I could. I thought things were great. What more could I have done?" She shot a scared-looking glance at Lacey.

Lacey could tell she was worried she'd said too much. Her face was red. Lacey stared at the worn-thin pile of the carpet. The shame nearly buried her.

"Maureen—can I call you Maureen?" Ms. Bray said, then continued without waiting for an answer. "It's important to understand that addiction can catch anyone, from any walk of life. We don't really know why it chooses who it does. There's no one reason." She folded her hands on her desk and leaned into them so her cleavage poked up over the edge of her shirt. "What Lacey needs right now is your understanding and support. She cannot recover from this disease on her own."

Lacey had wanted to yell at Ms. Bray then and tell her that her mom didn't need to be scolded. It wasn't possible for her mom to be any more supportive than she already was. Her mom was right. She'd had everything and just pissed it away. She couldn't be trusted.

"It's normal for parents to have an adjustment period, to have to learn to trust again," Ms. Bray said now. "She'll come back to you, though. Don't give up on her."

Ms. Bray stared at Lacey until she said, "Okay."

Ms. Bray leaned back and folded her arms, feet propped up on the trash can. She was wearing old black combat boots with lumps where her big toes were. "It makes you anxious, huh? Your mom not being happy."

Lacey almost smiled. "Anxious" was an understatement. Anxiety could not be enough to explain why her throat tightened at home or why her back hurt all the time.

"That's a recurrent problem with you. Did the guided meditation help last time? Want to try that again?"

Lacey said sure. She closed her eyes and waited.

Chapter Fourteen

MAUREEN WAS STARTING TO see her breath. She turned the key in the ignition and cranked the heat again. On and off, on and off. She didn't like to think about what it was doing to the environment, but she also didn't want to freeze to death in the hour her daughter spent in outpatient treatment every week. She could've waited inside; she knew there were chairs at the reception desk. She didn't want to go in there anymore, though. Not if she could help it.

She studied the building. So much institutional brick surrounding Lacey's life. The adoption agency, the high school, and now this. Lacey was supposed to escape to Brown. That was where she belonged.

When Maureen first registered Lacey at the clinic, she felt about six inches tall. She'd gone home and taken to Lacey's bedroom door with a drill she found in their garage, disassembling the hinges until the door fell to the floor with a gratifying bang. And she began.

First, the drawers. She found a strip of condoms tucked under Lacey's T-shirts from sleepaway camp. So at least she'd done the sex talk right. God only knew who Lacey was using them with, though. She shuddered and shoved them back into place. The only other thing she found was an old locking jewelry box lying forgotten in one of the drawers. Maureen's own aunt had given it to her years ago. "A girl like you needs a place to keep her secrets," she'd said with significance as Lacey tore the wrapping paper. Maureen was about to ask her aunt what exactly she was talking about when Lacey cooed obligingly and threw her arms around her great-aunt's stout waist. Such a good girl.

She wedged the rusty latch open, but it was empty inside, nothing but dusty pink felt. Not even the locket she'd given Lacey at her graduation. She winced now at how corny it was. Lacey never even wore it. Not that it mattered. She kicked the box back into place and turned around, hands on her hips. According to the woman who'd done Lacey's intake, the bed was a pretty common hiding place. "Addicted teenagers aren't exactly reaching new creative heights," the woman had said in a bored voice.

She took a deep breath and stripped back the sheets. They were striped, flannel. She had let Lacey pick them out after Lacey'd finally admitted she wasn't really into purple anymore. Nothing there. She heaved the bare mattress up onto one shoulder.

Sure enough, there it was. A blue toiletry bag she didn't recognize, smashed flat. She grabbed it up and let the mattress fall. She knelt on the floor and unzipped it. Inside, there were several squares of foil, burned black. A lighter. A couple of straws. A plastic bag, heavy with pills.

It was true, then. She'd somehow hoped it was all a horrible mistake, the phone call and the hospital room and the intake forms. It was hard to explain this away, though. Impossible, even.

"Fuck," she said. "Fuck!" she yelled. She yelled until her throat hurt.

She should've seen it, she knew. Lacey's first counselor hadn't said much to dispute it. He'd steepled his fingers in front of his lips and said, "And what makes you think that, Maureen?" It was like a cartoon of a therapist, and Maureen glanced at Lacey to laugh at him the way they once would have. But Lacey just stared at the floor, her face gray and grim.

Ms. Bray, on the other hand, had admonished her outright. "Support her," she'd said, "and try not to think too hard about the why."

Maureen wanted to beg her to tell her what she was missing. Motherhood had always come so naturally to her, once she'd finally reached it. Nanny or day care, curfew or none—when she made a decision, she never looked back and wondered. She knew instinctively what would work best for her daughter. But there was no fix for this.

When she got home from that session, she looked Ms. Bray up on the clinic's website. In her staff photo, the light reflected off her glasses a little, making her face opaque and unsettling. With her hair tied up, she looked even younger. Her credentials were listed under her photo—it seemed impossible she'd been practicing for twelve years. Across the bottom of the screen ticked quotes from various staff members, set in italics: "As a recovering addict myself, I have unique insight into the many struggles our clients face, and I find great joy in helping them overcome the hurdles between them and sobriety."

Without thinking, Maureen clicked her tongue and whispered, "Never trust an addict." Her eyes widened to the point of watering when she remembered. She hastily clicked the browser window closed and walked away from the computer.

Her butt was going numb. She shifted around in her seat a little and turned the van back off. On the street nearby, a car slowed, then inched to a stop, its engine rattling. Probably a new patient getting dropped off. Despite herself, Maureen craned her neck to see his face. He had white-blond hair that reflected the sun.

Maureen gasped. It was Matt.

She had learned about Matt at one of their family appointments, only after Ms. Bray coaxed Lacey into talking about it. Her daughter had looked so miserable as she explained that she'd been ignoring his emails. She loved him, she said, even though he'd sold her pills. Maureen could've sworn Ms. Bray looked shocked and maybe a little accusatory when Maureen admitted she didn't even know Lacey had been seeing Matt.

Maureen hadn't seen Matt in years. She and Matt's mother had arranged a couple of playdates when the kids were small, but she'd found Mrs. Duvry to be a hard nut to crack, tough and unsmiling. One of those women who nodded instead of laughed, a distant look on her face. The pickups had just been too awkward, so Maureen had started to screen Mrs. Duvry's calls. She'd always felt a little bad for Matt, growing up in a house like that, and for a while, she kept an eye out for him when she picked Lacey up from school. But then the years rolled on, and she'd forgotten him entirely as he was replaced by Lacey's other friends in the back seat of her car.

She had a feeling Lacey'd found a boyfriend when she started disappearing after school at the end of her senior year. Her mouth had a dreamy quality to it at dinner each night. Maureen hoped Lacey would tell her someday, when she felt ready. She wanted to ask about him, but Lacey had a good head on her shoulders.

And now, there he was. Was he waiting for Lacey? Was he going to try to bring her back under with him? The rage took Maureen's breath away. She clutched her car keys, thinking, *it's his fault.* He'd always made her uneasy when he was younger, hadn't he? There was something feral in his eyes then. He'd lured her daughter in and trapped her with something sticky-sweet and irresistible. It had landed in Maureen's lap without warning: someone to blame. She reached for the car door, but before she could open it, Matt's car pulled away.

Maureen paused for a second. She couldn't seriously consider chasing down some teenaged kid. She thought of Lacey's pained face when she talked about Matt. No matter how much progress she'd made, Lacey would follow that boy right back down into the pit if he asked.

Maureen started the car. She drove in the direction he'd gone, her left knee bouncing against the car door. It didn't take long to catch up with him—he was driving so slowly. He might've even been high.

In the end, he didn't go far. Around four corners, a couple of miles at most before he parked in front of someone's house. It was a nice, tidy house, with clean white siding and blue shutters. Maureen stopped two driveways down and watched.

After a moment, he opened his door and stood up. He'd pulled on a knit cap at some point, and he tugged it down low over his eyebrows before walking up to the house. He knocked on the door in what could've been a special pattern of some sort; it was hard to tell from afar. The door opened almost immediately and swallowed him up.

Maureen tapped on her window, a tuneless rhythm,

the silver ring she wore on her middle finger with Lacey's birthstone rapping sharply against the glass. It only took a few minutes. Soon enough, Matt was loping back down the front steps. He fiddled with something in his sweatshirt pocket.

Time. Maureen sprang out of the car and hurried up the sidewalk, nearly tripping over the roots pushing their way up through the pavement. She got to Matt's car and was about to knock on his window when she stopped, her hand raised in a fist. She saw him. He didn't see her. He was clenching the steering wheel, a bag of something white and sinister pinched between his index and middle fingers. His head was bent over, and for a moment, she thought he was already gone, already nodded off. But he hurled himself back against the seat, once, and then again and again. When he finally stopped, the car was shaking, swaying back and forth like a cradle. He leaned his head against the headrest, eyes closed, and Maureen recognized something in his face that she didn't quite want to see. She backed away from the car just as he dropped the bag in his lap and jammed his key into the ignition. As he drove off and a cloud of exhaust wafted over her face, she couldn't look away. Couldn't even blink.

After his car had disappeared down the street, she turned slowly and, without thinking, walked up to the house. When she rang the doorbell, she noticed that her hands were shaking.

The woman who answered the door had a blunt soccer-mom bob and a dish towel thrown over her shoulder. Her face opened up with surprise, and Maureen's heart stopped. It was Ophelia Walsh.

"Maureen? What are you doing here? I didn't miss a meeting, did I?" She glanced worriedly at her watch while Maureen braced herself against the doorway, the wooden edge pressing sharp into her shoulder.

Maureen swallowed. "What did you give to that boy?" she said.

Ophelia froze. "What are you talking about?"

"I saw him. I watched him leave your house, and I saw him sitting in his car with a baggie of…something." Maureen felt stupid. Maybe it wasn't what she'd thought after all.

Ophelia still looked pleasantly puzzled, but when Maureen didn't apologize and retreat, Ophelia changed her mind. Her smile slipped from her face.

That was all the encouragement Maureen needed. She pushed past Ophelia with all the roughness she could manage and found herself in their living room. Ophelia had left nothing in sight. There was no obvious evidence on the coffee table. Maureen heard the front door slam as she began wrenching open the drawers in the TV console. Ophelia just reached the living room doorway when one of the drawers slid out with a treacherous rattle. Empty orange bottle after empty orange bottle with Ophelia's last name printed on them. *Some drug dealer*, Maureen thought faintly. Didn't even throw out her trash.

"So you found out," Ophelia said. "What are you gonna do? Call the cops on me? I could get your daughter in a lot of trouble, too, you know." She glared at Maureen, a dare.

Maureen's head began to pound. From Ophelia's drawer to Matt's palms to her daughter's bloodstream. This was where it all started. It had to be.

"How could you do this?" Maureen said. "You care about this town more than anyone I know." It wasn't exactly true, but it was close enough.

Ophelia broke her gaze and stared at the front door. "How could I not?" She looked back at Maureen. Her jaw was tensed tight, but her hands were working in and over each other. "My husband's fishing business is about to go under, though he'd never admit it. We're up to our ears in loan payments, and he hasn't broken even in two years. Meanwhile, he put this place up for collateral." She flung one hand over her head. "So if we can't make our payments, the bank will take it right out from under us. He's got this diagnosis. Chronic back pain from working on the boat all those years. He doesn't like to take the medicine because it makes him all fuzzy." She crossed her arms over her chest. "So I pick up his prescription without telling him."

Horror built in Maureen's gut. It was like Ophelia'd been looking for someone to confess it all to.

"It's covered by insurance. We've got a terrible policy that won't cover so much as a pelvic exam, but it covers the pills. People will pay fifty, sixty bucks a pill. Did you know that? So now I've got a bottle of sixty pills, sixty Percs, and that's a loan payment right there."

Maureen heard it as "perks" until she realized what she meant. Percocets.

"So you tell me. How could I not?"

"You could get a goddamned job is what you could do," Maureen said through clenched teeth.

Ophelia snorted. "Right. Sure. I've been raising kids full-time the last twenty years. Not a career woman like you." Her eyebrow cocked air quotes around "career woman." "I haven't had anyone pay me for my work in two decades. Who's going to hire me now?" She threw her arms out to the sides, and her eyes softened a bit. *Help me. Please.*

"They're just kids," Maureen whispered.

Ophelia's face hardened. "They're old enough to know what they're doing," she snapped. "Don't you think for a second that they're not. They're junkies, that's it. I'm not responsible for how the town junkies choose to spend their time and money. They're a waste of town resources as far as

I'm concerned. The sooner we let them kill themselves off, the better. Even if it means there's no one left to buy this shit from me."

Maureen's eyes widened. She struggled to take in this woman, this small and ugly woman to whom she'd served canapés on a cheap plastic silver tray.

"Now, I'll thank you to get out of my house." Ophelia planted one hand at the base of Maureen's back and steered her toward the door, her hand a sharp, bony knob like the nose of a gun. "I don't believe we'll be needing your services at our next Historical Society fundraiser after all," she said, her voice suddenly smooth and pleasant. "Or at the Friends of the DP Library events for that matter. I'll be contacting Rebecca shortly." She opened the door and gave Maureen one final push that left her stumbling down a step before she caught herself. The door closed firmly behind her.

It wasn't until Maureen's feet hit the pavement that she realized Ophelia had it all wrong. Ophelia wasn't the one who had the upper hand here. Maureen was. All Maureen had to do was tell the library's board—or anyone, really—that Ophelia was dealing drugs and the woman would at least be ostracized, if not arrested. This community that had lost so much to pills would not tolerate a dealer in their midst.

Maybe they wouldn't believe Maureen, though. Maybe, as the mother of an addict, she was no longer a reliable source in this town. She could leave an anonymous tip with the police, but Ophelia was probably already finding a new hiding place for the pills and coming up with a new rumor to spread to all the rest of Maureen's clients if she found out Maureen ratted. She opened her car door, the sun-warmed metal nearly burning her fingertips. She slid into the driver's seat and stared out the windshield. She felt utterly alone.

Chapter Fifteen

LACEY AND MAUREEN GOT back home just in time for Ella to get out of school. Lacey, heeding Ms. Bray's advice, had asked a few friendly questions over the course of the drive. When was their next event? Did Maureen think the weather would turn before then? But this time, her mom was the one with her mind elsewhere. She answered in single sentences that trailed off at the edges. Or at least Lacey hoped she was just distracted and not angry or upset. Maureen had plenty of reason to be angry and upset.

As they pulled into the driveway, Lacey said, "I'm going to meet Ella." Maureen turned to her, and Lacey was so relieved by her full attention that she had to tell the truth. "She doesn't believe her dad is gone or doesn't want to believe it. She asked me to help her find him, so we're just going around town asking people about him."

Her mom sighed and rubbed the wrinkles out of her forehead. "Lacey," she started.

"I know," Lacey said, flicking the handle of her door. "She's so sad, Mom. I don't know how else to help her."

Maureen leveled her gaze at her until Lacey looked away. "Okay," Maureen said then. "All right. Do what you gotta do. But make sure you're back by five, got it?"

"Yup," Lacey said as she tumbled out the door. The impact of her feet on the driveway sent a ringing buzz up to her knees. She steadied herself before walking on.

Ella was waiting for her at their corner. She looked more tired than a girl her age should ever be. Her hair had pulled loose from her ponytail, and her head was down, backpack keeled over at her feet.

"Hey, kidlet," Lacey said. "How was school?"

"The other kids are idiots," Ella said, glowering across the street at an unsuspecting tree.

Lacey hesitated before patting her shoulder. "Yeah, I know. Sorry about that. You wanna go somewhere and talk about it?"

Ella looked at her like she was crazy, her face almost comically scrunched. "We're going to the pawn shop! Did you forget?"

In spite of herself, in spite of all her doubts and the wriggling of the beetle, Lacey smiled. "Nah, I didn't forget. Let's go."

The man working the counter at the pawn shop was the same one she'd sold her locket to. His round belly strained the seams of his shirt so you could see every stitch, and he breathed out of a slightly opened mouth, fluttering the hairs of his mustache as he did. Lacey kept her eyes fixed on the wall behind him while Ella approached the counter, hoping against hope he wouldn't recognize her. He glanced at her only once before staring back down at his newspaper, impassive. A true professional.

"Excuse me, sir," Ella said, curling the fingers of one hand over the edge of the counter. "We're looking for my father. Have you seen him?" She pulled a folded photo out of her backpack, uncreased it, and pushed it across the glass.

"I can't tell you about customers," he said. "Confidential. Store policy."

Lacey could've sworn he looked right at her as he said this, but maybe she was imagining it. She stared down at the counter. It was a display case, with headless velvet torsos holding gold necklaces and turquoise chokers that had once meant something to somebody. She studied every piece, but of course, the locket wasn't there. The librarian had it.

"Please," Ella said, "just look at the picture. He's missing." She tapped the photo.

He puffed out his cheeks and held the photo up to the light. He recognized John—everyone in town would—and this time, he did look at Lacey.

Lacey smiled apologetically.

"You John Staybrook's kid?" he said to Ella, handing the photo back to her. "I'm real sorry to hear about what happened to him. Been watching the reports come in." He jerked his thumb toward a corner of the room behind him where there was a boxy TV mounted, its audio muted, black-and-white captions ticking across the bottom of the screen.

Ella shook her head firmly. "It's not what you think," she said. "He didn't take that tuna boat like they said. He left my mom because they got in a fight." She leaned in toward the man, elbows on the counter, feet on tiptoe. "He tried to sell his wedding ring to you, didn't he? We're retracing his steps."

Lacey blushed at the *we*. She was aiding and abetting this hunt that could only end in heartbreak.

The man studied Ella carefully, pulling at the skin under his chin. "Okay," he said. "Yeah. He came in here and tried to sell it."

Ella danced up and down on her toes.

"I didn't buy it, though. Plain gold band like that, all scratched up, isn't gonna get much on the open market."

Ella leaned in even closer, her feet practically dangling up off the floor. "Was he mad?"

He shrugged. "Nah. Seemed like he knew that'd be the case. Was acting all set to sell it anyway, actually, until I told him it'd probably end up getting melted down for cash at some point."

"I see," Ella said. "Did he say where he was going next?"

He shook his head and met Lacey's eye again.

"Thank you very much for your time, sir," Ella said, holding her hand out. He folded it into his own huge paw and was shaking it solemnly when she tore away and pointed at the TV. "Look! They're talking about him now!"

The man fumbled for the remote on a shelf hidden behind the display case and unmuted it.

"…have announced they're winding down on the search for the local fisherman, which began less than twenty-four hours ago," said Jane Montgomery, the area's news anchor.

The camera cut to a stern-looking man with a crew cut standing at the docks, seagulls swooping behind his head. According to the ticker below his face, he was a Coast Guard lieutenant. "My guys have looked as hard as they possibly could," he said. "Generally, in cases like these, it's almost impossible to find any trace of the missing man. The ocean is a big place, and we simply don't have the resources to keep going on every search." If he showed any remorse or sadness at this, the camera shut off before it was captured.

"A tragic end to a story that's become all too common in our community," Jane said.

The man behind the counter eyed Ella and muted the TV again.

And now, Bill is here to give us an update on this weekend's Haddock Holidays festival, Jane said silently.

The man shook his head.

Lacey reached out to touch Ella's shoulder, but when the girl turned around, she was grinning. "Did you hear that?" she said. "No trace was found of him. That's because he wasn't fishing that night!" She sauntered over to the door.

Lacey exchanged glances with the man and opened her mouth to say something. What the lieutenant said was true: most of the time, if a fisherman went missing, he was never found. The wakes had no caskets, just blown-up, grainy photos of the man, usually ones where he wasn't quite looking at the camera. He would forever be in the wide, gray sea.

"You coming or what?" Ella shouted from across the shop. She held the door open with her hip and crossed her arms. "We've got a lot more work to do."

"Yup, coming," Lacey said.

"We've gotta go find Jess next," Ella said, scrolling through her phone. "She was probably the last person to see him, even if she is lying about what he did. I bet she would, to protect him."

Lacey closed her eyes. The cold sunlight shone red through her eyelids. "Hey, kidlet," she tried gently. "Do you think maybe we should call it a day? We've already got a lot of stuff to think about, right?"

Ella raised one incredulous eyebrow. "No way. I'm on a roll here. We've gotta figure this out before it's a cold case," she said.

Lacey chewed on the inside of her cheek. "He never would've left you without saying goodbye, Ella."

Ella looked away. "You didn't hear him yelling at my mom," she said. "He was really, really mad. I think he just got carried away." She turned back toward Lacey, fear on her face. She still wasn't ready for the truth.

Lacey nodded. "If you say so."

Ella marched ahead down the sidewalk. Lacey wondered

fleetingly if she should call Mrs. Staybrook and have her retrieve her daughter. She was probably dealing with enough, though, with funeral arrangements and wills on top of her own grief. Ella clearly needed to do this in order to deal with what had happened to her dad. And Lacey had to be there for her when she finally accepted it.

Lacey rolled her shoulders back three times, hoping to knead out the ache lodged near her spine. It didn't work. She followed Ella down the road.

As they expected, they found Jess on the docks. She wasn't working on the *Diane & Ella*, though. She stood a little ways back from it with her hands hanging limply by her sides. The other fishermen moved around her, their voices quieting as they approached, then crescendoing again as they walked on. None of them stopped to talk to her. If she happened to catch someone's eye, they nodded at her, once, respectfully. An understanding.

Ella broke through it all, of course. As soon as she stepped onto the pier, everyone surrounded her with their hearty voices, offering her tours of boats she'd already seen and bags of fresh seafood she didn't need while they mouthed things worriedly to one another over her head. She smiled patiently at them and skirted through to Jess. They watched her go.

The dock swayed unpleasantly as Ella grew closer. Finally, she tapped Jess on the shoulder, and the older woman pulled a smile across her face.

"Hi, Ella," Jess said, wrapping her arms around her in a hug. Ella allowed it. "How you holding up?"

Ella stepped back and slipped her hands into her back pockets. It looked like a pose she'd been practicing in front of a mirror. "I'm fine," she said. She looked quickly up and down the dock. "You can stop lying now," she said more quietly.

Jess's forehead furrowed. "Lying? About what?"

"I know my dad didn't go out on that tuna boat. I know he just ran away from us. It's okay. I forgive you for covering for him. I know you're his best friend after me. But now we're looking for him"—at this, Jess noticed Lacey for the first time, lingering behind Ella and giving an embarrassed little wave—"and we're retracing his steps. So where did you *really* last see him?"

Jess's breath stopped for a second. Where had she even come up with such a thing? "Honey." The pet name sounded unnatural coming out of her mouth. She knelt to the ground. Ella was taller than she remembered, so Jess ended up squinting at her from below, the setting sun flaring into her eyes. "Your dad never would've left you. He loved you so much. And your mom, too," she said. "I watched him get on that boat with my own eyes. I'm sorry," she said again and again and again. "I wish I could help you find him. Believe me, I wish he was still out there."

Ella took one step back, then another. She might've backed clear off the other side of the dock if Lacey hadn't caught her by the elbow. There was a scowl on her face. Jess braced herself for more of the blame.

"Why are you still lying?" Ella said. "I thought you were my friend. Don't you know I need him? I need to find him."

"I'm so, so sorry," Jess said. Her knees had started to hurt. "I should've stopped him from going out. I knew the weather was no good. But he'd made up his mind. I just… Will you tell your mom how sorry I am, too?" She hated how pathetic she sounded.

"He didn't go," Ella repeated. "Didn't you hear? The Coast Guard stopped looking and everything."

Jess's heart sank all the way down to the worn wood beneath her. She hadn't heard. There was a special brand of hopelessness reserved for those unresolved losses and presumed deaths.

"I can't believe you won't help me," Ella said. "You're a terrible person," she yelled suddenly, and Jess feared she'd turn and run, slip and fall on the wet boards. But she walked, dignified, toward the parking lot, Lacey following close behind. Jess watched them go, avoiding everyone else's stares.

Chapter Sixteen

July 5, 1998

ONE DAY IN JULY, Annie felt the baby kick for the first time. It felt like a misplaced hiccup. She sat up in bed, startled, and touched her stomach as if in reply. She still hadn't seen any doctors or had any ultrasounds like the ones they showed on TV, but she felt certain it was a girl. She rolled to the floor, one hand at her back.

Eve was in the living room. "It's kicking," Annie told her dazedly.

"Aww!" Eve dropped her book on the floor and reached out to press her palm to Annie's belly button, frowning when she didn't feel anything. The night before, when Eve was scurrying around the apartment getting ready to meet Sophia at a party, she confessed to Annie that she planned to be married with "at least two babies" within the next five years. The fact that she'd never even had a serious boyfriend didn't seem to trouble her.

"Just wait," Helen said at work. They were all standing around in the bathroom during one of those golden moments when there was a movie playing in each theater and no one was waiting to buy tickets or concessions. Annie sat on the counter between sinks and next to Sophia. Helen stood in front of them, leaning on her mop. She tilted the mop handle toward Annie and pointed. "Soon enough, the little demon won't hold still, and you won't be able to get five minutes of sleep without getting punched in the ribs." Helen had two kids, one and three.

"Looking forward to it," Annie said and exchanged head-shaking smiles with Helen. The truth was, every time Annie tried to imagine her life in the future—even just one week in the future—she drew a blank. Her mind wouldn't let her think about where this path was leading her. For now, all she could focus on was the occasional ripple in her belly.

The bathroom door swung open, and two middle-aged women walked in, glancing nervously at the three of them as they passed. Sophia sighed and hopped down while Helen helped Annie shimmy to the floor. They relocated to just outside theater four. After the theme music died down and the wash of people trickled out, they went to work.

"It's funny," Helen said. She groaned as she bent to pick up an empty cardboard bucket. The popcorn it once held was scattered across the floor. "They all sit here and clap for some dude on the screen who just saved the world, but they can't even manage to pick up after themselves. People in this town."

Annie snorted. "Not just in this town. It was the same in—where I come from, too."

"What are you going to name it?" Sophia said from out of the blue, two rows over.

"I'm not naming it anything. I'm letting her adoptive parents decide," Annie said slowly. She swept a gum wrapper into her dustpan.

"So you're actually going to give it up?"

Annie paused and stood up straight. "Um, yeah. I'm not cut out to be a mom, not right now."

Sophia walked down the aisle toward her, gum snapping in

her mouth. She stood before Annie and chewed. She shook her head. "I can't imagine doing that after going through all this." She pointed at Annie's stomach. "I mean, aren't you going to regret it? Letting someone else raise your child?"

"She's—it's not going to be my child," Annie said. She set her jaw and resumed her sweeping. "It'll be someone else's. Someone who can give her a better life." She'd read that phrase in the welcome folder the adoption agency had given her. *A better life*. She liked that phrase. She held it close.

"I don't know about that," Sophia sniffed. "A baby should be with its mother is what I think."

"Hey, numbnuts," Helen called. "You done with your section yet, or am I gonna have to do that one, too, while you stand around and *think*?"

Sophia walked back to her broom with a huff. Helen winked at Annie and smiled sadly.

Eve was the one who found the adoptive mother. Annie had left the stack of files on the floor of her room weeks before when the agency gave them to her. She hadn't gotten around to sorting through them yet. Truth be told, even on top of the strange, unmanageable weight of picking parents for her child, the folders themselves made her a bit squeamish. There were so many dreams and wishes tucked into those manila folders.

Eve seemed to love it, though, and cooed when she first saw the pile. "Just think," she said, "the little one's parents might be somewhere in there."

Annie let her have at it while she flipped through a magazine one night. She studied Eve's face every time Eve opened a new folder.

"Ooh, gonna have to say no to this one," Eve said, tossing a folder across the floor. "Both of them are teachers, which means they'd probably go broke with a kid. Plus, you don't want it to grow up with that kind of academic pressure."

Annie laughed and flipped back the cover to scan the paperwork. She could picture them in her mind's eye: a couple in pale button-downs, smiling. She pushed the folder under her bed with the dust bunnies. That one was a maybe. Teachers loved kids, right? She laid her magazine on the floor next to her and caught another folder as Eve tossed it in her lap.

"Nope," Eve said. "One of their hobbies is getting new tattoos. Can't be good for job prospects."

They got almost all the way through the pile this way. Eve had an uncanny knack for picking out the ways each would-be parent would ruin the baby's life. Too religious, too many other kids (Annie filed this one away with the two teachers), shifty-sounding, mentioned "a warm and loving home" one too many times. "I mean, your home would be warm and loving, too," Eve scoffed. "It's just that you'd be broke all the time."

Annie looked down and flipped another page in the magazine while its pictures blurred.

And then, on the second-to-last folder, Eve paused. "Oh!" she said. "This one's a former ballerina! Isn't that romantic?" Eve laid the folder on her lap and stared off at something over Annie's shoulder. "Can't you just imagine it?" she said dreamily. "Being a little girl with a dancer for a mother? I bet she tells the best stories."

"What's the rest of it say?" Annie said.

Eve flipped the pages back and forth. "I don't see her husband anywhere. Ah." Her face fell. "Single parent. Next."

The folder skidded across the floor and hit Annie's knee.

She picked it up. Her mother spent so much time accommodating her father, making his appointments and his dinner, letting him watch his favorite sitcom every Tuesday night even though Annie knew for a fact her mother hated that show. Maybe a single mom wouldn't be such a bad thing. She could focus all that time and energy on the baby instead.

Annie opened the folder. The woman's essay sounded warm and genuine with a hint of a sense of humor. She lived in Minnesota, which was good—Annie would be able to picture her baby living a better life without having to worry about actually running into her and screwing everything up for the kid. The essay went on to explain that she'd been working the adoption circuit for two years with no luck, which was why she had filed with an agency way out in Massachusetts. She didn't sound apologetic about it, though.

"And this couple says they were born and raised here and never left from the sounds of it. Who would want that for their child?" Eve dropped the last folder and sighed. "Just a whole pack of losers. You'd better ask the agency if there are any other files you could look at." She jumped to her feet and ran her hand over her own flat belly. "Back to studying for me. See you at dinner?"

"Yup," Annie said. When Eve had closed the door behind her, Annie tucked the dancer's folder under her pillow. She'd been on the floor so long, her back was sore, but she stayed where she was, sitting butterfly-style, her legs cradling her stomach. She rested her head against the edge of her bed and closed her eyes.

***

That one October afternoon, it was surprisingly cold. Annie had spent half the night before sweating, her sheets twined stickily around her legs. She'd been having cramps ever since dinner that night, almost like she was getting her period. For a split second, she worried that she was losing the baby, but she was almost nine months along. It must've been the tuna noodle casserole. She'd tried to make dinner for her roommates that night, but it came out chunkier than she'd remembered, and even Eve had trouble finishing her plate.

When it was finally time to get up, Annie's back and neck were so wet, you'd think she'd just run a marathon. She wiped at her forehead with disgust and got in the shower as fast as she could. She dressed for the unseasonably warm fall weather they'd had the day before, throwing on a cardigan at the last minute just in case. But as she walked to the theater, cool air pinched at her ears. She wished she were wearing something she could close over her whale of a body.

"New England, right?" Helen said when Annie finally pushed through the double doors. Helen drained her coffee cup and chucked it into the trash. "You okay, honey? You don't look so hot."

"Thanks a lot." Annie rolled her eyes, and Helen chuckled. "I didn't get much sleep last night," she admitted. "I was wicked hot, and I had these cramps? Like, right around my belly."

"Probably Braxton-Hicks." Helen nodded. "They're fake-out contractions. I had 'em for weeks with Dom. Sorry, babe." She rubbed Annie's back briskly. "Hey, guess what the little shit did this morning? Dropped my toothbrush in the toilet. On purpose, I swear. He's lucky my mouth was full of Listerine at the time. Couldn't cuss him out."

Annie laughed. She suspected Helen told her these horror stories to make her feel better about it all. She wasn't sure if it was working. Once, Helen invited her to an early dinner at her house before their evening shift. Annie sat perched on the couch and turned down Helen's husband's offers of a soda. The baby stood on the floor and walked his uncertain way along the edge of the couch, clutching the cushions as he went. His bare feet slapped against the hardwood. She winced as his legs twisted around each other, finding the next step. When he reached her, he leaned against her knees and smiled proudly up at her. She clenched her hands together as tightly as she could and braced them against her stomach.

The pain grew worse over the course of the day. Once or twice, a cramp came while she was taking tickets and she had to stop in the middle of tearing off stubs. When she looked up, the customer was there, hand held out, staring at her middle. She handed the stub back to them and recited the theater number that was printed right there on it, as if they couldn't read it themselves.

And then, when she and Helen were mopping out the bathrooms in the middle of one of the matinee blocks, Helen did a spot-on impersonation of their manager, and Annie laughed so hard, she felt something warm and wet spread between her legs.

"Dammit," Annie said, straining to look at her pants. "I think I just peed myself. I swear I just went a couple minutes ago."

Helen stopped short and stared. Dirty water dripped from her mop to the floor. "Maybe those weren't Braxton-Hicks after all. I think your water broke."

"My what?" Her throat closed up before she could say any more.

"You'd better get yourself to a hospital. This is no place to have a baby."

"I don't have a car," Annie whispered. She'd planned to take the bus when the time came, but they hardly ran at all in the middle of the day.

Helen calculated something silently before fixing her hand to the crook of Annie's elbow. "Come on," she said and steered Annie toward the door. "We're gonna make like a leaf and blow this joint." They dropped their mops and let them fall, clattering, to the floor. Helen found Sophia giggling into the pay phone in the lobby and told her to tell the manager they were going to the hospital and that there was a mess in the bathroom she might want to clean up. Sophia looked stricken, and Helen laughed after they walked out the front door. "Don't worry." She squeezed Annie's arm. "None of your water made it to the floor. I just wanted to see the look on her face."

Helen drove a tiny old sedan. The back seat was cluttered with hulking plastic car seats and primary-colored balls. In that moment, when the pain took her body in a wave, Annie wanted nothing more than to lie back and stretch out. She folded herself into the front passenger's seat.

"Let's go to St. Augustine's," Lacey said when they were both buckled in. She'd looked it up on Eve's computer. St. Aug's was forty-five minutes to the west. Devil's Purse Hospital was thirty to the east. They were the only two hospitals around unless you wanted to drive into Boston.

Helen snorted and wiggled her gearshift into place. "Like hell. You're not giving birth in this car, either. Can't you see I just got it detailed?"

Annie laughed weakly. She clutched at her stomach as Helen took the first ramp onto the highway, revving the engine so high, it threw them back into their seats a little.

It took an eternity for them to get to the hospital. In the maternity ward waiting room, she collapsed into a chair while Helen collected forms from reception. Annie glanced around the room, but she didn't recognize anyone. Which made sense, she guessed. Everyone in her grade was now starting their senior year or maybe getting jobs. And their moms were long past done with having babies. What would any of them be doing in this wing of the hospital?

"How can I help?" Helen said, handing her a clipboard.

Her mother would've wanted her to say, "I'm fine, thanks." Helen had done more than enough already, and Annie should send her on her way. Annie took the clipboard and said, "Call the agency?" She handed Helen the card she kept in her wallet.

Helen nodded once and was gone.

Annie had only managed to fill out two questions on the form by the time Helen came back. She couldn't figure out if it was better to bend over during a contraction and curl into it or to sit up straight and grip the armrests as tightly as she could, so she'd been alternating between the two.

"The adoptive mom will be here to fill out the agency's paperwork as soon as the baby's born," Helen said, settling into the chair next to hers. "Apparently, she's been shacking up in a hotel in Boston for two weeks in case you went into early labor." She paused and squeezed Annie's shoulder. "You're making someone very happy today, Annie-Girl."

Annie nodded through another contraction, her eyes screwed shut.

Helen took the clipboard off her lap. "Well, I see you know your name and date of birth, so that's good," she said. "I think they're gonna need more than that to go off, though. Mailing address?"

And so they filled the endless forms out together, with Helen reading out the questions and writing down whatever answers Annie could manage. A couple of times, she didn't bother reading them out loud, just grunted her disapproval at the question and checked the box herself. They handed the forms back with the insurance card Annie had swiped from her mom's wallet before she left. Annie told herself she'd pay her parents back for the copay, but then a contraction wiped away all her thoughts.

Nearly an hour later, a rigid-faced nurse showed them into a room with a bed. Annie had to stop in the hallway once, one hand on the wall and the other braced in Helen's, and she could've sworn she saw the nurse tapping her foot. As soon as she'd eased Annie into bed, the woman was gone, and it was just Annie and Helen again. Helen busied herself with collecting ice chips to slip into Annie's mouth and smoothing the bangs off Annie's sweaty forehead. As the pain jammed itself further and further into her and she began to feel like every organ in her body was going to get wrenched out her bottom, Annie found herself wishing for her mother. Or at least some imagined version of her mother who would've marched straight into her apartment and made her come home, who would've told her what to expect every month and taken her to the doctor's and dug up all the little sweaters she'd knit for Annie when she was small. The type of mother she hoped this baby would grow up with.

"I'm gonna go check on those damn nurses. You've gotta be getting close to active labor by now. They should be giving you an epidural," Helen said, pushing her chair back from the bedside.

"You mean all this shit hasn't even been active?" Annie said through clenched teeth.

Helen laughed on her way out the door. "That's my girl," she said, but Annie, twisting back and forth on the bed, wasn't sure she got the joke.

From there, things were mostly a blur. They put the

medicine in through her back, and suddenly everything went blessedly, terrifyingly numb. At some point, Helen explained the situation to the staff and told them about the adoptive mother waiting nearby. Annie thought they were rougher with her after that, more severe, wrenching her legs open to check her progress.

And then it was time to push. She made sure to do exactly as the doctor ordered. She pushed only when he poked his head up from between her legs and told her to. For a second, she thought absurdly of *The Exorcist*, which she'd watched with Eve a few weeks before. "Get out, get out, get the fuck out," she muttered, or maybe it was a scream.

Finally, finally, it was out. "A girl," the doctor announced briskly before the nurses whisked the baby away.

Annie felt triumphant and tragic. She'd been right. She'd known her daughter, if only for those few months when they shared a body. And now it was over. There were tears in Helen's eyes as she watched the baby get passed from hand to rubber-gloved hand.

One of the nurses reached over the side of the bed and started kneading Annie's still-sore belly. It was an odd way to comfort someone. Annie shied away. "It's for the afterbirth," the nurse said as if that explained anything and forcibly rolled Annie back over and continued to work. Somewhere, a baby wailed. Annie's chest ached.

A tiny girl appeared at her shoulder, maybe a couple of years younger than Annie, carrying a pink plastic jug with a thick straw sticking out the top. She held the jug up, and Annie peeled her cracked lips apart and sipped. "Don't you want to see your baby?" the girl asked while the ice water slipped down Annie's throat.

Annie swallowed, closed her eyes, and shook her head. A nurse whispered in the girl's ear, explaining.

At some point later, Helen leaned over into Annie's face and said, "All right, kiddo, I've gotta head home. Don't trust my husband to manage to get the kids in bed before midnight. You'll be fine, okay? You did awesome." Helen's breath smelled like old coffee, but Annie needed her to stay there, inches away, give her something to focus on. She was gone before Annie could so much as nod. Based on the blackness outside her window, Annie guessed it was late.

She was alone. She lay on her side with her knees tucked up to her chest and her hands stuffed up under her pillow, the way she used to when she was little. She wasn't sure why she couldn't stop crying. She didn't feel whole anymore.

The girl was back. "Hey," she said, sitting down in the chair next to the bed. "Your—the baby's sleeping with her new mom. They both look really happy together. Really peaceful."

Annie kept staring at the wall. So much of her was tied up with making that other woman happy.

"Well." The girl put her hands on her knees and stood. "I just thought you might like to know."

Annie nodded and glanced at the plastic ID badge dangling around her neck.

Rebecca.

Chapter Seventeen

Friday, November 10, 2017

REBECCA LOST HER BREATH when Addie told her the whole story that morning. "Did you hear about what happened to John Staybrook?" she'd said in a fake whisper. "Have you heard anything from Diane?" When Rebecca stared blankly at her, a light went up behind Addie's eyes. If there was one thing she loved more than hearing gossip, it was telling it.

It didn't seem real. She'd just seen John the week before. He'd slipped her an extra twenty on her way out his front door after watching Ella, which she didn't find until she'd gotten home and counted the small folded pile of bills. She had the twenty in her wallet, ready to give back to him the next time she saw him.

She had to sit down. She landed in one of the cheap wooden chairs they kept behind the circulation desk. To her credit, Addie murmured in sympathy and ran across the street to the Dunkin' Donuts, returning with a coffee that she left on the desk for Rebecca. Rebecca stared at the Styrofoam cup. The coffee grew lukewarm while Addie chatted with patrons in hushed tones, her voice occasionally rising for an "I know!" or "Can you believe it?" followed immediately by a worried glance in Rebecca's direction. At the end of the day, Rebecca dumped the coffee in the trash.

On the drive home, all she could think of was Ella, inhaling that book on the floor the day before and asking unanswerable questions about Lacey. How had Diane told her about her dad? Had she cried? Rebecca imagined she must have and was glad she hadn't had to see it.

At home, she walked slowly up the steps to the bedroom. The room was dark; they kept the curtains drawn so Mack could fall into bed, no matter what time of day he got home. The covers were still taut across the mattress where she'd tucked them that morning. He wasn't back yet.

The closet door, swollen since the house was built, had to be jiggled just so before it would moan open. She pushed aside the dresses and skirts hanging there. Behind them was a space barely large enough for her to curl up in. She climbed back and let her clothes fall together behind her, closing her in.

She sat on the dusty floor and squeezed her eyes shut. It was childish, she knew, but she'd always liked small spaces, nooks and crannies that held her in and couldn't surprise her. She brushed one hand out across the floor. And there were the boots. She pulled one into her lap. It was impossibly small—the sole fit into one hand. They were brown, the brand name long ago worn away.

They'd been hers when she was a kid. She'd toddled after her father and older brothers in them almost every afternoon when her mother would drop her off at the boat and cheerfully proclaim that she needed a break. Rebecca had taken them home in a burst of optimism over two years ago when she and Mack had first decided they were ready to try. They'd gone to her parents' for the weekend, and her mother had smiled knowingly when Rebecca came downstairs with the boots in her hand. Rebecca had blushed, but then she'd smiled, too.

She'd kept them in the front hallway at first, lined up with Mack's Xtratufs. Then up in the bedroom, then here, in the back of the closet. Where she didn't have to see them. It was like that with the second bedroom downstairs. When they'd moved in, she knew instantly that it would be the nursery, but of course, she couldn't decorate it as such. Over the months, the years, it accumulated boxes of old dishes and Mack's hunting rifles. Now, it was little more than a room-sized closet.

She shimmied her fingers inside one of the boots until she found the roll of money. Squinting in the dim light, she counted it once more. She almost had enough to cover their annual deductible, which they would surely need if she were going to start seeing specialists. She was almost ready to show Mack.

A door closed downstairs. Rebecca stood up, slamming her head against the ceiling. She tumbled out of the closet, hand clamped to the spot that already rang with pain, as footsteps creaked up toward the room. And then there he was, finally Mack, standing in the doorway, the light from the hallway spilling around him.

"You're home," Rebecca cried as he wrapped his arms around her. He kissed her nose while she kissed his chin, then they swapped positions before their lips met. Their ritual. She burrowed her face into his neck and breathed him in, the fishy, gas-fumed air of him. In the coming days, he would shower over and over again until the scent finally left him. And then he'd leave again.

"Sorry I'm a little late," he said. She felt his voice rumble up through his chest. "Heard about what happened to Johnny on the radio on the way in, so I stopped at the Break to pay my respects."

Rebecca almost burst out with everything she'd been thinking that day before she remembered that Mack didn't know how well she knew John because of the babysitting. She shouldn't be any more affected than she was by the other losses Devil's Purse had endured over the years. She pushed back from Mack and ran her fingers through the snags in her ponytail. "I heard that, too," she said. "How awful."

"I can't believe it." He shook his head and scratched at his stubble. "One of the best around, and he leaves behind a wife and child. You gonna bring them anything?"

"Oh," she stammered, "sure." She tried to come up with a suitably detached sympathy dish that wouldn't make Mack suspicious. Ella loved her chicken tetrazzini, but was that too intimate?

Before she could say anything more, Mack's face lit up. "I was wondering where you'd put these," he said.

Rebecca turned to watch him bend to pick something up behind her. It was one of the boots. The blood froze in her veins. She must've dropped it in her rush to get out of the closet.

"Can't believe these fit you once," he said, smiling as he held it up to his face. He shook it slightly, and his eyebrow raised. Rebecca's toes curled under. "There's something in here," he said. "Hope it's not a mouse living in your closet. Danny was telling me they got a real infestation over at their place this year." He peered into the boot, and she held her breath tight in her chest.

He pulled out the cylinder of rolled cash and looked at it quizzically. "Is this your money, babe?" he said, as if he almost hoped it wasn't.

"Sure is," Rebecca said, stepping closer. No sense covering it up now. "I wanted to surprise you with it. I've been babysitting for Ella Staybrook off and on while you were away. I think I've got enough now for us to see a fertility specialist. Theoretically." She waited for him to tease her like he always did for using a ten-dollar word when "supposedly" would do just fine.

He said nothing. He flipped the money over and back between his fingers, staring at it. "You got a second job without telling me?" he finally said.

A spot of anger flared in her throat. Who was he to tell her what she could and couldn't do while he was away? For God's sake, it was babysitting, not anything illegal. She folded her hands together. "I didn't want you to have to worry about it," she said. "I know those things can get expensive, and our budget is…what it is."

Mack nodded, but he still wouldn't meet her eye. "We can't keep it."

Of all the things she expected him to say, this was the very last on her list. "Of course we can," she said.

"Diane's husband just died," he said. He tossed the cash onto the end of the bed where it rolled to the floor with a sad little thump. "We can't keep her money."

She blinked. Diane had one of the best jobs in town. They bought a new station wagon and a new pickup truck every five years.

Rebecca opened her mouth, but Mack put his hand up, palm out. "Can we talk about this later? I'm beat. I need to get some sleep before I say anything stupid."

"Arguably, you already have," was what she wanted to say. She turned on her heel and left the room in peevish silence, swinging the door shut without caring if it slammed.

She fixed herself a frozen dinner, spiraling the gummy fettucine alfredo around her fork. Mack could fix his own dinner if he saw fit to come downstairs. She ate in front of the TV and hastily clicked past the local news channel—they would be talking about John, she was sure of it—before deciding on a marathon of police procedurals. For three hours, she watched, focusing on solving the mysteries before the detectives so she wouldn't have to think about whether she should've told Mack from the start.

Her eyes began to close as a millionaire got dragged, weeping, off to jail while the detectives shook their heads. She curled up on the couch and fell asleep.

Chapter Eighteen

A S IT DID EVERY time a man went missing, the Breakwater was closed to the public that night to allow John's buddies some time alone to talk about him. When Jimmy went to check on the yellow paper sign he'd taped to the window, no tourists were waiting. It seemed even they'd heard what happened and knew to stay away. He shouldered back through the crowd and took up his spot behind the bar.

The night had started out pretty quietly. The news from the Coast Guard was always the final nail in the coffin, so to speak, turning rumor into a funeral. Things picked up soon enough, though.

"Still can't believe he'd've done something so stupid."

"Remember that hurricane a few years back? Irma or whatever? Winds blowing at forty, fifty, and he keeps driving down to the docks to check on his boat. He called me to tell me my mooring's loose. I said, 'Johnny, you really think I'm leaving the house right now? Are you crazy?' He kept threatening to fix it himself till I finally told him I'd be right there."

Loud laughter, beer glasses clunked down on cardboard coasters.

"I tell you, when he first hired Jess, I thought he was smoking something. Scrawny thing like her. Two of them together made quite a pair, painting the boat like some Mark Twain bullshit."

"She turned out all right, though."

"The boat or Jess?" More laughter.

"Both, I guess. Mostly Jess." Everyone nodded and drew gulps of their beer.

"You hear she's getting the boat?" Ben O'Malley said to nobody in particular.

"No shit. Really?"

"Yep. Overheard Tommy talking about it. Guess he was in the lawyer's office filing some paperwork for his divorce when they were calling up his wife about the will."

Silence. Someone whistled low through his teeth.

"That's a damn fine boat."

"No way she could've afforded it on a crew wage, that's for sure."

"You don't think she could've—?"

"Of course she offed him," Sammy Mitchell yelled from the back. "I would've!"

"Can it, Sammy." Everyone rolled their eyes. "She probably didn't even know about his will before today anyway."

"Diane must be pissed," Will Feeney said, drawing out the last word so the air briefly rang with it.

"Can't imagine. Almost feel sorry for poor Jess. She was never one to stick herself in a fight."

"Think she'll show tonight?"

"Who, Jess? Who knows. Seemed pretty hung up last night, might be lying low."

"Nah, meant Diane."

"Diane? Diane Staybrook? Now you're the one smoking something."

"She hasn't stepped foot in here since the two of them got married."

"Too busy working."

"Something like that. And then they've got the kid, too."

"Jesus, the kid."

Each of them nodded and stared into their glasses, remembering the first time they saw Ella. John had taken her out to the docks a few times when she was just a newborn, strapped to his chest in a baby carrier, the soft pink sphere of her head peeking out over the top. "What happened, Johnny?" they yelled from their boats while they unloaded the day's catch. "You run outta paternity leave already?" They heaved skates and dogfish into the tubs waiting on the dock, soon to be dumped into a huge metal lift that would load and file it all into the processor's cold trucks.

"Nah," Johnny said, grinning. "Figured I'd give Diane a break so she could grocery shop. Gotta show the new intern the ropes." He cupped his hand over Ella's scalp, mist already collecting on the fine hairs there.

When the men finished loading, they jumped down to say hello. They clicked their tongues at her and let her grip their grease-blackened fingers while they joked about her strength. Some of them hung back, smiling sideways from a safe distance. All of them saw her eyes, gray, wide open, staring. Even the single guys among them had known it was early for her to be so alert, that it was unusual in one so young.

Jimmy reached for an empty glass and filled it. The foam spilling up over its edge seemed to break the silence in the bar.

"She's looking for her dad, you know. Ella. Doesn't believe he would've gone out like that."

"Fuck me."

"I know. Bob over at the pawn shop told my cousin Rick that she stopped by today, and we all saw her with Jess. Put them through the wringer, sounds like."

"Just like her mom. Johnny, too, for that matter. Hate to be the guy who tried to pull one over on him," Gus March said, smiling sadly.

"Can't say I blame her though, you know? The kid. She's right. It's downright odd he went out in that."

"When my old man went overboard, I spent a year thinking he'd swim up to shore any day now. Scare all the sunbathers at Oyster Beach, staggering out of the water in his survival suit."

"What's she gonna do when she finds out the truth, that he's really gone? You think she's gonna lose it?"

"Probably won't ever get the truth. No closure in this game."

"She'll just accept it one day. That's what happened to me at least."

The men were quiet again. They'd all lost somebody, somewhere along the way, and it was hard not to think about them on a night like this.

"Shit, man, what if she comes to one of us? What am I gonna tell her?"

"What do you mean, dumbass? You tell her what you know, which is jack. Give her a hug, maybe, or pat her on the back. Sucks to lose a parent. She's gotta deal with it in her own way."

"I dunno. There's a reason I never had kids. If she starts crying on me, I don't know what I'd do."

"You'd say 'I'm sorry' like a normal human being. Jesus, Danny."

Danny shrugged and shook his head like it still seemed impossible. He looked down at his beer.

"Any of you notice who's helping Ella out on this search?"

"Who?"

"Maureen Carson's kid. Lacey."

"You're shittin' me."

"Nope. Kid can't leave well enough alone. She should know better."

"Isn't that one of the steps? Quit messing with innocent kids' lives?"

"Hold on now. She's basically no more than a kid herself."

"Not sure any of the steps took with that one, though. You seen her lately? Looks strung out to me."

"It's sad is what it is. Way too much of that going around nowadays. I know so many kids turned rotten with that shit."

"Don't care if it's sad or not, she's a danger to the town and especially to that poor kid. She'll stay away from Ella if she knows what's good for her. I know you know what all went down at that methadone clinic over in Mayberry."

"Let 'em all die is what I say! They'll do it to themselves eventually! Kids nowadays."

"Easy, Sammy. There was plenty of dope to go around in your day, too."

"He's right, though. It's gotten worse the last few years."

"Can't even find a sober crew anymore."

"Abe had someone OD on him in the middle of a trip last month."

"Was wondering what those ambulances were doing at the pier."

"Yup. Kid fell over on the deck right as they were hauling in."

"Damn. They revive him?"

"Not sure. He was an out-of-towner."

"You think Diane knows?"

"That her daughter's hanging out with an addict?"

"Probably. She's a smart cookie, that one. Might be she just can't deal with it right now, with her grief and everything."

"Yeah. Your wife bringing her anything?"

"Oh yeah. There was a second lasagna already in the oven when we were eating dinner."

"I should check with Ophelia. She's usually pretty good with that shit, but she hasn't mentioned anything."

"Poor kid. She really loved him. You could tell."

Chapter Nineteen

Saturday, November 11, 2017

REBECCA WOKE THE NEXT morning with a sharp crick in her neck. She sat up on the couch and groaned, turning her head from one side to the other. There was cold coffee in the pot on the kitchen counter and the house was silent, which meant Mack had probably gone down to the docks already. Just as well. She didn't know what she was going to say to him. In the meantime, she had to get ready for his sister's baby shower.

A "sprinkle," they called it, for their third baby, though it wasn't clear how it was any different from a shower. When she got to her mother-in-law's house, there were just as many loud family members, and the mound of pastel-wrapped gifts was just as large as when they'd thrown a party for their first. It was going to be a long three hours, she knew from experience. She fixed a smile on her face as the room cooed over tiny onesies and her sister-in-law feigned excitement while unwrapping the same board book four times to shrieks of drunken laughter. "Oops! Guess it's a popular one!" She clapped politely when Mack's second cousin won baby shower bingo and hoisted the prize bottle of wine over her head, her safety-pinned name tag slightly askew.

And when the other guests weren't talking about babies, they were talking about John.

"I can't believe he's really gone," one woman at Rebecca's table said to her neighbor. "I mean, I know there's a risk in this business, but Danny was always so impressed by him. He said John was one of the best out there."

"He was," her neighbor replied. "Everyone makes mistakes, though." The women exchanged a glance. Both of them were thinking about their own husbands. Rebecca knew because she was, too, in spite of her fight with Mack. Her thoughts always ran reflexively to him in conversations like this.

"And that poor little girl." The two clucked their tongues in sympathy. "I just couldn't imagine."

"You've heard Maureen Carson's daughter is helping her look for him, right?"

The other woman gasped. "No, really?"

Her friend nodded.

"Honestly, what has gotten into that girl? Lord knows, my son went through some rough patches when he was a teenager, but if I'd ever caught him interfering with a grieving family…"

The two nodded. One leaned in closer and muttered, just loud enough so Rebecca could still hear, "She was adopted, remember. I'm not saying that's why things went south for her, but…"

"Oh, come now," the other said. "That can't be the only reason."

And maybe it was the setting, or maybe it was her third cup of spiked punch slicking its way down her throat, but Rebecca let the thought settle in—the one she usually steered herself away from because it was so bitter, it was almost cruel: Why were some women—teenagers, even—allowed to have babies just to wash their hands of them and give them away for adoption when she couldn't even get pregnant? Where was the sense in that?

She shook the thought out of her head and took another sip of punch, the high-fructose corn syrup and rum coating the inside of her mouth. By the time the party had ended and she was helping her mother-in-law fold chairs, her burps were a little acidic.

"Thank you so much for helping, Becca." Her sister-in-law appeared at her side, touching Rebecca's arm.

As if in a dream, as if of its own accord, Rebecca's hand reached out and pressed itself against her sister-in-law's stomach. It was taut as a trampoline. The baby kicked obligingly, and she felt it like an earthquake.

"You know," Rebecca said from far away, "I often think of these as bulbs"—she nodded toward her hand, the baby— "like the kind you plant in the garden. They're just the right shape, and after a few months, something beautiful sprouts out of them."

Her sister-in-law glanced at Mack's mother, who had paused midfold to take in the spectacle, and burst out laughing. "Oh, honey," she said, wiping tears from her eyes. "It's nowhere near that poetic. You'll see for yourself if my brother ever gets around to knocking you up. Excuse me. I've gotta go pee for the hundredth time today."

Rebecca's phone rang. Mack. Desperate for something to do besides crawl into a corner and die from embarrassment, she picked up.

"Hi," she said flatly lest he forget their last conversation.

"I know you're still mad at me and there's some shit we need to work out," he said, "but I'm down at the pier, and one of the guys found something."

"What? Like a turtle or something?" Mack's mother was still staring at her. Rebecca turned her back.

"No, actually, it's—" He hesitated. "You should just come see it."

Rebecca had half a mind to refuse him. What could it possibly be? But then, anywhere was better than her mother-in-law's house at the moment. Besides, the pier was a few blocks away and would give her a chance to walk off the rum punch before she had to get back in her car. "All right. I'll be there in a few minutes," she said, waving goodbye to his mother.

Down at the docks, the men stood clustered around something, murmuring to each other. The first prickle of dread grew in Rebecca's abdomen. Their faces were solemn, and the usual noise of the pier was gone, no shouts or laughter or loud whumps of rope hitting wood and metal.

Mack saw her and motioned her over. The men shuffled apart to let her in.

In the center of their huddle, lying on the dock, there was a boot.

"I found it doing a quick tow on my way out to the channel," Danny Colbert said. "Sometimes, the currents, they push debris around. Can't predict where anything will end up."

"It's John's," Mack said, placing one hand on the small of her back.

"How could you possibly know that?" Rebecca said. "You all wear those boots."

Mack pointed at a white scrawl on the rubber, near the toe. Rebecca squinted and leaned in. The markings were half worn away, but up close, they coalesced into letters. A name. Not John's. "Oh," she breathed.

Mack laced his fingers with hers. "Danny wants to bring it to the Coast Guard, but it doesn't seem right. Diane should have it," he said. "We were thinking, since you'd been spending time with the Staybrooks and all." There was no trace of their fight on his face.

Rebecca closed her eyes. What else could she do? "I'll bring it to her," she said.

Chapter Twenty

MOM! YOUR PHONE'S RINGING."

Even in her sleep, Diane's heartbeat sped at the sound of her daughter's voice. She pulled herself up from the couch, ratty blanket falling to the floor, but Ella was already gone. Diane watched her feet disappear up the stairs. Those ridiculous slippers. They were stuffed sharks, and the openings were their mouths, so you put your foot in through a ring of pointed felt teeth. John had given them to Ella last Christmas, and the two of them had giggled at them all day. It was a wonder they still fit her.

The phone was, in fact, ringing. She shook the sleep from her head and picked it up.

"Good morning, ma'am. I'm sorry to bother you on the home phone like this. John gave me your cell, too, but it kept going straight to voicemail."

Her cell phone sat on the coffee table, its face dark and lifeless. The battery'd died at some point yesterday. "Who is this, please?"

"Oh, right. Sorry. My name's Burt McGovern. And, uh, this is a little awkward."

She found her eyebrows raising.

"You see," he continued, "I owned the boat. The one

John took? I hired him to run it, but I hadn't heard from him since he left. I was starting to worry, and then his crewman, or crewwoman—Jess? Jen?—called and told me he'd gone missing."

Bile rose in her throat. She sat back into the couch as the chilly truth settled over her. John really had taken another boat out. A bigger part of her than she cared to admit hadn't really believed it. But here it was. There was no foul play here. Jess hadn't pushed him overboard or failed to rescue him when he'd tripped and fallen. She hadn't made up this unbelievable story to cover it up. There was no one to blame. It was just bad luck. Stupid, reckless choices.

"First off, I'm real sorry to hear what happened," this man was saying. "Such a tragedy." He paused. She begged him silently not to go further. "But secondly, well…uh… see, I'm trying to file an insurance claim. For the boat. And they're asking me all these questions I can't answer. About John and such."

She swallowed a laugh.

"I wouldn't bother with it at all, except the boat wasn't cheap, you know? I was wondering if you could maybe help me out with some of these answers."

Diane straightened the shirt she'd been wearing since Thursday night. In her sweetest, most patronizing voice, she said, "Listen. Burt, was it? I'm very sorry for your loss. Do you think maybe we could revisit this at some point in the future? Perhaps after we've had time to hold a funeral for my husband?"

She hung up on his backpedaling apologies and laid the phone gently back on its cradle. She picked up a throw pillow from the end of the couch, dented from her sleeping body, and began to fluff it. Dust flew through the air and up her nose. John always threw every pillow to the floor before stretching out on the couch, his body filling the space almost perfectly. Every night, when she followed him up to bed, she picked the pillows up, perked them back up again, and placed them in the corners of the couch just so.

She pressed the pillow to her face, the nubby fabric rough on her skin, and screamed and screamed and screamed.

Chapter Twenty-One

ELLA WAITED UNTIL SHE'D heard the door of her parents' room close before she crept back down the stairs. She needed time to plan today's schedule before she met with Lacey, and she always did her best thinking outside. The colder the better.

Today, they were interviewing more of her dad's friends, who might've heard him talking about his wife and any escape plans he'd made. She'd been up half the night, or at least until eleven, brainstorming the names of men they should find. She wrote them down in the back of her assignment book, her head ducked under the covers with a flashlight in case her mom appeared in the doorway.

As she eased open the front door, she dug in her pocket to make sure the list was there. So she didn't see Rebecca at first. She stood on the front steps with a beat-up box in her arms. Her mouth was open like she'd forgotten what to say.

"Hey, Rebecca!" Ella said. "We're not hanging out until Monday, remember?"

"I know." Rebecca looked down at the box. "Is your mom here?"

"She's up in her room. Someone just called, and she got really mad at them. What else is new. She's always mad at someone." Ella rolled her eyes, but Rebecca didn't laugh. "Is that for us?" Ella pointed at the box.

Rebecca backed down a step. "Well, it's for your mom."

"I'll take it up to her!"

"Oh, I—"

Ella reached down and grabbed the box.

"Ella, wait—" she said as Ella opened the flaps. "Danny went out on a trip, and his net came up with it," Rebecca said, so softly it was almost a whisper.

Danny Colbert the slacker finally took a trip! Ella couldn't wait to tell her dad. She peered into the box, and everything stuttered.

It was a single brown boot. The bands of beige around the top and sole had worn down to brown, too, but there were blotches of white paint all over it. A flowering vine and a butterfly. They were nearly unrecognizable now, beaten down by the sand and stones rolling along at the bottom of the sea. But she knew what they'd once been. She'd put them there.

Last year, she had watched her dad yank his boots off in the front hallway while she sat on the couch. Her mom had gotten home early and was in the kitchen, fumbling and using curse words Ella had never heard before as she tried to make a pot of John's famous chili.

"How come everybody wears those same boots?" Ella said as John sat down at the end of the couch.

John pulled a pillow out from under his tailbone and tossed it onto the armchair nearby. He turned to scrutinize the offending footwear with her. He'd forgotten to put them on the special tray her mom had got him, and they dripped water onto the tile floor that would dry into mysterious white rings by the morning. "Good question," he said. "I guess because they work well, and no one wants to risk wasting money on a pair that doesn't."

"But they're so…" she said. "Ugly" was what she thought, but she didn't want to hurt his feelings. She tried again. "What if you get them mixed up with someone else's? And then you're wearing shoes with someone else's foot juices in them." She wrinkled her nose.

He laughed. "We don't exactly sit around with our shoes off at the docks, Ella-Bella, so I can't say I've ever heard of them getting mixed up."

The next morning, he came whistling into the kitchen. "Come with me," he said. "I've got an idea."

And she went without a second thought, leaving her bowl of Cheerios behind to grow soggy in its milk.

He'd spread out newspapers across a patch of the concrete basement floors. Usually, the deep dark down there made her shiver deliciously before running up the stairs, but he'd set up one of his shop lights. She could see every dust bunny.

"I thought about what you said last night," he said, "and you were right. Those things could use a face-lift. Go ahead and make 'em mine." He held his hand out toward the newspapers. His boots were there, wiped clean of sand and salt, along with a brand-new can of marine-grade paint.

"Seriously?" She'd been dying to try out some of the new techniques she'd learned in art class that month.

"Sure. All they had was white paint, but I figured you could still do some damage."

"Is Mom okay with me painting down here?"

"You kidding? She's the one who bought the paint. Oh, and this." He pulled a paintbrush from his pocket and held it out to her. "Put anything you want on there. My one request is that they be signed by the artist."

She took the brush from him, grinning, and ran the clean white bristles over her palm. "Okay," she said.

She worked half the morning away, the light buzzing overhead as she chewed her lip. Painting on bent rubber was a lot harder than painting on the giant pads of paper they used in art class. Sometimes, a stray grain of grit would appear and mess up her stroke. When she finished, she stood back, hands on her hips. A thorny stem twined its way around the shaft of one boot, topped with a thousand-petaled bloom. The other boot had ladybugs, butterflies, and other nondescript insects dotted all over. She'd even flicked blades of grass around the soles. Near the toe, she'd written her name in her best, most ornate cursive.

She wondered suddenly if it was too girly. Maybe they'd make fun of him down at the docks. But when her parents came downstairs to check on her a few minutes later, her mom held Ella's shoulder, and her dad kissed his fingertips. "Perfection," he said.

He let her come along the first time he wore them to check on something on his boat. She sat in his truck while he sauntered down the dock. Every time he stopped to talk to someone, she watched through the dirty window as he pointed back at her.

All that week, he came home with orders for her. "Danny was wondering if you could do a striped bass," he'd say, or, "Jess said she wants a pair just like mine, only in color."

She sighed. "That defeats the whole purpose, Dad. If everyone had painted boots, they'd all look the same again."

He nodded seriously. "You're right, you're right. I'll let them down easy."

She turned the boot over in her hand and shook it. Two bits of dried seaweed fell out, crackling, along with one of the skate eggs the town was named for. A devil's purse. With its fat middle that held the baby skate and two spindly legs almost like fangs at each end. Lying black on their front steps. She stared at it.

"Mom!" she finally screamed.

Her mom appeared in the doorway right away. "What's going on?" she said. "Ella?"

At the sound of her name, everything leaked out of Ella. She turned and collapsed into her mom. The boot fell to the ground.

"It's John's," Rebecca said.

Ella felt her mom's chin bump against her scalp as she nodded into Ella's hair. "Oh, honey," her mom said.

"I'm so sorry." Rebecca touched Ella's back and rubbed it in small circles.

"Go away," Ella said. She buried her head into her mom's shoulder like that could make it all disappear. "Please."

After a moment, Rebecca's hand fell. Ella heard her footsteps move back down the walkway. Her mom pulled her inside.

Chapter Twenty-Two

REBECCA WAS STILL WIPING tears from her eyes when she got back home.

Mack sat on the couch in their silent living room. His head was buried in his hands, and he looked up when he heard her. "How'd it go?" he asked.

"Awful," she said. She dropped down onto the opposite end of the couch. She couldn't summon the strength to be angry with him anymore, but things were still not easy between them. She didn't know who owed forgiveness to whom. She wasn't about to apologize for the money.

"Did Diane—" Mack swallowed. "Was she upset?"

"She already knew he was gone. But Ella…" Rebecca drew her knees up to her chest and tucked her head down. "She saw it first," she said. "I tried to comfort her. She just needed her parents." And no matter how close Rebecca grew to Ella, she would never be her mother. Rebecca's breath caught in her throat. How absurd it was of her to think it. "She might not ever want to see me again."

"Come on, babe." The cushion shifted under her as Mack moved closer. "I'm sure she'll forget about it soon and you can babysit her again. I know it's important to you."

She was quiet. He took a deep breath and pulled her close with one arm. She held her body rigid.

"It's not really about the money for you, is it?"

She looked up and shook her head. "I knew we needed the money for treatments, but if you didn't want to do that, then I thought—" She paused. "I thought maybe I could be a sort of parent in another way. By helping to raise Ella," she admitted with a grimace. "What nonsense."

"No. It's not nonsense." He curled his hand around her elbow. "You worked hard for that money. You should keep it. Or spend it, I mean. On the doctors."

She released her legs, and her feet fell to the floor. "Are you sure?" she said, studying his face. "I know it's hard for you," she said, "going in to get tested. I know you're afraid something could be wrong with you." She didn't know this, not really, but a lot of women online said their husbands felt that way about fertility treatments. It seemed like something that could be true for Mack.

He said, "That's not why I hesitated." He rubbed his face. "I keep thinking about them. John's wife and that little girl. Or any of those guys who went before John."

Rebecca stayed very, very still. This was the most he'd ever said on the subject without telling her it was all going to be okay.

"What if we have this baby and something happens to me? I'm always careful, but so was John. I couldn't leave you alone with a kid." He stared up at the ceiling.

She shook her head against the thought of it. She remembered Diane's face when Ella turned into her arms. In spite of all the pain, there was relief spread across it, like she was suddenly whole again.

"If…that…were to happen," she began haltingly. "Don't you think I'd need someone else? Someone who was half each of us, someone who was our family?"

"I guess." He sighed. "And what about when I'm away

on trips? I don't want to leave you a single mother for weeks at a time."

"We'll figure it out," she said with a certainty she didn't quite feel. People did this all the time, didn't they? There were days it seemed she couldn't turn around in Devil's Purse without seeing a woman pushing a stroller on her own.

He gently pulled her over so her head rested on his shoulder. "You really want this."

She looked up at the outline of his chin. Part of her wanted to ask him what he thought they'd been doing all this time if she didn't really want this and why these concerns of his had never come up before. The other part of her understood: somewhere along the line, a child had become less and less of a possibility with every negative test. If they saw a doctor, it seemed like the child they'd been imagining could suddenly, finally be real.

"Yes," she said. "Very much so."

"Okay, then," he said resolutely. "Let's do it."

Chapter Twenty-Three

ELLA LAY IN HER parents' bed. She was never one of those kids who climbed in with them when she had a bad dream—they had such nasty morning breath, and she hated waking up with that in her face—but now, she needed the weight of her mom's arm across her back. It reminded her that her mom was still here. She wasn't completely alone.

It was time to meet Lacey. "Mom?"

"Yes? What?" Her mom snapped up to sitting, out of her nap.

"I gotta go meet Lacey." Lying about it seemed pointless now.

Her mom's forehead wrinkled.

"She was helping me look for…for Dad." Her eyes filled with tears. She sniffed them back and rubbed at her face. "I gotta go tell her the search is off."

"Oh, sweetie." Her mom sighed and touched Ella's shoulder. "Don't worry about that. I'll call her mom and tell her."

"No," she said too forcefully. "I really need to tell her myself. Please? I'll be back in a few minutes, I swear."

Her mom nodded slowly. "Okay. But call me if you need me. I'll drive straight there and get you."

"Thanks, Mom." She leaned in and pecked her mom on the cheek before scrambling off the bed.

Outside, the sun was way too bright. Ella picked up a stick and started whacking it against trees and fences as she passed for no particular reason. When she reached the corner, their corner, Lacey was already there.

"There you are," Lacey said. "You ready to go?"

Ella noticed she'd put makeup on. Her cheeks were pink, her eyes all fancy and smudged. Something unfamiliar gurgled up inside Ella. She thought maybe she was furious. "How could you?" she whispered.

Lacey stopped. Her eyes widened so far, you could barely see her eyeshadow. "What?" she said.

"You let me think he was alive. You took me on these stupid interviews to find him. But he's not. He's not. He's dead." She was yelling now, and it felt good ripping through her.

Lacey was flushed all over. Ella threw the stick as far as she could, not exactly at Lacey, but away, away.

"Ella, I—"

Lacey reached for her, but Ella couldn't stand to see her face anymore. Why didn't she just tell Ella her dad was gone like everyone else? Ella turned away and went back home.

It was painful, running, but a relief, too, to find that she could still do it; her knees didn't bend the wrong way, and her ankles didn't collapse under the weight of her. Lacey knew she was trying to leave the beetle behind, just as she knew it wasn't going to work, and still, she ran. Her breath came harsh and her head pounded whenever her feet hit the pavement. Sweat trickled down under the arms of her jacket.

She knew people were staring at her, running down the street in her suede boots and her nicest jeans, the ones she hadn't worn in months and now slipped down over her ass. Mrs. Wall, who always put up her Christmas decorations before they'd even hit Thanksgiving, stopped stringing lights along the railing of her front steps and shook her head when Lacey passed. Matt would've told her to fuck 'em if he'd been there, and maybe he would've kissed her on the temple, right near where the beetle lived. But he wasn't there.

And there was home. Her feet fell to an awkward, slapping rhythm as she slowed to a stop. Maureen's van was gone. She'd probably decided to take advantage of her afternoon off from nannying Lacey and go buy supplies for her next event. Mrs. Staybrook might call her soon, though, and tell her Ella's search party was off. She didn't have much time.

She thundered up the stairs to her room. She washed her face, hot water stinging her sinuses as she splashed the makeup off. She shouldn't have bothered. The mirror hung above her, daring her, but she turned away from it. She stripped off her jeans and folded them carefully back into their drawer before retrieving a pair of leggings from her hamper of dirty laundry. She pulled on a sweatshirt and tugged it over her hips.

She would go to the library. Her mom wouldn't find her there, and Lacey wouldn't have to see her sad, clear eyes. Everywhere else was too risky. She might run into people, people who knew, people who told her the beetle was right.

She ran again. Down the stairs, out the door, she forgot to lock it, but then they left it unlocked half the time anyway, not something to worry about in this town. Down the street a mile, two, trees whipping by around her, above her, the perfect joy of the sidewalk underfoot, her sneakers beating the beetle's tongue into the earth. She barely stopped at crosswalks, waved at the cars that stopped for her without looking at them. When she got to the library, she bent over next to a bush, her hands on her knees, her heart an enormous thudding. It was an effort not to puke. There was pain everywhere, everything hurt. She hurt. She remembered Ms. Bray talking about PAWS, what a silly name for this, like a kids' TV show.

She rubbed her sweatshirt sleeve across her forehead and licked the salt from her lips. She stood up tall and walked into the library, wiggling with impatience as the automatic doors wheezed open. The librarian was frowning down at something on her desk, twisting that locket, her locket, around one finger, and didn't look up when Lacey passed.

She stopped in front of the bathroom door. They'd never gone in there, her and Matt and his friends. Public restrooms, in libraries and fast-food restaurants, were for homeless users who didn't have cars or bedroom doors to close themselves off with. Her mom had gotten rid of her bedroom door, though, and she'd never had a car, only Matt's, so. There she was.

She pushed the door and was surprised by how easily it swung open. It didn't fight her, didn't throw the slightest weight against her arm. The greenish fluorescent lights inside made her squint, as did the industrial peach of the floor tiles. Just like the ones at the clinic. No, not here. Not with those floors.

The study room. It was quiet there and always empty. She knew because she and Amanda and Chloe used to go there after school. They'd spend hours there, talking and laughing.

Sure enough, the room was empty. She closed the door behind her. She sat down in a carrel in the corner, its half walls protecting her.

There was shame, there was fear, there was the beetle,

fastidiously noting everything she'd ever done wrong, even helping Ella, especially helping Ella. It was all too much, too much. There was the bag in her sweatshirt pocket, the last thing she'd grabbed from her bathroom vanity before she'd started running. She'd forgotten to put the diary back in the wall in her rush, and Maureen would probably find it and see the photos tucked inside it, the ones from the locket.

The bag slipped from her fingers to her lap. She picked it up again. The pills were white white white. They weren't a challenge, not anymore. They were all she had left.

Maureen had gotten rid of her kit. Obviously. She would have to snort it. Her tolerance would've lowered while she was sober, so she pinched a single pill out of the bag. She laid it on the desk before her and stared at it. If she took it, she knew, that would be it. Her mom would never forgive her. She couldn't claim to be sober anymore. Ms. Bray would probably smell it all over her the second she saw her. What did she have to lose, though, anyway? Her family didn't want her anymore. None of her old friends did, either, and she couldn't see her new ones or Matt. College was a pipe dream.

"Snap out of it, Carson," she muttered, the way Coach Johnson used to when she was daydreaming in the outfield.

It was so morose, so self-absorbed, like those videos they used to show in health class. A black-and-white image of a girl in an outdated hairstyle staring out into the middle distance, chin resting on her fist, with a voice-over that said mournfully, "If you or someone you know is suffering from thoughts of self-harm, please, seek help." And then the teacher would turn the lights on to reveal the doodling, the texting, the occasional good old-fashioned note being passed from desk to desk: "Would bang girl in video Y/N."

She swept the pill into her palm and folded it into a dollar bill. She put the bill on the desk and placed her school ID flat on top of it. She brought the heel of her hand down on the pile hard, three times, checking after each smack to make sure the dollar hadn't spat the pill out across the table. When she brought it back up to her face, the pill was not quite crushed, chunks of it still there, powder clinging to the creases in the bill. She pressed her thumbnail against the larger fragments, tried to break them up further, squeezing the dust back out from her nail bed. She held the bill up to her face. It shook a bit. She inhaled through her nose, as deeply as she could. And waited.

Chapter Twenty-Four

October 25, 1998

ANNIE MADE THE RIGHT choice for herself and for the baby. She knew that. In her best, strongest moments, she even believed it.

The hospital sent her home after two days with a handful of maxi pads and a plastic thing that looked like a bed pan. "It's a sitz bath," the nurse said when she hesitated to take it and then left before Annie had time to ask what the hell that meant.

Walking into the apartment felt strange. The last time she'd been there, she was two, and now, only one. It seemed like a decade had passed. She put a hand to her stomach before she opened the door. Her flesh jiggled now like it'd been formed out of Jell-O.

Eve was waiting on the couch where she always was. Annie was starting to wonder how she managed to pass her classes when she never seemed to actually go to them.

"Hey," Eve said gently, the way you'd talk to a runaway dog. "Your coworker stopped by and told us what happened. You okay?"

Annie looked out the window behind her at the sullen brick buildings across the street. "Yeah, I guess," she said. "Fine."

Sophia walked out of her room, high-ponytailed and red-faced. "Oh, hey!" she said. "Baby-free?"

Annie turned to display her profile, though what they never told you is that you still look pretty damn pregnant after giving birth.

"Sophia!" Eve hissed.

"What?" Sophia said. "She didn't want to keep it, did she?"

Her closed bedroom door only partially muffled the arguing that followed. She fell into her bed and rolled herself in her comforter and tried to sleep.

She spent the better part of two weeks there, mostly alone. Her breasts grew hard as rocks, and she cried out whenever she accidentally rolled on them. There was a girl in her class, Shawna. She'd disappeared one summer, no one knew where, and when she came back, a boy she hooked up with bragged about her "solid tits," not realizing such things weren't the norm. The prevailing rumor was that she'd gone off to get a boob job—and done something to her nose while she was at it—but now, Annie wondered. She wished she had Shawna's number.

The space between her legs was what hurt the most. It was so alarmingly painful, she peeked down there once and instantly regretted it. Eve taught her how to use the sitz bath, reading off instructions she'd found online from the other side of the bathroom door. And Helen came by once with some sort of magical frozen maxi pads she'd whipped up. She left them on Annie's nightstand, saying, "You know what to do." Mostly, Annie just limped from the bed to the bathroom, changing her pad when she bled through one and slurping down the soups Eve brought her in bed.

On the fifteenth day, Sophia appeared in her doorway. "Phone's for you," she said.

Annie held out her hand for the receiver, but Sophia tossed it onto the foot of her bed.

It was her mother. "You said your due date was around now, didn't you?" she said. "I wanted to call and see how you were doing."

"I did it." Annie inhaled. "I delivered the baby. Two weeks ago, actually."

"Oh," her mother said. "Well. How did it... How was it?"

"It went fine. Baby was healthy." Because she didn't think she could stand waiting for her mother to get to it, she added, "She's with her adoptive mother now. She's a really nice lady," she said, though they'd never actually met in person. The only thing she'd seen of the woman outside her file was her signature on the adoption papers.

"I wish I could've been there," her mother said softly, and it almost knocked Annie back into her pillow. "Well, don't worry," she continued. "Your father and I will cover all the medical expenses, of course. You just tell the hospital to bill us through our insurance."

Annie sat very still. All the resolve she'd had at the hospital to pay them back was gone now. "Thanks, Mom," she said quietly.

Her mother paused. "In any case, there's another reason I'm calling. Your father and I are moving to Vermont. It's been a dream of his for a long time, and we thought we could use a fresh start. We've found a house in a sweet little town and are hoping to sell ours in the next few months. I'll give you our new phone number when the time comes. And, well. You're always welcome to come visit. Any time."

When her mother hung up, Annie lay back, the phone held loosely in one hand. This was it, then. There would be no returning home to wake up in her old bed and pretend nothing had happened. She found she was okay with that. At some point in her pregnancy, she'd begun to sense that there would be no going back. She wasn't the same person anymore.

That night, she wedged herself into her favorite pair of pre-pregnancy cargo pants and a sleeveless turtleneck that clung unflatteringly to her midsection. She lined her eyes and swept glittery gel over her cheekbones, hoping it distracted from the rest of her.

Her roommates were still in the living room, fueling up for the night ahead with store-brand mac and cheese. There was an *SNL* rerun on, and Sophia turned to look just as the audience laughed.

Sophia raised an eyebrow. "You off to a rave or something?"

Annie stepped closer. "Actually, I was hoping I could come out with you guys tonight."

"Really?" Eve's head popped up over the edge of the couch. "You sure you're up for that?"

Annie shrugged. "Sure. Why not?"

Eve stared.

"Okay," Sophia said. "We leave in twenty."

On their way out the door, Sophia ran a paper towel under the kitchen faucet and used it to scrape the glitter off Annie's cheeks. She stood back and studied her for a second and said, "There. That's better."

When they got to the party, Annie was glad Sophia'd done so. She'd imagined college parties would be so glamorous, like they were in the movies. There should be a shimmering turquoise pool and a live band made up of moody upperclassmen, cold weather be damned. But this was no different from the parties she'd been to in high school. It was at a frat house, and people milled from room to room, nodding their heads to Destiny's Child and Backstreet Boys booming from the stereo. At some point, someone would probably yell out a complaint and switch it over to Third Eye Blind.

No, the only differences from the high school parties she knew were that the house was a fair bit messier and the plastic cups of alcohol were left scattered across every possible surface. No one sat hunched over their drinks, holding them close, ready to hide them at a moment's notice.

"Punch?" Sophia held a cup out for her, sloshing with red juice and undoubtedly some sort of vodka.

Annie gulped it down as quickly as she could. Over the past few months, she'd forgotten how satisfying that burn at the back of her throat could be.

"All right!" Sophia slung her arm around Annie's neck. "New kid can party!"

A tall boy in a backward cap offered her another drink, grinning as he held a cup out toward the nearby keg. His smile reminded her so much of her ex-boyfriend that she had to turn away. She filled her empty cup with a couple inches of rum and topped it with a splash of Coke. She'd always preferred rum above all other offerings at her high school parties for the sharp sweetness of it. In no time at all, she'd downed that drink, too. And then another, and another. Closing her eyes as the room spun and blurred around her. She couldn't see her ex's face anymore or hear the weak echo of her mother's voice. With the drinks, her head pounded, but her mind was finally quiet.

She woke—or resurrected, rather—in her room the next morning with no memory of how she'd gotten there. Her hair was plastered to her cheek, and there was a wet continent of drool on her pillow. But she hadn't woken up in the middle of the night with aching in various parts of her body or been kept awake by cries from a phantom baby. Even if she couldn't remember it, she'd been alone at last.

She stumbled out into the living room.

"Morning, sunshine!" Sophia said and pressed a mug of black coffee into Annie's hands. "You really went all out last night. Nice work!"

Eve wouldn't meet her eyes.

It was the same that night and the night after that. She started working at the theater again that week. She'd never noticed before how many babies and toddlers were around. Pushed in flimsy strollers, begging their parents for candy, bounced in patient arms outside theater doors, screaming. Just everywhere. There was a sickening seize in her chest whenever she saw someone venturing out with a newborn. What if it were hers? She didn't even know the baby's name.

The next weekend, they partied again. This time, she drank even more. She winced, sometimes, as the alcohol cut its old path down into her, but she kept going, stumbling right up to the point where she could stop thinking about her parents and the little kids at work and the past endless year. The rum dulled every sharp edge of her memory.

On the third weekend, Eve refused to come out with them. She sat on the couch, eyes fixed to the TV. She was watching a really good Lifetime movie, she said. She had to keep watching to see if the husband did it. Annie and Sophia carried on without her.

On the fifth weekend, Sophia and Eve both stayed in. Finals were coming up, so they had to cram. Annie went out alone. She stood by the stereo in that same frat basement, her eyes lowered so she wouldn't have to see people wondering who the hell she was and what she was doing there. She made sure she always poured her own drinks and that her cup was always full. She drank rum and Cokes until she couldn't picture that hospital room anymore, so her mind's eye could stop hunting for any trace of the baby, its toes or a finger flailing out beyond the turned back of the doctor as he walked away with her.

Both roommates went home for Christmas break. Eve stood in Annie's bedroom doorway and asked haltingly if she wanted to come with her to her parents' house in Connecticut. Annie looked away and declined. She'd enjoy having the apartment to herself, she thought. That whole week, she used the computer whenever she wanted and watched whatever she pleased on TV. She drank the bottle of rum they kept in the kitchen without the Coke when she was alone, letting it spill uncut through her every night. The forgetting was faster that way. She woke up the following mornings with headaches so fierce, she couldn't focus on anything else. And if Sophia and Eve noticed that the bottle was nearly empty when they returned, neither of them said anything.

The first time she went to work drunk, she tripped over the broom while she held it in her own hands. She laughed it off with Sophia while Helen watched silently. The second time, the empty popcorn tub wasn't quite where she expected it to be, and she dropped a full scoop of freshly popped kernels on the floor.

Helen pulled her over to the ICEE machine. "Your boozing is showing, kid," she muttered.

Annie turned her back to hide her blush and carefully centered a super-size cup under the dispenser, then filled it with neon blue slush.

After that, she cooled down. She reserved drinking for weekends only, even if she felt a little wild-eyed when she came home from her Friday night shift and asked Sophia where she was going that night. It sort of worked. She could hardly sleep at night, and she had trouble focusing at her job. Her attention was always drawn to the infants in the theater.

At least her roommates and Helen didn't seem so worried about her anymore, though.

One morning, she was sipping her coffee in front of the TV when a jewelry commercial came on. A woman opened a velvet box to reveal one of those ugly, twisting necklaces that looked a bit like a diamond-encrusted seagull turd. A toddler threw himself into the woman's arms, and she smiled beatifically at the man standing behind him, like the Virgin Mary herself. "This Mother's Day," the voice-over said, "thank her for everything she does with our beautiful Family Links pendant."

Mother's Day. She'd completely forgotten about it. All that week, she couldn't get away from it. Shop windows were papered with posters for last-minute gifts. Restaurants advertised special three-course meals, sure to get you home in time to tuck the rug rats into bed. Her roommates called home from behind closed doors, crooning to their mothers and promising to send flowers, the biggest bouquets they could afford after they'd paid their rent at the end of the month. Annie began sneaking sips straight from the replacement handle of rum in the kitchen at 3:00 a.m. when everyone was asleep, just so she could close her eyes and not think for a while. It was such a cliché, moping around on Mother's Day, but what could she do? Her own mother preferred Annie not call them in Vermont. It was an intrusion into their new life, Annie could tell. Her daughter would be six and a half months old on that very Sunday. For the rest of her life, she knew, she would measure time by how old her daughter would've been. How old she was, somewhere.

On that day, she locked herself in her room with a bottle and allowed herself to get carried away while the others studied. Her eyelids drooped low and her limbs loosened, and everything felt so, so far away. Her brain fuzzed up in the way it always did when she needed it to. At nightfall, she heard their voices growing louder and rowdier. She stumbled into the kitchen and dropped the empty Captain Morgan into the recycling bin in front of both of them, brazen.

"Dude, I've been looking for that!" Sophia snatched the bottle out of the bin and waggled it overhead. The remaining half centimeter of rum sparkled. "Did you drink this whole thing?" she said. "Not cool."

Annie shrugged. "My bad," she mumbled. "I'll give you cash when I get my next paycheck."

"We've been meaning to talk to you about this," Eve said, walking over with her arms crossed. "We think you have a drinking problem, and we think you need help."

Annie snorted. "And I think you've been watching too much Lifetime. I'm fine. Just a normal party girl, right?" It was only when she saw the hurt in Eve's eyes that she realized Eve was being serious. Annie sighed. "Whatever. If you guys aren't going out tonight, I guess I'll just head to bed."

When she tried to pass, Eve reached out and caught her arm. And it wasn't the way she'd done it a hundred times before, to support her, to guide her, to comfort her. It was firm; it was hard. It meant to take Annie somewhere she didn't want to go.

Panicked, Annie swept her free hand across the counter. The only thing she came across was a table knife, the dull blade coated with a film of old peanut butter. She gripped it in her fist and held it up in Eve's face, only thinking: *let me go*.

It worked. Eve screamed and Sophia gasped and Eve dropped her arm. Something about the way Annie had lunged unleashed a flood of nausea that rose from her stomach, and then everything was dark.

Chapter Twenty-Five

Saturday, November 11, 2017

AFTER HER TALK WITH Mack, Rebecca went upstairs to change for her afternoon shift at the library. As she pulled a dress off its hanger, she stumbled over her old boot, lying small and forgotten on the floor.

She dressed without looking at it. She twisted to zip up her dress and scooped her hair up into a clip. Before she walked out the bedroom door, she leaned into her closet, groping past her hamper and discarded sandals, and found the other boot. She lined the two of them up in front of the closet, neat as you please, and left.

On her way to the library, she remembered Addie's sympathy cup from the day before and stopped at Dunkin' Donuts to order coffee just the way Addie liked it: large caramel latte, three Splendas.

"Afternoon, Addie," she said as she slipped the warm cup onto the research desk.

Addie eyed the coffee, then Rebecca. "You feeling better today, Becks?"

Did it show on her face, what Mack had said? But no, Addie took a sip, wiggled her shoulders with pleasure, and said, "I know you and the Staybrooks were kind of close or whatever."

"Oh, yes," she said with a gulp. "Well." She couldn't come up with anything else, so she turned back to her own desk. "It's so terrible," she said as she walked away and felt rather than saw Addie's shrug.

How was she going to make it up to Ella? What could she say that would possibly make any difference? She googled sympathy messages on her computer while looking up fertility specialists on her phone. Every time the door opened, she looked up only to see the usual parade of tired weekend parents and their broods. No sign of Ella.

It took a couple of hours for her to remember the money. John's twenty, the extra one he'd slipped her the last time she saw him. She took her wallet out of her pocketbook, and there it was, kept separate from the rest of her cash in a tiny pocket she'd never found a use for so that she could give it back to him. This one, she would return. She'd leave it in her mailbox or stick it under her front door. Not because she thought it'd be any help but because it seemed somehow to be unequivocally his.

"Hey, Becks," Addie called.

Rebecca shoved the wallet back into her pocketbook.

"You hear something in the study room?"

"I didn't, no."

"There was definitely something, like a big thud. You mind checking it out? I'm a little busy here."

Indeed she was. A woman stood at her desk, her hand on a little boy's shoulder, perhaps six, seven years old. "Now, tell the nice librarian your question," she said.

"How do people make sex?" he asked. "And how come it's so loud in the movies when they do it?"

Addie shot her a wide-eyed, panicked look as the woman smiled sheepishly. Checking the study room for puking kids or homeless adults seemed tame in comparison. Rebecca held her breath against the inevitable smell as she swung open the door.

Rebecca almost didn't see her at first. She was halfway across the room before she realized there was a body on the floor. It was coiled under a carrel on the far side of the room. She hurried over. When she saw the face, acid filled the back of her mouth. Lacey Carson. She knew in an instant from the gray of the girl's face exactly which rumors had been true.

She ran back to her desk and tried to catch Addie's eye. She was still talking to the boy, making unsettling motions with her hands. There was nothing for it. She found the lockbox under her desk and spun the combination. It took her four tries for the lock to release. She snatched the plastic bag from it and ran back to the study room. "Call 911, please," she said through her teeth as she passed Addie's desk, as discreetly as she could.

The bag's seal was difficult to break, and its contents spilled out onto the floor as she shoved her way back into the study room. She knelt down and gathered them into her trembling hands, the vial, the applicator, the cheery yellow cap.

She could hear the crackling of the walkie-talkie on the paramedic who'd trained her on Narcan use as she jammed the vial into the applicator. They hadn't ever needed to use the Narcan since they'd gotten it. In Devil's Purse, people chose other climate-controlled places to nod off, like fast-food restrooms and cars.

God, she hoped she was doing it right. She tilted Lacey's forehead back, shuddering at the clamminess of her skin, and shimmied the applicator up one nostril. Impossible to tell how far back to push it. She bit down on the inside of her cheek and squeezed the plastic trigger.

After one moment, two, Lacey's eyes fluttered open. One hand rose slowly, as if through a thaw, and pawed at Rebecca's necklace. "Mom?" she croaked.

The pendant must have been dangling in Lacey's face. Rebecca sat back on her heels and tucked it under her collar. "You're at the library, Lacey," she said. The paramedic had said something about talking to the patient and asking questions to keep them awake. "I can call her. Do you want me to call her? Should I use your phone?"

These were things she should've said more firmly, in short, clear sentences. She could think of nothing else to ask.

Lacey shook her head, still slow, the weight of her skull grinding her hair into the tile floor. Her eyes screwed shut, and tears pooled in the inner corners.

Rebecca found her hand on Lacey's forehead, brushing the hair back over and over. "It's going to be okay," she said. No more questions. "You're going to be fine."

The door slammed against the wall. Rebecca turned, dazed, and there were three or four men there. One of them held a bright orange board. Addie was behind them. Her eyes darted anywhere but the floor, the back of one hand pressed to her mouth. The men shuffled in and, counting down to each other, heaved Lacey onto the board and strapped her in. One of them asked Lacey stern questions to which she nodded or shook her head. Rebecca shrank back against the wall as they carried her past.

Out in the hall, Addie hadn't moved. "Is…is she…" Her mouth collapsed.

"She's conscious," Rebecca said. She touched Addie's arm. "I think she'll be okay since you called an ambulance."

Supplying the library with Narcan had been one of the biggest scandals the town had seen in years. The members of the Friends of the Devil's Purse Library in particular had been beside themselves. "Pearl clutching" didn't even begin to cover it. Rebecca had brought it up at their monthly meeting, slipping it in under "other business."

"Wait a minute," one woman had said, smacking the flat of her palm against the table to interrupt Rebecca. "Narcan. Isn't that that stuff they use to revive junkies? Here, in our library. When there are kids around?"

"It doesn't make any sense really," another one said. "I watched a story on this, on YouTube. It just enables them. They keep overdosing and then going back for more when they wake up."

"Besides, I can't imagine we'd actually need this. In our town?"

Addie, sitting beside Rebecca, snorted. All the members' heads swiveled toward her at the impertinence. "Sorry," she said, "and no disrespect, Mrs. Loom, but look, I went to high school with your son. If you think the twenty-five-year-old man living in your basement is clean, then you must be on something, too."

Mrs. Loom's face flushed while the others held back snickers, and Rebecca loved Addie in that moment. The board agreed to authorize the Narcan if it was kept hidden and locked away, to be used only when necessary.

Now, the patrons gathered against the windows, watching the flashing red lights. One of the EMTs came back to ask her questions she couldn't answer while another lumbered out of the study room. A plastic bag of pills unfurled from the fingers of one hand while the other opened to reveal an ID card and a dollar bill.

The first man sighed and scrubbed a hand through his crew cut. "You probably saved that girl's life, you know," he said, but there was something ambiguous to his voice.

Chapter Twenty-Six

THE RESTAURANT SUPPLY STORE was a relief. Maureen wandered through the aisles with her cart, allowing herself to study the things she usually hurried past to get back to Lacey in the van: vats of Crisco, packages of smoked salmon longer than her arm, and liter bottles of red food coloring. She watched other carts roll by and tried to guess if they were for cafeterias or overpriced restaurants.

It was wrong, she knew, to think of Ella as a good influence on Lacey. That was too much of a burden to load on a little kid's shoulders. She could only imagine what the townies thought about the two of them hanging out. They didn't see the look on Lacey's face when she talked about Ella, though, or the wrinkle between her eyebrows when she learned about John. Lacey cared about that girl even when she didn't care about much else. Including her own self. Maureen knew that Lacey would not relapse around Ella. It was maybe the only place she knew she wouldn't.

So when the phone rang while she was unloading her spoils, Maureen's first thought was that something had happened to Ella. She cradled a plastic bag of apples in the crook of one arm and tucked the phone to her shoulder.

"Lacey?" she said. "Honey, is that you? What happened? Did Ella find something bad?"

"Uh, no," an unfamiliar voice replied. "This is Rebecca. Rebecca Holmes, at the library?"

Maureen's face grew hot thinking of Ophelia. Word must have spread to the rest of the board, and they'd sent the librarian to scold her for accusing one of their members.

"I hope it's okay for me to call you," Rebecca continued. "Lacey's phone fell on the floor, and I guess she doesn't keep it locked."

At the mention of Lacey, every part of Maureen tensed. "What is it?" she demanded.

Rebecca's voice became strange and muffled. She was probably cupping her hand around the phone. "She's okay, I promise. I found her in the study room here. I believe it was an overdose? The ambulance just came to take her away."

And there it was. Every worst-case scenario she'd conjured up over the past few months—hell, every one since she'd first held Lacey in her arms, red-faced and wailing and perfect. She took down the name of the hospital and thanked Rebecca for calling and for offering to meet her there with more details, all while watching herself from somewhere far away, a kitchen on another planet. When she hung up the phone, an apple fell out of the bag and onto her foot before rolling under the sink, and she was surprised she could feel it. She looked down and saw that her fingers had dug into the bag and her nails had torn the plastic, flimsy and frail.

She made two phone calls from the van, staring at the road as it unspooled before her. The first was to the clinic.

"Lacey overdosed," she told Ms. Bray, quickly thankful for the brutal workloads that kept caseworkers at the office on Saturdays. "I don't know what on. I swear I cleared her room of everything, and I don't know when she would've seen her boyfriend—her dealer."

"Goddammit," Ms. Bray said.

Maureen winced at the bald anger in the word. She should've known better. She should've done better. Her daughter.

"She's in an ambulance right now. On her way to DP Hospital. Would you—"

"I'll meet you there," Ms. Bray said and hung up.

Maureen breathed. That woman probably saw things like this all the time. She would know what to do. She'd be like a priest in confessional, telling Maureen what came next and meting out justice and blame where it belonged.

Maureen hesitated before calling the second number. It would lay nuclear waste to what remained of what was once her closest friendship. She dialed anyway.

"Is Ella with you?" she said as soon as Diane picked up.

"Yes, she is."

Maureen's hands finally loosened a little.

"She's actually asleep in bed right now. Since you sound so worried, I'm guessing you knew what she and your daughter were up to."

The chill in her voice made Maureen shiver. "I can explain," Maureen said with a sigh. "Or maybe I can't. I don't know anymore. I thought it was good for Lacey to help Ella through this. It'd been so long since I saw her have a purpose, and I know you think she's dangerous and she made her bed, but she's my little girl, Di, and I just—" The words cracked as they left her mouth. "She overdosed. I'm on my way to the hospital."

"Oh, no," Diane said, and it sounded sincere. "Oh, how awful. Was it at home?"

"At the library. That librarian called me, Rebecca? Half the town must be talking about it by now." She ran a red light. She blinked at the signal, glaring at her from her rear-view mirror.

"Well, I'm really sorry to hear that. Truly, I am."

"Thanks."

"You let me know if there's anything we—I can do, okay? Anything at all."

"Sure. Sure, I will." Maureen hung up.

Chapter Twenty-Seven

ELLA WASN'T ACTUALLY SLEEPING. When she got home, sobbing again, her mom had carried her up to bed like a toddler. Her mom tucked her covers around her just the way Ella always liked them.

The ringing phone woke her up. Even from upstairs, she could hear it, attuned as she was to the chirping of her mom's cell. At first, she watched the shadows from the tree outside sway across her ceiling. When she realized her mom was talking about her, she slipped out of bed and toward the doorway. That morning's revelation—the boots, Lacey—was still too sore to touch, so she focused on listening instead.

It didn't take her long to realize what had happened from her mom's half of the phone call. Ella was good at stuff like that. As soon as she heard her mom hang up and turn on the news, Ella ran down the stairs.

Her mom was curled up on the couch, clutching at the edge of the blanket thrown across her lap. When she saw Ella, she released the blanket and wiped the worry off her face. "Hi, sleepyhead," she said in the voice Ella knew she used only with her. "You want to join me? I'll make you a cup of cocoa."

It was tempting. Ella could almost taste the little fake marshmallows. She shook her head. "Was that Lacey's mom?"

"It was." Her mom turned back to the TV. "She wanted to check in and make sure you were doing okay." Her gaze was steady, but her finger twitched a little on the remote. She knew about Ella's special eavesdropping abilities.

"Something happened to Lacey," Ella said.

Her mom turned off the TV.

"She's sick, right? Like, something's really wrong with her."

Her mom studied Ella for a moment and nodded. "Yes. Yes, unfortunately, Lacey is very sick." She patted the couch next to her.

Ella climbed up, grabbing a pillow along the way. She held it to her middle, bracing herself.

"Do you remember," her mom began, "when we had to help your dad quit smoking? Just like how he quit drinking a long time ago?"

Ella squeezed the pillow closer at the mention of him, but she nodded.

"It was so hard for him, and he felt pretty bad a lot of the time."

"He was super cranky. Everyone stayed away from him at the docks." She giggled at the memory, and her mom smiled.

"That's right. Even though the cigarettes were really bad for him, it made him feel sick to give them up. That's called addiction, and that's what Lacey has, only it's not with cigarettes. It's with other things."

"Like drugs?"

Her mom faced her, startled. "How did you know about that?"

"I don't live under a rock, Mom. Don't worry, though.

206

I signed a pledge online not to take them. Only losers do drugs." Losers, she thought suddenly, like her best friend.

"That's good, Ella-Bella," her mom said, patting her on her knee. She moved on to say something about peer pressure and what to do if her friends started doing them, but Ella wasn't listening. She was too busy thinking.

She remembered helping her dad quit, it was true. She also remembered how, on some days, when he was stressed out or upset about something, she would find him at the docks after school, smoking alone in the shadow of his boat. He always flung the cigarette into the water before she got to him and waved his hand in front of his face, as if that did anything to get rid of the smell. She never told her mom. Secretly, the scent of tobacco smoke and diesel fuel always reminded her of him.

And today. When she threw that stick at Lacey. Lacey seemed upset. When she ran away, maybe it was to do drugs.

"Can I go see her?" Ella interrupted her mom.

Her mom sighed and stretched one arm across the back of the couch. "I don't think that's a great idea. We need to give her some space and let her recover."

Ella brought her legs up under her and turned to face her. "No, Mom, please? You don't understand. It's my fault. I need to tell her I love her." Her eyes welled up, and she wiped at them angrily before she realized the tears might help her cause.

Sure enough, her mom smiled sadly and reached out to touch her cheek. "You're such a sweet girl. Have I told you that before?"

Only about a million times, but Ella said nothing and waited.

"All right," her mom said finally. "Let's go. But we're only staying ten minutes, max, you hear?" She held up one scolding finger.

Ella nodded before springing to her feet. Another thing to fill the day.

The automatic doors to the hospital always took exactly five seconds to open. Even in Rebecca's high school volunteering days, it had been this way. She counted to five under her breath, then waited for an old woman on a walker to inch out. She smiled at the woman as she passed her on the way in.

A curmudgeonly woman sat at the reception desk, glasses on a beaded chain made of plastic suns and clouds around her neck.

"Hi, Martha," Rebecca said.

"Rebecca!" Martha's face broke along the smile lines that didn't show when she was grimacing at her computer screen. "How long's it been, six months, a year?"

"Something like that," Rebecca admitted.

"I can't believe what a lovely young woman you're growing into. How's Mack? And the library?"

"They're good, both good. I'm actually here to see a patient. Lacey Carson?" She leaned into the counter while Martha squinted at her screen.

"Ah, yes." She glanced up at Rebecca, then back. "She's in the ICU, room 224. If you go—well, you know where it is." Martha winked.

"I sure do. Thank you. I'll come by and chat on my way out, okay?" Rebecca stood straight and touched her locket, still under her sweater. No more delaying it. She'd told Maureen she'd be there.

Nevertheless, she took the long way there, winding her way through stale-aired halls and pretending to be lost.

When she got to room 224, Maureen wasn't there yet. It was just Lacey, unconscious, pale, and very small under the thin hospital-issue blanket. Rebecca stepped closer and dug through her pocketbook for the tube of lotion she kept there. Using just the tips of her fingers, she rubbed a bit onto the backs of Lacey's hands. She knew how the ventilation system in here could dry out your skin in an instant. Many patients left the hospital with cracked knuckles and stinging palms.

"Rebecca?"

She moved away from Lacey's bed quickly. "Hi, Maureen."

Maureen bent to one side to catch a glimpse of Lacey. "Oh, honey," she murmured and hurried over to the bed. She laid her fingers on Lacey's forehead, and Rebecca looked away.

Another woman had entered the room, unnoticed. "I'm Ms. Bray," she said with a tiny wave. "Lacey's caseworker."

"Hello." There was something so familiar, unplaceable about her blue-gray eyes and sweep of brown hair. Perhaps she'd been at the library recently.

Ms. Bray raised her eyebrows and Rebecca realized she'd been asked something. "I'm sorry, what?" she said, flushing.

"I said, do you know how long she was out for?" Ms. Bray said. "Or what she took?"

"Oh. A few minutes, maybe? And I don't know. Pills?" Rebecca fumbled.

Ms. Bray nodded and pushed her glasses up on top of her head. She moved closer to the bed, next to Maureen. There was no longer a place for Rebecca—almost literally, the room was so tiny. She backed out the doorway and walked away, wishing her shoes were quieter on the linoleum.

When she left the ICU, she took her necklace back out of her collar and started zipping the pendant back and forth along its chain. The sound filled her head, metal on metal, until she made it back to Martha's desk. Martha was explaining to a stressed-looking couple where they could validate their parking. They turned to each other and started to discuss which of them could possibly find the time to stop by the parking ticket window on their way back to the car. "Can't you just do it here?" the man said. "She's eight months pregnant."

"Afraid not," Martha said, lowering her eyes in remorse or boredom. She tapped her bright-red fingernails against the desk until the couple turned away.

"You're back!" Martha said when they were gone. "That was fast."

"Her family showed up, so they didn't need me anymore. Those two were delightful, weren't they?"

"Oh, them?" Martha flapped her hand dismissively. "We get their type through here at least three times a day. They're the least of our troubles." She launched into a discussion on the latest hospital dramas, departmental meetings missed, new policies ignored, feuds between doctors and nurses whose names Rebecca no longer recognized. Rebecca gasped and murmured in the appropriate places, said the types of gossipy things Addie might say.

Eventually, another man appeared behind Rebecca, fiddling with his parking ticket, and cleared his throat delicately. She said goodbye to Martha and let him take her place. Martha's face fell back into its usual pinched annoyance.

She was nearly to the door, already tallying up the groceries she'd have to buy for dinner, when she stopped. She planted one hand on the wall and the other on her belly. She sat down on one of the benches meant for those waiting for taxis.

She knew why she'd recognized Ms. Bray.

Chapter Twenty-Eight

May 10, 1999

ANNIE OPENED HER EYES to an industrial-looking ceiling, the kind with the tiles that have holes all over them. She could tell from the beeping, sucking machinery around her that she was in a hospital. She pushed herself up on her elbows, heart beating hard as she searched the room for evidence that this was St. Augustine's, not Devil's Purse, before she remembered her parents were gone. There was no one left to embarrass.

An envelope stood on the table next to her bed, propped up against a glass vase of sad red roses. Her name was written on the front. It was Eve's handwriting. She reached for it, wincing. The paper was smooth under her fingers. Inside was a thick cream note card rimmed with an embossed silver border, an elaborately scripted E at the top. Annie raised her eyebrows. Eve's family in Connecticut must be richer than she'd realized.

Annie read the note, skimming over phrases like "concerned for our safety" and "best for all of us" and "care deeply." The gist of it was that they wouldn't let her move back in unless she went to rehab. They'd give her a month before they started looking for another roommate, provided she still paid rent in the meantime.

Annie pushed her head back into the pillow and sighed. It was like they were searching for drama. Yes, she'd gone a little overboard that one night, but she'd seen much worse at the parties they frequented.

There had been a knife, though, hadn't there? She grimaced as she remembered the blade swishing through the air. She was not a violent person. She couldn't even watch action movies. She realized with a sinking feeling that she was beginning not to recognize herself. She pushed the thought away. She'd just gotten carried away, that was all.

The fact remained that their rent was cheap, and she wasn't sure she'd be able to find anything else in the area that she could afford on a minimum wage. Regardless of what she was or was not becoming and what she did or did not want to admit, she'd have to go through the motions until her roommates were satisfied.

The ER doctor recommended the regional youth rehab facility and said he thought they'd take her insurance. The taxi charged her an exorbitant amount to drop her off at the address the doctor gave her. She squinted at the meter and did quick calculations in her head to avoid looking at the bleak prison of a building. "It is what it is, babe," the taxi driver told her, and she wasn't sure if he meant the price or rehab in general. He looked down her shirt when she leaned forward with the cash.

At intake, she handed the woman behind the desk the new insurance card her mother had sent her in a slim envelope after her parents had moved. There had been a note with it: "You're still our dependent, so you shouldn't have to pay your own medical expenses." Scribbled underneath it in another ink color was, "We love you always."

The receptionist told her her parents' insurance would cover two weeks' worth of treatment. It didn't seem very long. She could get through fourteen nights in this place. She'd be fine.

All the other patients in the facility looked so young. Some of them dressed all in black and leaned against the outer walls of the building for cigarette breaks, leaving butts ringed with dark red lipstick in the ashtray bins. They were so bony, the bricks must've left bruises on their shoulder blades when they stepped away. Other kids were just sad, sitting hunched in the cafeteria in oversized clothes and scooping soup into their mouths without looking up. A few were loud teenagers, shouting down the halls at each other. Annie slept with her back to the room she shared with five other patients and her face toward the dull gray cement wall. She did not want to be popular here.

Every day was the same. Cereal in the cafeteria, individual therapy, art therapy, sloppy joes, spaghetti and meatballs. And groups. Session after session in group after group. When it was her turn to talk, she talked about her parents and how cold they were, how distant. When she was bored, she'd make up stories. Innocent stuff: they'd made her give away her puppy when she couldn't take care of it; she could only have sweets once a month. The other kids were half-asleep by then anyway. She picked at her chin when the session leaders talked about God.

Her individual counselor was a guy named Randy—no one even knew his last name, because he told them all to call him Randy—and he ran a few of the groups, too. He always stared at Annie for longer than she cared for.

On the eleventh day, during her individual session, Randy pushed his chair back from his desk and crossed his legs. "So, Annie," he said. "I had an interesting call with your mother this morning."

Annie stiffened. Her parents must've already known about

the rehab from the insurance bills, but she preferred not to think about that.

"Are you sure there's nothing more you want to talk about?" he said.

Annie shook her head.

Randy watched Annie's face closely. Annie looked right back, grinding her teeth together. She could tell her mom had told him about the baby, but she knew he wouldn't bring it up until she did. It was probably counselor protocol.

Her daughter's memory did not belong within these walls. For once, she was glad she'd never named the baby. There was nothing to call her by, nothing to tell him.

Finally, he started back in on his lecture on preparing for the outside world. She remained silent for the rest of the session. She watched him squirm. After a while, he stopped talking, maybe thinking she'd fill the quiet out of sheer discomfort. She didn't. They spent the remainder of that hour in their separate bubbles, him checking his files and her picking at her nails, the tick of the button on his mouse occasionally interrupting the silence.

When she checked out on her last day, she felt buoyant. She still didn't quite know if she was cured or needed curing, but she was free, and the air was crisp and early-summer new. Neither of her roommates had offered to pick her up, but that was okay. She'd taken a cab to the clinic, and she would take one away from it.

Sophia was gone when she walked in, off running errands or something, but Eve was there. She leapt up from the couch to greet her. "You're home!" she said. She embraced Annie tightly. "We've missed you." She stood back, her hands still clamped around Annie's biceps, and lowered her voice. "Listen, I know one of your steps is seeking forgiveness, but you don't have to worry about us. That horrible night is all water under the bridge now."

Annie smiled wanly. She mumbled a thank you and headed to her room to unpack the ill-fitting clothes Eve had dropped off for her at the clinic.

The theater manager let her come back only because he was shorthanded for the summer rush. Helen barely acknowledged her. Annie saw her glance at Sophia more than once on her first day back. When Annie asked her about her kids, Helen hesitated and said, "They're fine," before turning back to the popcorn machine. Sophia probably told her about the knife. By the end of her first week, Annie was exhausted and drooping, wondering always what her daughter would think of her.

The girls didn't invite her out with them that Friday. They swanned past her door in miniskirts while she lay in bed with an aching head. She knew better than to ask to join them. No matter; it was a college town. There were bound to be other parties going on. She had to do something about the pain.

It took her four tries to get sober—really sober. Sophia found her passed out in front of their door one morning, her face mashed into a bag of cinnamon rolls she'd bought from the bakery downstairs. Annie was still picking icing out of her hair when they dropped her off at the clinic, trying not to think about the frat boy who kept asking her about her family the night before. After that, she moved in with a bunch of girls from the clinic, all in recovery.

When she relapsed a second time, the rum took up most of her wages. There were no more college parties to supply her in this new part of town. She hid the bottles under her bed—the girls had a strict substance-free policy. One night, she lay on the floor, one arm outstretched to retrieve the half-empty bottle. The walls of her apartment were so thin, it was a mystery how they supported the weight of the building. She heard a baby wailing in the unit next door, and as its cries ripped through her and she brushed the dirt off her cheek, she realized she didn't like herself very much. She held the bottle in one hand and wondered if it would kill her.

No more. She tried to quit on her own that time, to see if she could, but the shakes and the vomiting quickly became too much. She checked herself back in that third time. The receptionist at the clinic told her without even a little bit of sadness that there were no beds available. She referred Annie to the adult facility nearby. At eighteen, she qualified for treatment there.

The adult clinic was somehow even bleaker. The patients were all worn down, strung out, given up. Nobody yelled in the hallways. Nobody bothered. A lot of them had kids they weren't allowed to see, and in group, some of them talked about how the only thing getting them through was that they needed to get out and see their daughters again. She checked herself out after a week and needed a drink just to forget what she'd seen.

The fourth time, she went because she was just tired. Tired of herself and of the effort it now took to get a buzz. She went back to the youth clinic, since she still qualified as a teenager. She resolved to tell Randy everything this time, every little detail, but Randy wasn't there anymore. Her kind-eyed new counselor said he'd transferred to a facility in North Carolina to be close to his family.

By rights, it shouldn't have stuck that time. She had no

friends, no family—her mother had written her a letter shortly after her first stint in rehab and said they would pay for treatments as long as she liked but asked her to please not contact them any longer. She had no job, either, and no energy. All things the group leaders said were crucial to a successful recovery.

"What would you like to do with your life, Annie?" her counselor asked her one morning. "How do you envision your future?"

Annie's eyes darted around the room. "I want to survive" seemed like it might raise an alarm bell or two for this sweet woman. She said, "I want to be a drug counselor," and both of them raised their eyebrows in surprise.

That night, she stared at the ceiling, kept awake by the rattling snore of the patient she shared a room with. Maybe it could work. She could be matter-of-fact like Helen, nurturing like Eve. She would never, ever force her patients to admit something they weren't ready to face. She would be like the mother she hadn't been able to be.

And so by some miracle, she was. She got her GED and went to night school for her bachelor's in psychology while she worked days in a coffee shop around the corner. She studied for exams on public buses and on sticky tables in the window of the café on her breaks. She discovered she had an extraordinary capacity for reading when surrounded by noise. Whenever she needed a drink—which was often in the beginning and still once or twice a week a few years later—she studied instead, even when her head pounded and her hands shook and every part of her told her "you cannot." She went to a couple of AA meetings, but all that talk of God and a higher power still made her fidget, remembering the hard, unforgiving pews of her childhood. Her higher power was studying so ferociously, she lost track of herself. Giving herself no breaks, ever. Was that healthier? She didn't know. She went to her graduation despite not having anyone to invite, and when she walked across that rubberized stage, she glowed.

She went back to her own rehab clinic to apply for a job. She could have gone anywhere, to any state, and she shivered a little as she climbed the steps to its front door. But she wanted someone to recognize her and see how far she'd come. Of course, none of the caseworkers she remembered were still there—turnover rates were high. The field as a whole tended to chew through idealistic new college graduates, spitting them out into gentler careers. She thought she saw the receptionist glance twice at her face while she filed her orientation paperwork, though.

Working at the clinic was both far better and far worse than she'd imagined. Sometimes, she got letters—not emails but real, honest-to-God letters—from former clients who were now out, living cleaner lives. They wrote to her to thank her for her help. She kept those letters stacked in a drawer in her bedside table, and sometimes, late at night, she took them out and read them all, even the ones whose names she barely recognized, even the ones who she remembered as reticent and near silent during their sessions.

But then, working with teenagers was often a special kind of thankless, with their mood swings and their all-knowingness. But then, there were the deaths. So many. Over the years, the alcoholics and marijuana users were replaced with painkiller and heroin addicts. They were hooked on Oxy and Percs. They would finish their treatments and walk out the door, and the staff would watch them go. Even the receptionist could tell they weren't ready. And what could Annie do? Insurance covered what insurance covered, and that was that. Sometimes they got calls from parents weeks later. They were distraught, angry, tragically grateful. Their kids were missing, relapsed, dead. The staff developed a sort of gallows humor about it to protect themselves. They called each other by their last names, like soldiers, and never admitted to each other when they'd gone home to cry or scream or drink. She was "Fitzpatrick," which eventually got shortened to "Patty," even after she married and became a Bray.

One day, Annie walked in her apartment door and found her husband, Terry, dumping several glugs of vodka into the tomato sauce bubbling on the stove. "I know, I know," he said. "I'll pour the rest down the toilet when I'm done. It's just been one of those days."

Annie made a mental note to eat her pasta dry that night. The alcohol would cook off, but the flavor would still be there.

"You got a letter, by the way," he said, pointing over his shoulder with the sauce-dipped spoon. "Doesn't look like it's from a client or anything."

Well, of course it didn't. Client letters went to the office, not to their home address. Annie picked up the envelope from the counter and immediately dropped it. She wiped her hands on her legs, shook out their shake. Fear shot through her belly. Terry stirred away, but he was no doubt watching out of the corner of his eye. He'd specified what the letter was not because he was curious about what the letter was. There, in the upper left-hand corner, in staid, black font, was the name and address of the adoption agency.

She took the letter into their bedroom and checked twice to be sure the door had closed behind her. Terry knew about the adoption. One of the things she loved most about their marriage was that he'd never once mentioned having kids of their own. She couldn't bear the thought. As far as she was concerned, she hadn't earned another shot. No matter how understanding Terry was, though, she wasn't ready to share whatever this letter had to say.

She sat on her knees on her braided rug and slipped her finger under the envelope's seal. She felt seventeen all over again. Everything she had was slipping away.

Her daughter had just turned eighteen and had requested identifiable information about her birth parents. Would she be willing, the letter asked, to release that information?

Every year, in October, she googled stock photos of five-year-olds, twelve-year-olds, fifteen-year-olds, and tried to imagine those generic faces with her own features on them. She read articles about what to expect from your child's development during that year. And then, that one night a year, she took a sleeping pill before bed and refused to think.

She'd known this day would probably come from the moment she chose a closed adoption against the agency's disapproving advice. Birth parent reunions were a staple of daytime talk shows now, and she clicked the TV off whenever one appeared.

It wasn't that she didn't want to meet her daughter and see what she'd become. She ached for it. But she also couldn't bear to think of the look in the girl's eyes when she learned who her mother was: a recovering alcoholic who never even left the state. Better that the girl live in the dreamy life of possibility Annie picked out for her, where her birth mom could be an actress or an astronaut. Better that she keep the clean slate Annie had given her. Lord knows, Annie had cluttered her own slate up plenty. Better for everyone.

The letter had the agency's phone line listed in the last

paragraph. Annie pulled her cell from her coat pocket. She already knew what she was going to say.

Ten months later, Lacey Carson came to the clinic for residential treatment.

"New clients in today," one of her coworkers said, pausing in the doorway of Annie's tiny office.

"What's their substance?" Annie said, not looking up from her computer screen.

"Heroin and Percs. Wanna come meet 'em?"

Annie sighed and pushed back from her desk.

"Tell me about it," her coworker said. "Never thought you'd see the day when you hoped for an alcoholic client, huh?"

Her fellow caseworkers knew about her addiction, but they never treated Annie delicately. Annie liked that about them.

The two new kids were waiting in the reception area, under that tone-deaf motivational poster. Annie reminded herself to see if she could find a cheap replacement to send her supervisor's way. One of the kids was staring down at his feet and kicking the toe of one sneaker against the sole of the other. The second kid looked up, and Annie's heart shuddered to a stop.

It was her old boyfriend's face staring right at her. A more feminine version, beautiful actually, with long eyelashes and a thinner nose. But his eyes, his mouth, his dark hair.

Impossible. She didn't know much about the adoptive mother, but she knew she was from out of state. No, her daughter was living a perfect, happy life somewhere far away. She wasn't an addict.

Annie's fingers began to tingle. She was going to pass out if she didn't take a breath soon. She smiled brightly. "Hi, I'm Ms. Bray," she said, "one of the caseworkers here." She held out her hand, and the girl took it.

"Lacey," she said.

Annie glanced at her coworker, who was busy trying to extract a name out of the boy. "You from around here, Lacey?" It was a totally normal thing to ask, she told herself.

"Thirty minutes or so away. Devil's Purse," Lacey said.

The air released slowly through Annie's nose. Of course. The town was so small, this was probably a niece or a third cousin of Simon's. She was pretty sure he'd had a large extended family. She ignored the tremble in her knees. This could not be her daughter. Her daughter was from Minnesota.

"No shit?" Annie said, trying to find her usual delight in the teen's slackened jaw. New clients never pictured this as a place where swearing was allowed. You couldn't even wear T-shirts with logos on them, but her supervisors never cared much about language. "That's where I'm from, too. Come on, hon. Let's get you settled in." She hoisted one of the bags at Lacey's feet—she'd have to inspect them, but that could wait a few more minutes—and led her down the hall.

Lacey wasn't assigned to Annie. Annie had a full load of clients already, so she went to Calvin Cole, whom all the rest of the staff teased for having a name that sounded like an underwear designer. She did see Lacey around the halls, of course, and a shiver went down her neck every time they passed each other.

Lacey was in one of the groups she ran as well. She

leaned forward whenever the girl spoke, not taking notes, transfixed. She always had to correct herself and duck her head toward her notepad. Favoritism was obviously frowned upon here. Even though this wasn't her daughter, maybe this was what her daughter looked like now. It was better than anything she'd dreamed up before.

During one session, she asked the kids to go around the room and describe their families. It was a pretty standard prompt, really more of a venting session meant to bring them all together than anything else.

A couple of kids passed, looking down at their hands. When it was Lacey's turn, she shrugged and said, "It's just my mom and me." She grinned. "She's pretty great, though. She used to be a dancer, but now she owns her own catering business."

Annie's notepad tumbled to the floor. She bent to retrieve it.

Lacey continued. "I'm adopted, so I don't know much about my bio family."

She said it so easily. Annie's ears began to ring.

"We don't see my extended adoptive family much since we moved out here, but they kind of sucked anyway. So that's me."

Annie could hear nothing more. She barely managed to pull herself back upright in her chair. She watched as the boy sitting next to Lacey began to talk, to take his turn. Lacey's legs were crossed, and she bounced one foot up and down, over and over.

It was no use. Annie stood. The boy stopped talking. A dozen pairs of eyes followed her. "Sorry," she said. "Sorry. I'll be right back. Just take a quick break."

She hurried down the hall to her office. She imagined the kids all turning to Lacey and using their precious unsupervised time to ask her questions: had she tried to find her bio parents, did she know where they were from, did she feel like she belonged. The cheap rubber soles of Annie's shoes squeaked against the linoleum. When she reached another office door, the caseworker was already looking up from his computer at the sound of Annie's feet.

"Hey," Annie said apologetically. So many apologies. "Do you mind covering for me in the group in 12B? I've got a…thing." She put her hand on her stomach.

He shrugged. "Sure," he said. "I'm getting bored with this paperwork anyway."

"Thanks." Annie didn't explain what prompts she'd had planned or what they'd already talked about in the group. She shuffled down the hall to her own office, trying to look pained. Though she was tempted to lie down on the floor as soon as she got there, she made sure to walk all the way to her desk before sitting down. She scooted her chair in. She pushed herself so far into her desk that its edge dug into her ribs.

And so. Her daughter was here. Here, in this place Annie'd worked so hard to keep her out of. It seemed like the most terrible coincidence, that her adoptive mother had chosen to move back, that she would fall prey to one of the deadliest drugs in an area where there was only one youth rehab facility. Annie's facility.

For a moment, Annie was furious with her daughter. Not with the eighteen-year-old who sat in that room but with the newborn whose bald, red scalp she'd glimpsed only briefly before turning away. Why had Annie gone through so much shit only to look back and find this girl, the one she'd tried to save, all mired in it?

Annie shook her head firmly, dislodging the anger. She'd been trained over so many years to see this place as one of hope, not of failure or of shame. It wasn't right to blame the client, no matter who she was. Addiction wasn't anyone's fault. There were so many factors involved: environment, mental illness. Genetics.

She knew what she had to do. Ethically and professionally, she was required to disclose her connection to her supervisor. It was a conflict of interest. Annie would be removed from Lacey's care. She pulled up a new email to her supervisor and started to draft her message. "I have recently learned…"

But no. That was not what she had to do. Calvin Cole was known to be a bit of a hard-ass with his clients, maybe to make up for all the teasing he endured from the staff. His scared-straight bit would work with some kids but not with Lacey. Annie had seen it in Lacey's eyes, the ones that reminded her so much of her ex. Of Lacey's father.

No, Lacey needed someone gentler, more empathetic. All that girl's life, Annie had been utterly incapable of giving her what she needed. Even last year, when the only thing Lacey wanted was to know who'd given birth to her. Annie told herself it was for Lacey's own good that she not find out, but it had to have been hard for Lacey to receive that no. Annie shuddered imagining what would happen now if Lacey somehow discovered who she was.

It was a risk Annie'd have to take. Because here, finally, was something Annie could give her. She was a good caseworker, she knew it. She was everything she'd decided to be back in that last trip to rehab. She knew deep down that only she could help Lacey back onto the path she was supposed to be taking. Back to her adoptive mother. Away from all this.

Annie clenched her hands. It was a terrible risk she was taking, but she had to do it. She had to help. She deleted her message, letter by letter. She typed up a request for a client transfer.

Chapter Twenty-Nine

Saturday, November 11, 2017

REBECCA SAT ON THE bench for what felt like a very long time, trying to decide what to do. She knew Lacey had been adopted in this town and she was around the right age and had, according to rumor, never found her birth parents. But then, how many children were adopted each day, perhaps in that very hospital? And the woman seemed familiar with Lacey and her mother. It could be they each already knew who the other was to them and had somehow kept it hidden from the rest of the town.

Still. In all her time of candy striping, that was the only time she'd seen an adoption. It was why she remembered it so clearly now, though she was embarrassed to realize she hadn't thought of that lonely, anguished mother in the hospital bed in years. If she were Maureen, she'd want to know if there were the slightest possibility. If she were Lacey, she'd want to know. She thought of Lacey's eyes, so lost as the paramedics carried her out of the library.

Decision made, Rebecca stood, straightened her sweater, and walked back toward Lacey's room. Martha watched her curiously as she passed. Rebecca smiled quickly at her and said nothing.

She paused outside the door and listened to the voice

of that woman, the stranger who perhaps wasn't a stranger. "I suspect she has generalized anxiety disorder, though she resisted talking about it with me," it was saying. "That would've made it hard for her to manage difficult news like that without reverting to her old coping mechanisms."

When she stepped into the room, Ms. Bray and Maureen both turned. Rebecca stopped. Now that she was here, she had no idea how to ask the question tactfully. "Sorry," she said for some reason. "I—"

Ms. Bray raised her eyebrows.

Rebecca drew another breath and tried again. "By any chance, were you at this hospital in 1998?" She glanced behind Ms. Bray at Maureen. She didn't want to be too explicit in case she was wrong. There was no need to upset things further.

Maureen looked back and forth between Rebecca and Ms. Bray, the picture of confusion.

"As a patient, I mean?" Rebecca finished.

She expected Ms. Bray to scoff and say she didn't know what Rebecca was talking about. For a moment, she looked ready to do just that. Rebecca exhaled. She must be wrong after all.

But then, Ms. Bray's eyes darted toward Lacey in the bed. Ms. Bray's face slackened, and she looked so tired. "Don't," she said softly. She looked back at Rebecca with a raw pain that made Rebecca fall back a step. "Please."

Chapter Thirty

DIANE LED ELLA THROUGH four separate waiting rooms before they finally figured out where Lacey was. In each one, people sat, young and old, staring at their hands, flipping listlessly through outdated magazines. Diane found herself viciously, perversely jealous of these people who could study an X-ray or look into a doctor's eyes and know with some certainty what was taking their loved ones away. Ella squirmed out from under Diane's hand when her fingers clamped more tightly around Ella's shoulder. She smiled tentatively up at Diane and linked her arm with Diane's. Diane smiled back.

Admitting defeat, they stopped to ask a cranky-looking receptionist where they could find Lacey Carson. The woman directed them down a series of hallways to a room they'd already walked past.

"You wait here," Diane instructed, pointing to a molded-plastic chair stationed outside the door. She pulled one of Ella's books from her purse, and Ella's eyes lit up just like she knew they would, in spite of everything. "I'll come get you when they're ready. I promise."

She stepped into the room as Maureen said, "What do you mean?"

There was a third woman standing there, and when Rebecca stepped aside and Diane saw her face, rage grabbed at her.

"You," Diane said.

The woman's mouth fell open. Annie Bray.

"Diane." Annie came one step closer, then another.

Diane pinched her lips closed, distantly aware of Maureen on the other side of the bed looking confused and Lacey lying unconscious in the middle of it all.

"What are you doing here?" Diane asked, but of course she knew. Annie was Lacey's caseworker. Maureen probably hadn't known where else to go.

And Annie, she had the gall to ignore the question and say, "I was so sorry to hear about John. Really, so sorry."

"It was your fault, you know," Diane hissed. It made her think of that first terrible morning with Ella, the accusations her daughter had thrown. This one, though, was true, and Annie knew it.

Annie raised one hand, calming an animal. "Hold on," she said. "I don't think—"

"Oh, you don't think! You don't think!" Diane's voice was high, mocking, shrill. "I know you don't, and that's the problem, isn't it?"

"Wait a sec," Maureen said. She nearly had to shout in order to be heard. "What's going on? How do you two know each other? And what happened in 1998?"

It had been a Wednesday. Diane remembered because John had come home with their weekly takeout—sushi that time—and Diane felt guilty throwing the plastic containers away. "Just chuck 'em," John said as he passed her, paused over the garbage can with the stack. "You know you'll never use 'em if you keep them."

"You're right," she sighed and stepped on the can's foot pedal. Through the window, she saw a car idling in their driveway. Based on the amount of exhaust puddled behind it, the car had been there a while. She wiped a smear of soy sauce onto her jeans, unthinking. She'd have to fit a load of laundry in somewhere tomorrow. She was about to point the car out to John when it turned off and a woman stepped out of the driver's seat. She squinted at their front door and tucked her hair back once, twice. She turned back to her car and opened the door. She stood for a moment in the glow of the interior lights before closing the door again and walking to the house, head down. Her waffling was almost comical.

Finally, the doorbell rang. Diane opened the door. The woman looked to be around their age, with dark, shaggy bangs that made her appear much younger at first. Diane peered behind her at the car once more, but she saw no Mary Kay sticker in its window, nor did the woman launch into any sort of sales pitch. She just stood there, gawping.

"Can I help you?" Diane prompted.

The woman blinked. "Oh. Yes. Is this John Staybrook's house?"

"It is," Diane said, angling her body to block the view inside. It was a little disturbing that this stranger knew her husband's name, but then it was easy enough to find a home address online these days.

"Is he home?"

Diane looked her up and down and considered saying no when John came barreling down the stairs.

"Confirmed, kid is asleep," he said and sidled up to her. "We can watch that slasher movie you've been dying to—oh, shit. Annie Fitzpatrick."

The woman—Annie—looked unabashedly relieved. "John. It's Annie Bray now actually. Can I come in?"

"Sure, sure," he said, guiding Diane away from the door. "Sorry to make you wait out here." He avoided Diane's stare. "Had to make sure my daughter was all settled."

"You have a daughter?" Annie said, surprised.

Diane racked her brain and tried to come up with the name of John's only ex-girlfriend. She was almost certain it wasn't Annie Fitzpatrick. She could've sworn it started with an N. Maybe there were others, though.

But then Annie's crow's feet crinkled. "That's awesome," she said and slipped out of her shoes. Her feet were bare, the toenails painted an electric blue. John's boots had left puddles of brackish water on the tile floor. Annie picked her way around them as she followed John into the living room.

"Can I get you anything? A snack?" Diane asked. It was an empty offer; the whole point of takeout night was that there was little food left in the house at this point in the week. On Thursdays, Diane went grocery shopping with Maureen during her lunch hour.

"Oh, no, I'm fine," Annie said. The three of them settled in, John and Annie on the couch, Diane on the armchair. Diane watched Annie pat Ella's teddy bear, the one she claimed she was too old for, propped up in the corner of the sofa.

"So what've you been up to all these years? You just passing through?" To Diane, John said, "Annie here was a year or two behind me at DP High, but there were so few students that we still had one class together. What was it, gym?"

Annie smiled faintly and nodded. She seemed to be collecting something from within herself, gathering.

"That's nice," Diane said to fill the silence.

"And I dated your brother for a while there," Annie said quietly.

"That's right!" John hooted. "Simon. What a wild man."

Diane nodded. She'd never met Simon. She and John had started dating shortly after he'd returned from Alaska, after they met at the Blockbuster between her college and his hometown. Simon was someone she'd pieced together with stories from John and from all the others in Devil's Purse who had a thing or two to say about him.

"I assume you know he passed," Diane said and then wondered why she had. The boy probably didn't mean much to Annie, and if she hadn't already known he was gone, Diane might've ruined a sweet memory of hers.

Annie reached up and touched John's arm, draped across the back of the couch. "I wish I could've come to the wake," she said. "I didn't find out until months later."

John waved her off. "Eh, don't worry about it. The wake was mostly for the old folks. What you really missed out on was the after party." He winked at her, and she laughed.

"He had a lot of life to celebrate, didn't he?" she said, wiping at her eyes.

"Oh, yeah. I gotta say, I know you guys weren't together for that long, but man, seeing you is really bringing back some memories," John said.

Annie's smile faltered, and she looked down into her lap.

"All good ones, of course," he added.

"There's actually something I need to talk to you about," she said. She lifted her chin and turned toward Diane. "To both of you."

Out of the corner of her eye, Diane saw John glance at her. "What is it?" she said when Annie didn't continue.

Annie planted her palms on her knees. "Well," she said, "the thing is." She took a deep breath. "I had a baby.

When I was seventeen. She was Simon's." She turned back to John.

His face was intent, patient, but his hand was gripping the arm of the sofa, the fabric rippling under his fingers.

"He didn't know," she continued. "No one did really. I know now that I should've told him before he… The fact is, I was just a kid. I didn't know any better. I was scared shitless. Anyway, I gave it up for adoption. I gave her up." She was no longer looking at either of them. She was staring off at something else.

Diane thought of Ella and the beeping L&D room where her tiny, wrinkled body was first laid on Diane's chest. John had leaned over her shoulder, cooing, while Diane worried that the fabric of her hospital gown was too rough for their daughter's brand-new skin.

"I gave her what I thought was best for her. A new mom, a new life far away. But apparently, her mom decided to move back to Devil's Purse a few years back. Help her find her roots or something." Annie's eyes refocused, jumping between Diane and John. "I work in the teen rehab place a couple towns over. You probably haven't heard of it. Anyway, I think I found her. There. She's a client of mine."

Diane began to shake her head. She felt terribly ill. John, for his part, had let go of the sofa and clamped one hand over the bottom of his face. It did nothing to hide the tears collecting in his eyes. She knew he was thinking of Simon.

Annie said, "She's kind of in bad shape. I mean, obviously. She's in rehab. But I think she needs help. She needs family."

John nodded vigorously. "Of course she does. What can we do? Can we meet her?"

Annie sighed. "I don't think so. Not yet. The situation is delicate. I don't want to upset the balance when she hasn't yet recovered. I haven't even told her that she's...what I think I am to her. I can't believe I'm here actually. This breaks just about every rule in the book." She laughed an empty laugh, and a miserable look flashed across her face before she brushed her bangs out of her eyes and adjusted her glasses. "Her insurance is only going to cover a couple more weeks of inpatient and six weekly outpatient sessions. I truly believe she needs at least twelve sessions after she checks out, but the clinic is not cheap. It's highly inappropriate for me to say so, but I'm at my wit's end trying to make sure this girl has a chance. I don't think her mother can afford to pay out-of-pocket. Her adoptive mother, I mean."

"We'll cover it," John said before she could go any further. "Whatever she needs, we've got it. She's my niece. Right?" He looked at Diane. Diane, who watched it all from far away. Waiting for the other shoe to drop.

"Oh, thank you," Annie said. She clasped her hands in front of her chest like some Precious Moments figurine. "You don't know what a relief that is."

"What's her name?" John said.

"Oh, I couldn't tell you that—" Annie said just as Diane finally broke in.

"John," she said.

He turned to look at her. It took a few seconds, but eventually, his eyebrows raised. There was only one girl in Devil's Purse who fit the description. It was stupid of Annie to think they wouldn't be able to figure it out.

"Oh, shit," John finally said. "Lacey."

Annie coughed, choking on a dry throat.

Diane closed her eyes.

And there it was. This town. This fucking town.

Later that night, when John had recovered, he explained the extraordinary coincidence to Annie. "I knew it," he kept saying, though of course he hadn't. "I knew there was a reason I trusted her on sight. Must've been because she looked so much like my brother." He retrieved the photo of Simon from its place on the mantle and held it up next to an old picture of Ella and Lacey on his phone, showing them to Annie, though of course Annie already knew what Lacey and Simon looked like. The resemblance between Simon and Lacey was there, it was true, but it was the kind you only saw if you were looking for it. They had the same coloring. Simon got it from their mother—Lacey's grandmother, Diane supposed—while John was a carbon copy of his father. Ella was a different matter altogether. She'd always taken after Diane.

At one point, John offered Annie a beer or a glass of wine, a toast to "newfound family." She shook her head and asked for water, averting her eyes down and away. It was a look Diane recognized from John, in the early years, when their dates took them only to ice cream stands and small restaurants with no liquor licenses.

"How many years sober?" Diane asked, more harshly than she'd meant.

"Seventeen," Annie said without hesitation, without having to calculate.

"Good for you," Diane said sincerely.

Annie and John clinked cans of seltzer while Diane sipped her tea. And then, when Annie's can was empty, she went through a show of pulling out her phone and noticing the time. "I'd better get going," she said. "Today was my day off, and showing up late the next morning is not a good way to make friends on the staff."

At the door, John grabbed Annie into a hug. She met

Diane's eye over his shoulder, and Diane tried to smile at her. She knew the precise outlines of that hug, how John hooked his arm around the back of your neck so the crook of his elbow pressed your face close into his chest, how he placed his feet along the outer edges of your own. John didn't do polite acquaintance hugs.

"We'll all get together when Lacey gets out, eh?" John said when he released her.

Annie's eyes widened. "Oh, please, you can't tell her."

John looked back at Diane, as if she could explain this.

"Just, it's not the right time for me to let her know who I am. Not until she's better," Annie said. "I'll call you as soon as I tell her, okay?"

John stared at her for a long moment.

"Helping out with her treatment is the best thing you could do for her right now. I promise." Annie touched John's elbow.

Diane wanted to smack her hand away. John nodded.

When Annie's taillights had receded from view, John closed the door and put his arm around Diane's shoulder, his disappointment hidden. "Isn't that amazing?" he said. "We have a niece now. Simon had a kid."

"Mmm-hmm," she said as he jiggled her back and forth.

She washed her face and changed out of her clothes with John puttering around in the background, humming some unidentifiable song. She slid into bed and could no longer hold it in. "So we'll look at the budget tomorrow, then?"

"I guess so," he said, pulling on a clean undershirt. "I wouldn't worry about it, though. We'll manage."

"Will we?" She sat up, but he wouldn't look at her. She bit her lip and thought about what John's accountant had told her the last time he'd called.

"Sure we will," John said. He got into bed and kissed the top of Diane's head. "We always do, don't we?"

"John, your business is not doing well," she said.

He lay down and kicked the covers back.

"You're on the verge of declaring bankruptcy actually. Which you didn't even bother to tell me."

"Lacey is family," John said, his voice hardened. "And we will support our family. Period." He turned his back to her. Within minutes, his breath was rhythmic with sleep.

Diane stayed upright in their bed. After a time, her jaw began to ache. She'd forgotten to wear the mouth guard her dentist had given her. At the rate she was grinding, he'd warned her, she would be out of teeth before she'd even retired.

Another family member. Another person for John to worry over and look out for and text Diane about while Diane cooked and cleaned and cared for and supported his actual family, his daughter. They'd both wanted more kids, a whole drop-leaf table full of them, but she couldn't afford to quit her job for more than a year, and they couldn't afford day care for more than one toddler. So John had looked elsewhere, stretching the fabric of their family just as far as it could go to cover anyone who needed it. Whenever Diane and Ella read that Jan Brett story, *The Mitten*, Diane secretly felt sorry for the mole who'd first found the mitten in the snow and eventually found himself crammed in there with all variety of woodland creatures.

It was only when the blue sunrise light began to fill the room and Diane's eyelids began to droop that she thought of Maureen. Maureen, her very best friend, whom she was supposed to meet at the grocery store tomorrow—or rather, later today. Maureen, who'd called her in tears a year ago, saying something about how Lacey's biological mother didn't fill out a form and therefore wouldn't tell them who she was. "It's funny," Maureen had said, sniffing. "My worst fear used to be that her birth mother would want to take her back from me. Especially when we moved here, I'd have nightmares about it. But now, I just want her to know her whole family, you know? I want the kid to know how love-able she is, how loved she is, by more than just me."

"Don't be silly. We all love Lacey," Diane had said, and Maureen had sniffed and muttered that she was right. Later that week, Diane had taken her out on a spa day, picking up the tab for pedicures and hot stone massages at the over-priced resort in town that no local would be caught dead in.

She used to wonder what Maureen saw in her. Maureen laughed without covering her mouth. She danced in such elegant movements in the Staybrooks' living room at every holiday party. She swept through the kitchen with equal grace and knew with a single waft what every dish needed. She always did the fearless thing and did it with a smile so wide and genuine that a trail of friends followed her there. The fact that it was always Diane she called, chuckling when Diane said the wrong thing and coaxing her into the right one, filled Diane with pride and confusion. Even waiters at restaurants looked a little disappointed when they turned away from Maureen's flirtations to take Diane's order. She felt so prim and buttoned-up in comparison.

But now, she understood. Her role was to clean up after Maureen's storms. To murmur soothingly, to arrange escapes, to call the clinic. To pick up the slack, to be an adult. And now, apparently, to pay the bills as well.

John shifted awake with his usual groans, the mattress shaking with his movements. Diane pulled the covers up to her chin and pretended to sleep. In a few hours, she would text Maureen with an excuse as to why she couldn't grocery shop today.

That night, John came home especially late. Diane had already told Ella it was time for lights-out and called through her door thirty minutes later to turn her flashlight off.

"There you are," Diane said as John hung his jacket in the hall.

He said nothing. He sat next to her on the couch, kneading his fingers into his scalp. "I ran the numbers today," he said.

She laid her book down on the arm of the couch.

"You were right. There's not much wiggle room."

Diane nodded, though she knew he couldn't see it.

"That check," he said, looking up at the ceiling. "The one your parents give us for Christmas each year."

"It goes toward Ella's summer camp."

"What, all of it?" He dropped his hands.

"And then some."

"Jesus." He fell back into the couch and sighed. "Okay, so I'll buy a snowplow rig for the truck. Get some extra income in the winter. There'll be snow on the ground before we know it."

"Those things cost at least a couple thousand dollars." Carol Zane down the street had spent last Christmas without her husband while he plowed out peoples' driveways in time for their holiday suppers. John had insisted on inviting her and the Zane boys, nightmarish eight-year-old triplets, over for a meal. Ella's bedroom door still bore the marks of Nerf gun fire.

John growled with frustration and yanked a pillow out from under him.

"I really think we've done more than enough already," Diane said quietly. "It's not our place to—"

"Of course it's our place." He shook his head. "She's our niece, not to mention a close friend of the family. What's wrong with you?" At last, he looked at her, his face twisted with disgust. Like she was nothing.

She stood. "Well, I'm sorry," she said. "I just happen to think that our family, the three of us, should be your first priority. Not this girl you've just discovered you're related to. Who, by the way, already has her own mother. Two of them, in fact." She turned and left the room, her eyes burning.

In the end, they hadn't been able to pull together the money. Lacey was released. And John was desperate to find some way to help Lacey. Diane knew he needed to make up for the fact that he couldn't so much as walk up to her and tell her who he was. He wanted to find the money to pay for additional treatment, though how he planned to explain the donation to Maureen, Diane didn't know.

So when the opportunity arose to do something dangerous but potentially lucrative, he had seized it. Diane could picture exactly how it had happened, despite her initial denial. She could see the light and relief in his eyes. He could finally solve a problem for this person he loved. For Lacey.

Chapter Thirty-One

ANNIE RECITED THE WHOLE story, or her side of it at least. Diane stared out the window at the roof of the hospital building next door. The HVAC exhaust fan whirred and blurred. Still, she felt Maureen turn to face her when Annie finished.

"You knew," Maureen said with a wrenching incredulity. "You knew, and you didn't tell me? After everything we'd talked about? After I—"

"It wasn't my job to tell you," Diane said, looking pointedly at Annie, who was studying the pulse readout on one of the machines by Lacey's bed.

"Bullshit. You were my friend, my best friend."

Diane's heart sank a little at the past tense.

"Of course it was your job. Or were you worried it'd mess with your perfect little life?"

"And it did, didn't it?" Diane said.

Maureen bit her lips closed.

"I think we all know now why John went out on that boat. We were stretched too thin as it was, but he was bound and determined to pick up your slack when you couldn't do your job as her mother."

"If I may." Annie cleared her throat, her eyes bouncing

back and forth between the two of them. "I understand that this news is upsetting for both of you, but I really think we should focus on—"

"Oh, honey," Maureen said in a voice that actually made Annie gasp. "I haven't even gotten started on you. You're a recovering alcoholic, right?" Maureen crossed her arms. "I saw that quote on your employer's website, out there for anyone to see, but you refuse to tell the one person who really matters. Addiction is hereditary, and if only you hadn't been too chickenshit to respond to us when she turned eighteen, we would've known. We could've—"

"What?" Annie said. "Given her the life she was supposed to have? A safe life, a healthy life, far away, one that made giving her up worth it for me?"

Maureen's shoulders slumped.

Annie swallowed. "Genes are one factor, yes. But it's complicated. We don't really know if an alcoholic can pass down an addiction to something else. And there are a whole host of other factors. It's impossible to know in any given case what contributed—"

Maureen wasn't done. "And you tried to get to know her, didn't you?"

Diane wanted to cheer as her friend pulled herself back up.

"You tried to sneak around and become buds with the girl you abandoned and become important to her. You couldn't even manage to explain yourself to her, your own flesh and blood."

"You think it was easy for me?" Annie said. "I got to hand my baby over and then go on my merry way, right? Right?" She had shed her caseworker voice and was close to shouting, close to tears. "Why do you think I started drinking in the first place?"

"There are plenty of birth mothers who manage not to become alcoholics," Maureen hissed. "Who go on to have functional relationships with their biological children."

The two women stared at each other, tensed, coiled. Diane reached out and touched Maureen's shoulder, ever so gently. Maureen didn't move away.

None of them noticed when Rebecca slipped out of the room. She closed the door behind her and leaned against it. Her head spun with everything she probably shouldn't have heard. Annie. Lacey. Maureen. Diane. John.

"Hey, Rebecca," came a small voice to her right.

"Ella!" Through it all, Rebecca still smiled at the sight of the girl's face. Then, she remembered that morning. The boot. She crouched down next to Ella and said cautiously, "How are you doing?"

Ella shrugged. "It was stupid." She put her book down. "I can't believe I thought he was still alive."

Rebecca sighed. "No, it wasn't. It's hard to accept these things. He loved you so very much, though."

Ella nodded, her face serious, and leaned forward to hug Rebecca so fiercely that Rebecca rocked back on her heels a little. She heard Ella sniffle as Rebecca gingerly wrapped her arms around Ella's shoulders.

"They've been fighting in there a while, huh?" Ella said when she drew herself back.

"They have," Rebecca said. "Could you hear what they were saying?"

"Yeah." Ella scrubbed at her runny nose. "Some lady in there is Lacey's real mom, and my mom thinks it's her fault my dad went out." She looked down and fiddled with her book.

"That's about right," Rebecca said. And then it dawned on her—the one thing that might make Ella happy in all this mess. "You know what else?"

"What." Ella dog-eared one page, then the next.

Rebecca put her hand over Ella's to still it. "Lacey is your cousin."

Ella's jaw dropped. Her eyes lit up. "Really?"

Rebecca nodded.

Ella jumped down off the chair. "I've gotta go tell her! I'll see you later, okay?" Before Rebecca could stop her, she opened the door and slipped inside.

Rebecca stood and considered following but stopped herself. Diane was in there. This wasn't Rebecca's responsibility anymore.

She turned away and saw an old man standing nearby with his head craned toward the shouting still coming from the room. She raised one eyebrow, and he harrumphed along on his way. She walked back toward the hospital entrance.

Her phone rang just as she walked through the doors. Still addled from everything, she didn't even check who it was before answering.

"Rebecca? It's Ophelia Walsh." Ophelia's voice already trembled with rage.

Rebecca closed her eyes and told herself not to sigh. As a library board member, Ophelia was effectively Rebecca's employer. It would do no good to brush aside whatever small complaint Ophelia was calling her about, no matter how inconvenient the timing. "Hello, Ophelia," she said. "How can I help you?"

"I've just heard about what happened with that girl at the library," Ophelia said. "And you—how could you—it's just atrocious," she continued, so affronted she tripped over the words.

"Yes, it's terrible what's happened to her."

"What happened to her?" Ophelia's voice rose. "What's happening to our *library*? Druggies are just passing out on our floor now? This is a community space! How can our children continue to use it the way it's intended when they're surrounded by addicts?"

"Well." Rebecca sucked in her breath. "I hardly think there's a crowd of addicted—"

"And her mother!" Ophelia cut in. "Her mother caters our functions! That doesn't seem appropriate now, does it? I demand that we find another caterer. Someone more fitting."

The air stuck in Rebecca's windpipe. Maureen Carson, bent over Lacey's hospital bed, her worst fears written all over her face.

And Lacey, Lacey. So small in that bed. So pale and fragile. Rebecca knew administering the Narcan was not the only thing she could do for Lacey. There was so much more she should do—she could do—to help that girl recover. So: "No," she said quietly.

After a stunned, silent beat, Ophelia said, "I'm sorry?"

"No," Rebecca said, louder this time.

"I'm not sure you understood me. This was a demand, not a request. Our library cannot be seen as affiliated with—"

"And I'm not sure it's within your powers as a board member to determine who our library does and does not contract with." Actually, Rebecca was fairly certain it *was* within Ophelia's powers, but she kept herself steady and stared out at the cars in the parking lot as if daring them to do something about it.

"Well," Ophelia said. "Well then." It appeared she was finally at a loss, but it lasted only a moment before she said, "In that case, I will be resigning from the board immediately."

Rebecca raised her eyebrows. Was Ophelia bluffing? Was she trying to get Rebecca to give in? "That's a shame," Rebecca said. "We will miss your input," she lied.

"I—" Ophelia stuttered.

"I have to ask, though," Rebecca interrupted, "why it's so important to you that we cut ties with Maureen Carson. It seems to me that if we didn't allow anyone who'd been affected by addiction into our midst, we wouldn't have very many contracts at all."

Ophelia sniffed loudly. "It's a matter of principle." And then, there was just the dial tone.

Chapter Thirty-Two

ELLA'S MOM DIDN'T NOTICE when she snuck into the room. They probably didn't even know Ella could hear them arguing out in the hall. One old man in a robe and slippers had walked by where Ella sat at least four times, wheeling an IV bag behind him, his steps slowing each time he passed. He stopped just short of cupping his ear to the door. Ella glowered at him each time, but he just grinned right back at her.

Lacey was awake but lying down, her face still as she watched the three women fight around her.

Ella approached the bed and slipped her hand into Lacey's. Lacey squeezed her hand weakly. Ella could smell that she was wearing lotion, Ella's favorite scent from the store at the mall, the one that smelled like cherries.

"Hey, kidlet," Lacey wheezed.

"Did you hear?" Ella whispered. "We're cousins! Isn't that amazing?"

Lacey nodded. Her eyes were wet, probably because she was so happy. Ella looked down and patted her hand where the IV went in. They used pretty weak tape for those things, and it was already coming unpeeled.

"You're sick," Ella said. "Like, on drugs?"

"Yes," Lacey whispered.

"Sorry I got mad at you and made you go take them," Ella said. She bit her lip.

"Oh, Ella," Lacey said. "It's not your fault. I promise."

"You weren't really off visiting your grandparents in September, were you?"

Lacey shook her head.

Ella knit her brows together and bowed her head. It was still Lacey's hand beneath hers, bitten nails and all. "You're gonna go away again and get better, right?" Ella said. "For real this time? I've always wanted a cousin."

"Sure," Lacey said. "Of course."

And neither of them could tell if she was telling the truth. But Ella knew that Lacey wanted it to be true. Just like Ella wanted her dad to be alive. Maybe this time, Ella could help make it happen.

Chapter Thirty-Three

WHEN LACEY FIRST WOKE up to the sound of the three women arguing, she didn't know if she was dreaming or maybe it was a nightmare. Then again, maybe she had died and was watching the whole bizarre thing unfold from somewhere else. And then Ella had appeared, full of unfathomable forgiveness, and made Lacey feel real again.

After Ella had extracted her promise, she squeezed Lacey's hand and sat back to read her book. Mrs. Staybrook would probably be mad when she realized Ella was there, but Ella didn't seem to care. And the three kept going, arguing around and around again.

One of them was her mother, of course, as hopped up on anger as Lacey'd ever seen her. One was her aunt now. And the third was her bio mom apparently, the one some people insisted on calling her real mom, the one who hadn't wanted her, the one to whom—it stung to remember—Lacey had opened up about her fights with Maureen. Lacey wished she could take it all back. This woman didn't deserve to know her mother's weaknesses and flaws.

"Genetic or not," Maureen said or rather snarled, "it's a disease and one my sweet girl has been completely helpless before. We've both been helpless. It would've been nice to at least have a heads-up, to know what to look out for."

"Surely there's something we could've done if we'd known," Diane said.

Maureen glanced back at Diane.

"She thinks you're still sweet underneath there?" the beetle said. "I don't think so. Defective," it said. "Defective, defective, defective."

Enough. Lacey jammed the heels of her hands into her temples. "Shut up," she said. "Shut up, shut up, shut up."

It was loud enough to hear.

"Lacey?" Maureen said, suddenly quavering. "Oh, thank God."

All three of them moved toward the bed, but Maureen got there first. She swept her arms around Lacey and pulled her close. Lacey hugged her back as tightly as she could.

"Lacey, Lacey, oh, thank Christ," Maureen said into Lacey's matted hair.

"Hi, Mom," Lacey said, and then, more softly, "I'm sorry."

"No." Maureen pulled back and wiped the back of her hand over her face. She grasped Lacey by the shoulders. "This is not your fault, do you hear me? You're sick, and we just need to try again."

Lacey nodded slowly.

Annie stepped closer. "Lacey, hi," she said. "There's something I should tell you."

"I heard," Lacey said, settling her hands in her lap.

A small, trembling smile grew on Annie's face.

Lacey couldn't stand to see it. "Please leave."

"What?" Annie said, though all of them had heard her. "I was only trying to—"

"I need you," Lacey said, one word at a time, "to leave." The beetle was quiet, waiting to see what would happen.

Lacey's stomach turned, and she couldn't tell if it was out of anger or grief. Here she was, the woman Lacey'd been looking for all her life in one way or another. There was no treacly music or shy greeting at the airport. Instead, there was this: Lacey in a hospital bed and Annie with her eyes on the floor as she gathered her things.

The door closed behind her, and Maureen started to say something, her face crinkled with concern. But then she stopped herself and leaned forward to tuck a chunk of hair out of Lacey's face.

"Ella? What are you doing there?" Diane said, finally turning toward the chair next to Lacey's bed. Ella looked up from her book warily, but Diane just sighed. "I should've known you'd sneak in. How much did you hear?"

"Is it true Lacey's my cousin?" Ella asked in response.

Lacey held her breath. Would Diane deny it? She wouldn't want her daughter growing closer to someone like Lacey.

Diane touched Maureen's elbow and looked down at Lacey. "It's true," she said. "It's good to have you back, sweetie. And in the family, too."

For the first time all day, Lacey smiled.

Chapter Thirty-Four

DUSK WAS JUST STARTING to creep in around the edges of the white-bright hospital room. The buzzing of the fluorescent lights crammed Lacey's head. Everything ached in the usual way. Again, she pictured Ms. Bray—she refused to think of her as anything else, not "my bio mom," not "Annie"—her face twisted up and pink as she scurried out of the room. As she ran away again. Lacey wondered with a sickening lurch if she'd be going to a bar tonight.

Then, there was her mom, her mother, head bowed, sitting by the bed. Lacey finally begged her to leave. The beetle—or her "generalized anxiety disorder" or whatever Ms. Bray wanted to call it—was skittering all over the place, scraping its legs across the place where her scalp met her spine, hissing and spitting. "You've done it now," it said. "Shouldn't have made that woman go away. Neither of them will want you anymore. Your fault."

Now, in the empty quiet, she pressed her hands to her temples again, the IV tugging at her skin. Focus, she had to focus. She'd just found her bio mom, the woman she'd been looking for, consciously or not, willingly or not, for as long as she could remember. The woman for whom she'd been unwanted. The one who'd given her her brown hair and maybe the beetle and maybe the addiction but had also given her her real mom in some small way. Lacey wished she could be angry about it, but all she felt was emptied.

On the day her mom took her to the adoption agency, her friend Amanda had come over for a sleepover. Lacey sat at her desk, supposedly doing her math homework but really staring at the wall while the beetle made wide pirouettes. Amanda's bright voice—the one she used with parents—filtered up the stairs. She'd just started dating Derek at the time, and it felt like Lacey hadn't seen her in weeks.

Lacey heard her mother's low murmuring, and Amanda's voice dipped, concerned. Lacey winced. Her mom believed in collecting a team of women and using their wisdom and strength to problem solve together. It was progressive, Lacey guessed, but it meant her struggles and fights with her mom were never all that private. She hated it when that team extended to Lacey's own friends.

Sure enough, when Amanda got to her room, sympathy was scribbled in wrinkles across her forehead.

Lacey sighed. "She told you about what happened at the agency," Lacey said.

"I can't believe she won't release her info," Amanda said, flopping down onto Lacey's bed. "I mean, what kind of person gives birth to a kid and then never wants to see it again?"

Lacey shrugged and turned back to her desk. An ant was crawling slowly along the spine of her textbook. She flicked it away. "Whatever. It's not like I need her at this point anyway."

"But aren't you curious?" Amanda sat up and hugged a pillow to her middle. "Don't you want to know what she looks like or, like, what she does for work?" Her eyes were bright, like this was her own private mystery to solve.

It struck Lacey that they'd never talked about it before, not really. Just like everybody else, Amanda knew she was adopted, but she never brought it up. Lacey thought it was unremarkable to Amanda. To her, she wasn't the adopted kid. She was just Lacey. But maybe it was just that Amanda felt she needed permission to ask about it.

"Why would I want to find out about someone who doesn't want to know me?" Lacey mumbled.

"Oh, screw that." Amanda tossed the pillow aside and scooted to the edge of the bed. "She was probably, like, our age when she had you. She didn't know any better, and now she's being stupid and stubborn. Anyway, your mom was telling me—" She wrinkled her nose. "Um, your other mom. The one downstairs. She was saying there are other ways to find her. Private investigator type shit."

Lacey opened her desk drawer and pushed aside a pile of notebooks. She pulled out a small, white box and put it in Amanda's lap.

Amanda picked up the box and squinted at it, as if she could see through the cardboard. She tilted it from side to side. "What is it?"

"A DNA test." Lacey reached over and closed her bedroom door. Her mom was slamming pots around in the kitchen, probably getting ready to cook her feelings. "There's a cotton swab in there, and you get some of your spit on it and mail it in. They've got a whole database of people who've done it, and they can match you to anyone who's in there that you're related to. Sometimes, if you get in touch with those matches, they can tell you who your birth parents are."

"Whoa." Amanda picked at the flaps.

They opened easily. Lacey had already peeled away the tape, sifted through the box, and read the instructions.

She'd looked up vlogs online of adoptees who'd found their families.

She'd ordered the kit one brightly moonlit night before she'd sent her forms to the adoption agency, when everything still seemed possible and she'd felt undeniably optimistic, thinking she could meet her birth parents and find out about her extended family, too, while she was at it. Why not? The beetle was quiet that night as she lay awake in bed. Her bio parents would respond to her request with heartfelt letters explaining how they wished they could've kept her and they couldn't wait to meet her. Maybe they'd send her an old, beaten-up teddy bear they'd bought at the hospital when she was born and held onto ever since.

"You should do it. Definitely," Amanda said. She held the box clamped between her hands and nodded firmly.

"If she doesn't want to be found, she doesn't want to be found."

"What she doesn't want is *you*," the beetle whispered.

"Lacey." Amanda sighed, still cradling the box. "You deserve to find her."

Lacey opened her mouth to protest, but there was nothing left. There might still be extended family who wanted to meet her, even if her bio mom didn't. She could send in the test and find lists and lists of second cousins, aunts, great-uncles, her family ballooning right before her eyes in steady italics. Her mom would organize a family reunion, and their backyard would fill with masses of people with dark hair and freckles and honking, embarrassing laughs. People like her.

She'd seen the commercials for the DNA test. It could be true for her.

It was sort of a game after that. Amanda clapped when Lacey rolled the swab over the inside of her cheek, bouncing up and down with glee so the springs on Lacey's bed creaked. Lacey slipped the envelope under her shirt, the paper cool and smooth against her clammy skin, and they told her mom they were heading out to get ice cream. They giggled as they slammed Amanda's car doors behind them.

At the post office—Amanda insisted they mail it at an actual post office, not the drop box outside the grocery store, even though it was late and the post office was closed anyway—Lacey hesitated on the sidewalk.

"Come on, do it," Amanda whispered, planting one hand on Lacey's shoulder and pushing her forward.

Amanda probably imagined herself as the coach in an inspirational movie, with rain streaming down her face and a headset around her neck. The image made Lacey smile, and she focused on that instead of the sour taste of panic in her mouth as she stuffed the envelope in the mail slot.

"You have to let me know as soon as you get the results, okay?" Amanda said.

Lacey nodded. All the bubbly helium had gone out of her.

"Hey," Amanda said. She bumped her shoulder against Lacey's and turned back to the car. "You got this."

"Yeah, I know. Thanks," Lacey said. The beetle's feet tap-tap-tapped.

It didn't take nearly as long as she'd hoped it would for the company to get back to her. A few weeks later, she finally checked her phone after helping her mom at a town festival for the day, and there was the email. "Your Family Tree Is Here!" the subject line said, all perky.

"I'm gonna go upstairs and study," she told her mom, eyes fixed to the phone.

"Hey, wait a minute," her mom said and stood up from the couch.

Lacey froze. She'd found out. Did the company have a policy of notifying the parents? Had she given them her mom's contact info? The night was such a blur, she couldn't even remember. She'd have to come up with the perfect response for her mom, one that simultaneously reassured her that she was her true family and tempered her expectations about the results. It might be that she had no matches. She had no idea how many people out there had taken the test, and the chances seemed so slim that she was related to any of them.

Before she could say anything, her mom reached up and cradled Lacey's cheek. "Don't work too hard, okay? You busted ass for me today. Tomorrow, you're doing something fun. That will be strictly enforced." She raised an eyebrow until Lacey smiled.

"Aye, aye, captain," Lacey said, and it sounded weak to her, but her mom released her and walked back to the couch.

"Don't know what I'd do without you, kid," Maureen said. She folded herself back into the cushions with a happy sigh.

"Probably perish." Lacey turned away toward the stairs when her mom laughed.

By the time she sat down at her desk and opened her laptop, her heart was roaring in her ears. She dialed Amanda's number and pulled up her email while the phone rang. It rang and rang, and the beetle scratched circles in her head.

Meanwhile, there was the subject line, in bold. "Your Family Tree Is Here!" Next to it, a little pop-up box from her email host: "Is this spam? Yes/No."

Her mouse hovered over the email. If she closed her eyes, she could picture what was there: a list of strangers with unfamiliar surnames that her birth parents may or may not share. More opportunities for dead ends. "More people to reject you and to tell you you don't belong," the beetle said.

The phone went to voicemail. Amanda was probably with Derek.

And then there was her mom. Reading downstairs, coiling a chunk of hair around one finger, squinting because she still insisted she was too young for glasses. She was always so gung ho about finding Lacey's bio parents, but Lacey'd heard her talking about it with Mrs. Staybrook. She'd heard the thready fear in her voice. "Don't know what I'd do without you, kid," she'd said. It was Lacey's job to make sure they'd never have to do without each other. Her mom had to know she was all of Lacey's family.

She moved the cursor to the pop-up box and clicked "Yes." Yes, this was spam. With a whoosh, the message was deleted, unread. "You will no longer receive emails from this sender," another pop-up box announced. Lacey breathed out.

The memory played in her head over and over as the night wore on. She could barely answer the nurses when they came to check on her. They frowned at their clipboards, chalking her unresponsiveness up to the aftermath of her overdose, but she kept feeling the cotton swab against her cheek, kept seeing the cursor moving before her eyes.

She always assumed she'd see something of herself in her birth mother's face. There'd be physical resemblances, sure, but also some sense of recognition or understanding. They'd look at each other and know instinctively. They would know things about each other that no one else did, things that came from nine months of sharing everything, from the tiny cells of herself she'd once read still floated around in her birth mother's body like dust motes.

What a stupid thing to think. All she'd ever seen of Ms. Bray was a mask. The same plastic face of concern she wore with all her clients. Lacey knew next to nothing about her, and Ms. Bray had worked hard to make it stay that way—not just while Lacey was at the clinic but for years before then.

And Ms. Bray knew everything there was to know about Lacey. Lacey's chest tightened with humiliation when she thought about all the times she'd spilled her guts in Ms. Bray's airless office. The times she'd cried and Ms. Bray had passed the tissue box, calm as could be. At least she hadn't told her about the beetle.

Ms. Bray had told the Staybrooks God knows what about her. And John had died because of it. Not because of Lacey, but because Ms. Bray had made Lacey sound desperate for his money. Ms. Bray was the one who made him think Lacey needed his help.

His death wasn't Lacey's fault. Even the beetle didn't contradict her on that.

She should've opened that damn email. If she had, she might've seen "Bray" on the list and at least known to be wary around her. She might've learned John was her uncle, and she could've gone up and knocked on his door and told him. He would've been confused at first, disbelieving, maybe even angry. Not angry at her, though. Eventually, he would've hugged her and ordered a pizza for everyone, and they would've all eaten it together, the Staybrooks and her mom and her. She was sure of it.

Now, it was too late. She punched the plastic side rail of her bed until it rattled and her knuckles stung. "Stupid, stupid," she muttered, and the beetle echoed her. Ms. Bray had found the blue-black spot of loneliness at the heart of

Lacey and pressed, hard. No matter how sick Lacey was, no matter how loudly the beetle screamed, Lacey could never forgive her for that. She lay back into the bleach-smelling pillow and squeezed her eyes shut.

She woke up to a hand touching her wrist. "Matt," she whispered.

He smiled a little. "Hey, Lace." His face had grown hollower since she'd seen him, and the movement pushed his cheekbones out even further.

She cleared the sticky sleep from her throat. She wondered if he could feel her pulse thumping through the vein under his hand. "How'd you know I was here?"

He pulled his hand away and shrugged. "Mark texted." One of his friends—their friends. "He was at the library when the ambulance came. I had to see if you were okay."

She nodded.

He looked down at his feet and shoved his hands in his front pockets. "I sent you emails."

"I know," Lacey said. "I had to ignore them. They wouldn't let me—in rehab."

"Yeah. Yeah."

Lacey wanted to reach out for him and pull him in. Part of her wondered if he might've been the only person who ever saw her for who she truly was and loved her just the same. She'd even told him about the beetle one night, and instead of shrinking away or brushing it aside, he had swept the hair from her forehead and placed a kiss there. "Yeah," he had whispered. "Me, too."

So she'd hoped, just a little, that he would find her. And now, here he was. A million miles away.

"I tried to check myself in, you know," he said. "To rehab? I drove all the way there, and then I just…I couldn't. I wound up at Ophelia's house. How fucked up is that?" His laugh was short and bitter. "I have to get out of town, you know? Start fresh."

She bit her lip. How many times had their friends talked about it? They didn't need much to quit, they told each other. They just needed to get away from this shitty town, and they would all get better.

He met her eye. He looked at her like he was asking for forgiveness, though there was nothing for Lacey to forgive. None of it was his fault.

"You'll get treatment when you're ready," she said.

"Sure."

They stood in silence for a minute, staring at each other. He leaned in and kissed her on the cheek, swift and sweet, just like the first time she kissed him in the car. "Later, Lace," he said and turned to walk out the door. She wondered if she'd ever see him again. Maybe someday he'd come back and go to rehab. Or maybe his fresh start was a lot like the Fentanyl she'd kept in her wall: a promise to himself that he would ultimately break.

She knew what the people at the clinic would say about him. "Emotionally vulnerable," they'd call her. "Predatory enabler," they'd call him. But that wasn't all that they were. They were Lacey and Matt, too. And now, she was alone. "Everyone is gone," the beetle said.

But Ella. There was Ella. Ella was so excited. She wanted Lacey as a cousin, no matter how damaged and bruised and secondhand Lacey was. One day, when Lacey was better and they were all past the part of grieving when laughter seemed impossible, maybe they could be a family, Maureen and Lacey and Diane and Ella. There was that. That was something.

Chapter Thirty-Five

I T WAS QUIET IN the Break that night. Still packed with men standing sweatshirted shoulder to shoulder, but no one spoke above a murmur. Jimmy turned the radio down low. Hardly any tourists came by—a rarity for a Saturday night—and everyone was grateful for it. The tinkling of the bell over the door and the clueless laughter would've been too much.

"I heard the kid flipped out when she saw his boot."

"Shit."

"I mean, can you blame her?"

"I know."

"It's weird. I mean, obviously I know better, but still…"

"Yeah. I was holding out hope the Coast Guard would find him there, hanging onto a piece of the boat like that guy in *Titanic*."

"Didn't that guy die?"

"Whatever. Never saw it."

"Anyway, doesn't matter. Not like that's ever happened in the history of Devil's Purse."

"Yeah, but if anyone could pull it off—"

"It'd be him, for sure."

"Damn shame. What a loss."

"The wife's gonna be on me again to sell the business and get another job."

"Yeah, mine, too. She always freaks out when things like this happen."

"You ever think about…?"

"Nah, no way. Can't sit at a desk all day. My back's gone to shit after all those years standing at the wheel."

A small chuckle rumbled through the room.

"Guess there'll be a funeral soon, then."

Silence. Nodding.

"Maybe a wake, too. Wasn't he Catholic?"

"A recovering one."

"Aren't we all."

"I gotta give Diane the number of my sister's husband. Kinda creepy guy, but he runs a real nice funeral home."

"Guess you've gotta be a little odd in the head to own a place like that in a town like this."

"At least business is booming for him!"

"Jesus, Sammy."

"I'm just sayin'."

The men paused and sipped from their beers. A chirpy commercial for the local community college came on the radio. "When you're ready for a change, our night school programs are here for you!"

"You guys hear about what happened to the Carson girl?"

"Yeah, in the library? My deckhand's wife was there."

"I heard she almost died."

"Good Lord, I can't imagine."

"She's way too young to be dealing with all that, you ask me. Got her whole life in front of her."

"Should've been a damn good life, too. You know she got into Brown?"

"And the first one to get in there outta DP High in decades, I guess. They got some sorta grudge against us down in Providence."

"Think she'll still go?"

"She'd better."

"This point, all I'm hoping is she doesn't wind up dead."

"Yeah, talk shit about junkies all you want, but it makes you think when you see a young one trying to kill herself like that, you know?"

"She's a good egg, too. You ever met her?"

"Course I've met her. Met everyone and their dog in this town."

"Nah, but I mean really met her? I talked with her once over at the Dunkie's. Sweet kid, you could tell. Slipped me an extra Munchkin for free."

"Pretty sure they all do that."

"I know, I know, but she got all red-faced when I tried to give it back. She's modest, more than you'd think, considering."

"I feel bad for her, adopted and all that."

"Why's that? Maureen seems cool."

"Way better than my mom was."

"You think that's why she…?"

"Nah, no way. My aunt's kid is adopted, and he's just fine. Found his, what's it called, biological parents last year."

"It's just one of those things, I think, you know. Never can tell who's gonna get sucked into that world."

"Way too many kids dying of it."

"She going back to rehab?"

"Pretty sure. Maureen seems like the type to make her. Tough woman."

"Hope it takes this time."

"It's gotta take eventually. My nephew had to go three times, but now he's the best damn welder in the state."

"Hey, yeah, I forgot about that. Good for him."

"She'll pull through. We'll help her. Nice kid."

Chapter Thirty-Six

Wednesday, November 15, 2017

EVERY MORNING, JESS WENT to the *Diane & Ella*. She didn't take it out, of course. She needed a permit to do that. And it wasn't even hers yet; the paperwork was still being processed, and the boat was in legal purgatory. But no one questioned a longtime crewmember tending to the boat she worked on. Even if her captain was gone and lost.

She was scrubbing away at a stubborn rust stain in one corner of the deck when someone called her name. She poked her head over the side of the boat—almost her boat—and there was Frank Callahan, squinting up at her.

"Listen," he said before she could greet him. "I've been a little shorthanded since my kid went back to college. You interested in picking up a few trips here and there?"

"Oh." Jess's mouth opened, which was a mistake. The fumes from the bucket of cleaning fluid at her feet made her eyes water until she coughed. "Yeah, maybe," she managed. "I'll think about it."

Frank nodded and started to turn on his way when he hesitated. "And hey," he said, "if you're looking to get into another fishery, you could take your pick. There's captains all over this town would take you in a heartbeat. Lobstering, cod-fishing, you name it. World's your oyster."

"Thanks, Frank," she said, but he'd already started walking back to his boat. He raised one hand over his head in reply.

Jess sank to the floor, back against the deck railing. She pushed her fists into her eyes. Word must not've spread yet that the boat was hers and she could be her own captain now.

Or could be they did know and their pity was for another reason. They'd all done the math themselves over and over again for their sons and grandsons. It would be nearly impossible for her to find a permit she could afford to buy outright with the bits and pieces of her crew wages she'd socked away over the years. She didn't even have any assets she could sell for cash. She rented her apartment from the old woman who lived below her, and her truck was a piece of junk that she herself had bought used a decade ago.

There was only the boat. She looked from bow to stern. There was the dark spot where she'd cut her palm with a shucking knife while working through a pile of scallops. Shucking without gloves was a rookie move, and she was not a rookie at the time. Just distracted. She'd almost cried from the embarrassment, but John had pretended not to notice. He'd bandaged up her hand and pulled a rubber glove over it to protect the wound, not making a single joke about her incompetence. He insisted she spend the rest of the trip in the wheelhouse while he shucked.

And there was the spot he told her Diane was pregnant, smile wide. He'd been standing a few feet down from that when Diane called him to tell him she was in labor. He started running this way and that after he hung up, yelling nonsense instructions and hooking things that should've been unhooked. Jess followed behind him and corrected everything. She couldn't imagine a luckier kid, to have John as a father. She wished she'd told him that.

After an hour, she'd just about decided to take Frank up on his offer. She'd scrimp and save even more. She'd eat nothing but peanut butter sandwiches and hot dogs if she had to. She'd call the local permit broker at nine and four every day to ask if he'd seen any bargains lately. And in the meantime, she'd take good care of this boat. John's boat.

Her rear started buzzing. She was so lost in thought, it took her a moment to remember she'd stuck her cell phone in her back pocket. She grimaced a little when she saw Diane's number flash across its face.

"I've been thinking," Diane said when all the awkward greetings were out of the way.

Jess scratched at a fleck of paint that had embedded itself in the cuff of her sweatshirt. What was Diane going to accuse her of now? Not that Jess could blame her for lashing out when she'd gone by the Staybrooks'. Everyone grieved differently. She was just lucky Diane hadn't gone to the Break with her theories.

"What's up?" Jess prompted after several seconds of silence ticked by.

"I want to lease you the permit," Diane said, rushed like she was afraid she'd change her mind.

Jess had never heard her so flustered. Her heart hiccupped in her chest and began to lift in spite of itself. "Are you serious?"

"Yes." Diane exhaled. Jess could practically hear her resettling. "John was right." She paused again. "It should stay in the family."

It wasn't an apology. Not quite. But it was as close as she was going to get. "Wow," Jess said. She watched a seagull pick a shard of shell up off the deck. It turned to face her, yellow-rimmed eye sizing her up. It seemed unimpressed. It spread its wings and pulled its way up into the sky. Those birds' personalities used to crack John up. They were the pigeons of the sea, circling the boat at lunchtime. Jess almost told Diane about her visitor—it seemed like a good omen— but then she thought better of it. Maybe John didn't talk to Diane about the seagulls. Maybe that was just their thing, him and Jess.

"Anyway, what else am I going to do with the thing?" Diane said. "It felt like you and John spent half your time studying the markets sometimes. God knows that's not a hobby I'm looking to pick up."

Jess smiled. It was almost exactly what she thought Diane would say when she first learned about John's will. Diane snorted, and soon, they were both laughing, Jess covering her face with one hand. Helpless.

When they wound down, Jess wiped her eyes and said, "I can pay you at least fifty percent up front, I think. Got some savings ready to go, and I think the going rate is—"

"We can figure out the details later," Diane said. "Why don't you stop by our house on Saturday at around ten. We'll sort it all out then, I promise," she said and hung up.

Jess tilted her head back and looked up at the sky. It was blue, so blue. Nothing clearer than a fall New England day. She put her phone away and went back to work.

Jess chased Frank down before she left the docks on that afternoon. He was loading some gear into the bed of his truck, and she handed a couple of plastic bins up to him while she tried to think of how to ask. When everything was loaded, she still had nothing. He thanked her and was about to climb up into the driver's seat when she finally said, "Hold on."

He paused with his hand on the door handle.

"I think I might've found a permit of my own," she said.

"No shit." He raised his eyebrows. "Good for you."

"Yeah." Jess studied the toes of her boots. "There is one way you could help me out, though."

Frank said nothing.

"I could use a reference letter," Jess soldiered on. "So the person leasing it knows I'm trustworthy. That I can catch it."

"Sure." Frank opened the door and got in. "When you need it by?"

Jess looked up, startled. "Um. Tomorrow would be great."

"You got it. See ya, J."

———

For the rest of the week, she worried that Diane would change her mind. She worried right up until the moment Diane answered her door in a clean, white button-down and cuffed jeans with her hair swept back.

"Hi, there," Diane said. "Come on in. I'm afraid we'll have to chat back in the dining room," Diane whispered as she led Jess through the house. "I forgot you were coming by this morning, and I seem to have double-booked myself."

Jess's foot skidded across the floor. Even she knew that Diane was not one to stray from her schedule. John's phone used to vibrate every once in a while with the calendar reminders his wife had programmed into it. "I can come back later," Jess offered, though she didn't know if she could take another day of the uncertainty.

"Oh, no, it's fine," Diane said. "It's just Maureen and a mutual acquaintance. They can keep themselves occupied in the living room until we're done."

Jess did her best not to crane her neck for a glimpse of the sofa as they passed the living room door. Someone's elderly dad had overheard at the hospital that Lacey's biological mom had resurfaced, and stories had been swirling all week, but nobody knew who it was. Theories ranged from the new worker at the post office to DP High's most-hated math teacher to the governor's wife, though that last one was posited by Sammy, so no one paid much attention to it. Maureen and Diane were a pair, just the two of them, with no mutual friends that Jess knew of. The other woman in there must be Lacey's mom, the Devil's Purse mystery.

When they passed the living room, though, Diane shifted so she stood between Jess and the door. Jess dutifully kept her eyes forward under Diane's watch.

Jess paused in front of the dining room table. She'd only ever seen it covered with chafing dishes at the Staybrooks' holiday parties or occasionally tableclothed and set when John invited her to dinner, four place settings evenly spaced. Jess realized with a sudden ache how much she'd miss those nights, as stiff as they'd been.

Now, the table was bare save for a beige file folder lined up perfectly in one corner. Diane sat down before it and motioned for Jess to take the chair beside her. Jess's knees cracked audibly as she sat. She ran her hands over the wood tabletop. It was surprisingly dinged and scratched for such a formal room. She could imagine Diane chiding John for putting heavy, unwieldy things on there that didn't belong. The image warmed her up.

"Okay, so," Diane said. She opened the folder, and Jess noticed her nails were painted again, though their length looked bitten to the quick.

"I brought you a letter," Jess said before she lost her nerve. She retrieved the envelope from her pocket and held it out to Diane. "From Frank Callahan. About my fishing abilities and how I can catch the scallops. Just, you know, so you don't have to take John's word for it. I can make those payments."

"I see." Diane's brow furrowed as she took the letter. Jess had sealed it up without reading it, embarrassed, and part of her worried she'd see its contents written all over Diane's face as she scanned it, but Diane stuck it in the back of the folder without a glance. "I'm sure that won't be necessary," Diane said, "but thank you."

"Okay."

"Now, as to the lease." Diane pulled a sheet out of the folder and pushed it across the table toward Jess. "That's what I'm thinking in terms of a schedule of payments and totals. Does this seem fair?"

Jess looked over the typed columns and blinked. It was well below market price, spaced out into several installments.

"I know it's the middle of the fishing year and you two had already used up a good chunk of the scallops you were allowed to catch with that permit, is that right?" Diane said.

Jess swallowed and shook her head. "Even with that, the cost is too low." Maybe Diane had gotten the wrong pricing information. "Leases are going for at least twice as much right now."

"Yes, I know." Diane folded her hands on top of the table. "I also know this is a tough time of year to be fishing. John always started complaining around Thanksgiving." She smiled wryly, and Jess mustered a smile in return. "I don't want you to get in over your head with the payments. Or do anything foolish for the money, like John did." They both looked away. "So I came up with something that I thought seemed reasonable."

"But it's not enough," Jess protested. "John would've

wanted the lease to support you both." She held her breath. She might've overstepped.

"You'll notice the lease price gets closer to market in the new fishing year, once you've had time to get your feet under you. We can revisit that when the time comes, of course, and adjust where necessary. And not that it's any of your business"—she leveled her gaze at Jess, but there was mischief in her eyes, a look Jess recognized from John—"but I will be putting the income in an investment account. I've found one that's been doing very well lately, and the money will go toward Ella's education. Toward all our family."

Jess chose not to puzzle out the ambiguity in those last three words. She paused before she nodded.

Diane slapped her folder shut. "Good. This way, that permit can support all of us."

And it suddenly dawned on Jess that Diane was right. This, then, was what John truly would have wanted. For his business, his legacy, to help all the people he loved most in the world.

"Are you coming?" Diane asked from the doorway.

"Oh. Yeah." Jess pushed her chair back, stumbling over its spindly legs as she followed Diane.

"Sorry about that," Diane said. "I keep meaning to replace those fancy things with more practical chairs, but, well, they were a gift from my mother." Diane smiled wistfully.

Jess realized she knew next to nothing about Diane's parents. John had never said anything about them.

"You know your way from here, don't you?" Diane said.

"Sure," Jess said, though anything outside the dining room and the playroom was largely uncharted territory.

"Good. We'll see you soon, then." Diane put her hand on Jess's upper arm, more of a touch than a squeeze, and returned to the living room.

Alone, Jess finally let her posture droop. She took a wrong turn and found herself in the kitchen. Ella was sitting at the counter with the town librarian, their noses buried in a workbook spread between them.

"I have no clue what happened," Ella groaned. "I carried the two and everything."

"Sorry," Jess mumbled, though it wasn't like either had spotted her. She backed out of the room, but it was too late.

"Hi, Jess!" Ella said. "Rebecca's just helping me with this stupid math problem."

"Don't say 'stupid,' Ella," Rebecca said and smiled at Jess.

Rebecca. Jess tried to imprint the name on her memory, but she knew she'd forget it as soon as she walked out the door.

Ella sighed loudly. "Yeah, yeah. Hey, you want to come over for dinner next week? I'm collecting a bunch of stories about Dad for his party."

Jess glanced at Rebecca.

"His wake," Rebecca mouthed over Ella's head.

"Happy to," Jess said. "You sure you don't want to meet down at the docks? I don't want to impose on—"

"Mom already said it was okay. See you then!" Ella bent back over her book.

Jess had been dismissed.

Rebecca tried to concentrate on the numbers in front of her as Ella retraced her steps through the math problem, but there were a couple of things distracting her. For one thing, Annie was here. She'd reintroduced herself as Annie Bray the minute Rebecca walked in the Staybrooks' door, as though Rebecca could've possibly forgotten what she'd learned in the hospital room. Annie'd barely met her eye as they shook hands.

For two days after her visit to the hospital, Rebecca couldn't sleep. The scene from the maternity ward replayed itself over and over—the woman's face, her baby screaming while the doctor took its Apgar score, the plastic jug of water Rebecca clutched in her hands as a woefully inadequate comfort. This, then, was the one who'd managed to give up a baby, the most precious thing. It hadn't been as easy for Annie as Rebecca'd imagined in her darkest moments.

"Ugh, I give up," Ella said. "Can you help me?"

"How about you try from scratch?" Rebecca said. "Retrace your steps."

"I just did that twice. Hello, you were sitting right here? You do it."

"Let's see." Rebecca pulled the workbook closer and let her hair fall forward to cover her blush.

The other thing distracting her was this: yesterday afternoon, she'd gone to see the reproductive endocrinologist. His office manager had called her during lunch break. They'd had a cancellation, and would she be able to come in now? Rebecca had barely hung up the phone before telling Addie that she had to go home and would see her for the Saturday afternoon shift.

It began much like any other doctor's appointment. The nurse took her blood pressure and pulse and height and then started taking more and more from her, vials and vials of blood. With each one, the nurse explained what they'd be testing: thyroid, progesterone, something called an ovarian reserve that made her feel rather like a factory. The needle left a small bruise on her inner arm that they patched over with a square of gauze. "Good girl," the nurse said as she strapped it on with medical tape. From time to time, Rebecca pushed on the spot where the needle had been.

They did an ultrasound, too. Rebecca was readying herself for the gel to be spread across her abdomen when the technician came in and pulled out a wand. It was an internal ultrasound, she said with sympathy in her eyes. Rebecca gulped, and the technician positioned her feet in the stirrups and slipped the wand between her legs.

"There's one ovary," the technician said and pointed at one fuzzy spot on the screen with no discernible difference from the rest of the fuzzy picture.

Rebecca smiled in what she hoped was an encouraging fashion.

And then, finally, she was shown into the doctor's office. She sat in a pleather chair with her pocketbook on her lap. There was a small tray of sand with a rake on the far corner of the doctor's desk, and calm, tinkling music played on a speaker somewhere, like the kind of thing you'd hear in a spa. Rebecca stared at the Zen garden until the doctor bustled into the room.

"You're here alone today?" he said as he sat down behind the desk.

"My husband had to meet with his accountant. He'll be here for the next one," she promised.

"Hmm." He turned to his computer screen, already losing interest. "We'll need him to drop by and give a semen sample this week."

"That's it?" she said before she thought better of it. The plastic bin they'd filled with tubes of her blood, the pictures they took of her entire reproductive system, and all Mack had to do was masturbate?

The doctor barked out a laugh. "Don't worry," he said. "We'll start with that and then put him through the paces if necessary. You two have been actively trying for a year?"

"Two years and three months."

He pushed his chair away from the computer and folded his arms. "The clinical definition of infertility is twelve months of attempts without success. And as you've probably heard, a woman's fertility plummets after the age of thirty-five. So it's good you're here today," he said ominously.

Rebecca looked down at her knees. The doctor went on to say the ultrasound had shown no cysts on her ovaries. She knew from the frantic research she'd done on her phone in the waiting room that this was a good thing. Depending on the results of her blood tests and Mack's semen analysis, he explained, they would start her on pills to "kick start her ovulation." She would need to come in several times for blood draws and follicle scans over the course of her treatment, and their intercourse would need to be "carefully timed." From there, they might do IUI or maybe IVF. FETs or ICSI might come later. Rebecca could not even begin to think about how much all those acronyms would cost them.

That night, over dinner, Rebecca recited back as much of the conversation as she could remember to Mack.

He stopped shoveling meat loaf into his mouth and watched her intently. "Sorry I couldn't be there, babe," he said when she was done. He pushed aside the salt shaker and reached across the table for her hand. She gave it to him automatically. "It sounds like a lot," he said, "but maybe we'll get lucky and get a baby out of it."

The day before, she wanted nothing more than to hear him say those words. Now, though, she wasn't so sure. It was a lot: a lot of science, a lot of poking and prodding, a lot of bills. And no guarantees. This was not the way she'd imagined growing her family. There was nothing romantic about blood draws and speculums.

Then again, she thought as she leaned over Ella's math homework, perhaps nobody ended up with the family they imagined for themselves. Did Maureen Carson think she'd be a single mom? Did Annie Bray think she'd reunite with her daughter in a hospital room? Almost certainly, Ella and Diane didn't imagine they'd lose their third piece in the space of one stormy hour. Rebecca couldn't imagine it herself, though the possibility was always there. She'd tried to prepare herself for a call from a captain or the Coast Guard, but her mind would go no further than that.

Ella kicked at the legs of her stool and took a deep breath. Her cheeks were flushed and her ponytail askew. She looked defeated by more than just math.

Rebecca planted her palm below her belly button, around where she thought her uterus would be. "I see the problem," she said. "You forgot to include the fraction."

Eventually, Jess found her way back to the living room door. She was nearly certain she knew how to get to the entryway from there, but she paused to make sure she had her bearings.

And admittedly to peek in on the scene, now that Diane wasn't watching her. Maureen sat at one end of the couch, her back straight as a tall ship's mast. Diane was next to her, glancing periodically at the woman coiled in the other corner of the couch. She had dark, messy hair and wore a faded old T-shirt. Jess squinted at her until she could place her: she'd been a year or two ahead of Jess at DP High, though damned if she could remember the woman's name.

"Where is she now?" the woman asked.

"At home," Maureen said. She interlaced her fingers and held them so tight, Jess thought she could see her arms shake. "With Jude, one of my employees."

"And you trust this Jude?" the woman said. "He knows to call you if anything happens?"

Jess quietly sucked in her breath. She had balls, whatever her name was.

"Obviously, she trusts him," Diane said. Any warmth Jess had glimpsed in Diane during their conversation was long gone now. "She's only managed to hire two people in her career because no one else was good enough. And the second hire was her daughter."

The woman nodded and looked away.

Maureen smiled at the back of Diane's head and nudged her a little with her shoulder. "It's okay," Maureen said. "She's right to make sure. It was—is—her job."

Diane faced Maureen and nudged her back.

Her job? Jess was mistaken, then. This must be someone from the hospital or the clinic or something. Not the mother after all. But then Maureen met the woman's eye from across Diane, and there was something there that Jess couldn't quite name. Something sad and complicated.

"Do you think she'll make it?" Maureen said quietly. "I mean, in your professional opinion. Will the rehab work this time?"

All three of them watched the woman carefully, Jess from the doorway and Maureen and Diane from the couch. Maureen picked a chunk of polish off her thumbnail. They were painted the same color as Diane's.

"It's impossible to say," the woman finally admitted. "I've had kids who had everything going for them—nice family, plenty of money to keep them in rehab, good jobs waiting for them at their parents' company—and they just keep relapsing."

Maureen nodded, her chin buckling.

The woman ran her fingers through a knot in her hair at the nape of her neck. "On the other hand," she said slowly, "there have been some clients who look like they've got nothing, less than nothing. And in spite of that, they pull through. They live healthy, boring, sober lives. Hell, I do."

The room grew so quiet, they could hear Ella talking in the kitchen. She'd moved on from math to Spanish and seemed to be stumbling over every syllable.

"At the end of the day, she has to want it," the woman said. "And we can't make her want it." She looked directly at Maureen. "None of us can. But if she does decide she wants it, she's going to need help. From all of us."

"Maureen said you mentioned something about an anxiety disorder," Diane interjected. "Could that be the cause?"

The woman sighed. "Again, it's hard to say. It could be a factor, sure. And it definitely doesn't help. Self-medication is really common. Unless and until she gets honest about it, recovery is going to be tough for her." She chewed her lip and abruptly buried her face in her hands. "I just wish she would talk to me," she said, muffled. It was clear she wasn't talking about a patient.

"I know," Maureen said. Her cheeks were red, and Diane linked her arm through Maureen's. "But you're just going to have to wait." Her voice went rough. "She's upset, and rightfully so, and if there's one thing I know about my daughter—" She paused and let the word hang in the air, motionless and full. "It's that there's no getting through to her when she's like that," she finished.

"Okay." The woman nodded slowly and pressed her hands between her knees. "You're right."

Somehow, the tension in the room had burst like a soap bubble.

Diane untangled herself from Maureen and stood. "Anyone care for a snack?" she said. "I think someone gave me a block of cheese when they came by to pay their respects last week."

"Must've been Daryl," Maureen said. "Did he also leave a bag of tortilla chips to make his famous nachos?"

"He did!" Diane's eyes lit up. "I'll go preheat the oven." She walked out the other doorway, away from Jess.

When Diane was gone, Maureen turned to the woman, who was trying to look casual, like she belonged, as she scrolled through her phone. Jess was very familiar with the move, but the woman rubbed at her eyes intermittently, and it kind of gave her away.

"That's all it is," Maureen explained. "Tostitos and cheddar cheese. Nothing special, but you'd think from the way Daryl talks about them that they're God's gift to the Super Bowl party. Apparently, he now thinks it's an appropriate bereavement gift as well."

The woman smiled gratefully at her. Maureen looked away, and the two fell silent, staring at their respective feet. In that moment, there was no doubt in Jess's mind who they were. The woman reached up and fidgeted with her hair just like Lacey sometimes did, pulling her bangs back to reveal a widow's peak just like Lacey's. And Maureen let loose a small sigh as she crossed her arms over her stomach, just like Lacey had when Ella tracked Jess down at the docks.

Jess backed away from the door and tiptoed to the entryway. She slipped on her boots, praying the puddle beneath them wouldn't dry into a stain, and out she went. The guys at the Break would probably kill to hear about what she'd just seen. She would tell no one.

Chapter Thirty-Seven

Saturday, November 25, 2017

IT WAS TWO WEEKS before a spot opened up for Lacey in the clinic. During those weeks, she submitted to her mom's nervous hovering, opening her mouth for Maureen after swallowing her Suboxone. By the time Maureen pulled to a stop in the clinic's parking lot, it was a relief for both of them to see the squat, stolid building.

Maureen didn't turn the engine off. "Maybe I should've told you this before, but Ms. Bray—Annie quit. She's transferring to an adult facility."

Lacey stared at her. "You talked to her?"

Once upon a time, Maureen would've heard accusation and anger in her voice. Now, she recognized it as fear.

"She emailed me," Maureen lied. She couldn't tell Lacey about the meeting at Diane's house. She knew now how much Lacey still needed her protection. "She had my contact info from when you were...from when she worked here." Maureen brushed her hands over the steering wheel, giving Lacey a moment to collect herself. "She really wants to talk to you, you know," she said. "Get to know you."

"She already knows plenty about me," Lacey said, glaring out the windshield. "I don't know jack shit about her."

"I know. It was fucked up what she did, all of it. And I'm

not saying you have to forgive her, not ever, but if you want to, you could call her when you get out. In case you want to know about her."

Lacey deflated into the back of the seat. "I used to imagine what she looked like. Where she was, what she was doing."

Maureen nodded carefully, keeping her eyes forward, same as Lacey.

"It's just too much right now, you know? I'm kinda pissed at her still, and that's not…" She picked at a loose thread in the knee of her sweatpants.

"I know," Maureen said and squeezed Lacey's forearm. "If and when you're ready, Lace. I won't push you."

"Thanks," Lacey said. She leaned just a tiny bit into Maureen's hand. "It's so sad. He was my uncle, and I never…"

"Oh, honey." She pulled Lacey closer so their bodies tilted awkwardly over the center console. "You're grieving. Do you want me to talk to the counselor about it? Maybe it's not such a good idea for you to do this now. Maybe you should wait until after his wake."

"No, it's okay." Lacey sat upright. "I've gotta feel what I'm feeling. You have to let me."

"Okay," Maureen whispered after a pause.

"Do you think—" Lacey inhaled. "Do you think Ella looks like me?"

Maureen smiled and touched Lacey's cheek. "Spitting image. I can't believe I didn't see it before actually," she said. It wasn't quite the truth. Maureen had looked everywhere for faces like her daughter's after they moved to Devil's Purse. If Ella resembled Lacey, Maureen would've seen it. There was something in their eyes, though. They lit up in just the same way.

One corner of Lacey's mouth quirked up. "You and me and Ella and Mrs. Stay—Di. Built-in family, right? So crazy."

"Sure is. Guess I've got a niece now. And an...adoptive sister-in-law? This shit is complicated."

Lacey laughed like she used to. It spilled over Maureen's skin and felt like relief. But then Lacey's face grew somber again.

After a moment, Maureen gave Lacey's arm one last pat and released it. "You sure you don't want me to come in there with you, help fill out the paperwork?"

Lacey shook her head. "I've gotta do this one myself."

"Okay. If you're positive." She scanned Lacey's face, memorizing it. "I couldn't be prouder of you. I love you so much. You know that, right?"

Lacey paused for a moment and said, "I know. Love you, too."

She slid out of the car, and Maureen watched in the rearview mirror as she pulled her single suitcase out of the back of the van. They'd packed it together that morning. Maureen taught her how to tightly roll and stack her clothes to get the most space. Neither of them acknowledged that the neat rows would soon be torn apart anyway during the intake inspection.

And then Lacey walked away, getting smaller and smaller the closer she got to the clinic.

Chapter Thirty-Eight

Friday, December 22, 2017

T TOOK JESS OVER a month to get everything in order. The paperwork, the gear, the buyers. Ben O'Malley had referred one of his crew to her, claiming the kid was interested in getting into scalloping. The boy's surly silence on deck made Jess wonder how voluntary the change in employment had really been for him, but she'd take what she could get. It was possible to run a boat solo, but it sure wasn't easy.

"First trip as captain?" Will Feeney called from the docks.

Jess cursed under her breath. She would lose her place in her mental checklist, which she'd now gone through at least three times. She poked her head out of the wheelhouse and smiled quickly. "Yup."

"I'd wish you luck, but you don't need it," he said. "You know what you're doing." He pounded on the hull of the boat. The metallic ringing echoed across the pier. "She's a beaut."

"Thanks, Will," she said, her smile more genuine this time, though he didn't stick around to see it.

Jess asked her new crewman to take a couple of tasks off her list. In response, he grunted, but she watched him comply. He was quick and efficient. She couldn't ask for much else.

And then, finally, they were off, the dock receding behind them and the horizon widening in front of them. The kid stood at the back of the boat and lit a cigarette while she returned to the wheelhouse.

"Look at that, John," she whispered into the steady growl of the engine. "I can handle this after all." She glanced back to make sure her crew hadn't heard her, feeling foolish. But this was where John was for her, where he'd always be: in the salt air in her throat, in the hot smell of fuel, in the swooping, incredulous joy of a full haul.

When she'd showed up on the pier on that last evening, John had a kind of jangling energy about him that she'd never seen in him before. For a disloyal second, she wondered if he'd taken something. He looked like he hadn't slept in days, and his eyes jittered all over the place.

"You think maybe we should sit this one out?" Jess said, wiping the drizzle off her face. On cue, the flag hung outside the harbor master's office snapped in the wind.

"Nah. No can do," John said, scratching the back of his neck, head down. "Actually, I've got a favor to ask you."

"Sure," Jess said.

"I got in touch with this guy from out of state. Trying to hire someone to run his tuna boat." He pointed at an unfamiliar fishing vessel docked next to the *Diane & Ella*, all gleaming and white. "I told him I'd do it. He wants me to head out today."

"Are you insane?" Jess said. It was over one hundred miles to the nearest tuna fishing grounds, a ten-hour steam in the best weather. Some guys still did it—a single fish could get you $5,000—but you'd have to be either extremely cocky or extremely desperate to go out on a day like this. And John Staybrook was not cocky.

He laughed, then coughed. "I know, I know. My wife would kill me if she found out. Which is where you come in," he said. "No one's around now to see me leave, but if someone comes by and sees my boat at the dock, Di will find out I'm not where I'm supposed to be." He looked away. "Can you take out the boat and cover for me? Least till I'm out of shooting range?"

"You think there's a reason nobody else is here right now maybe?" Jess said. "Christ, John, this weather."

"Eh, you could handle it. You've seen worse."

"I'm not the one I'm worried about." Sure, she could putter around the bay for a few hours. But no one should be out in the open ocean today.

"The window for the tuna season closes real soon," John said. "Not much time to waste, owner's breathing down my neck. I spent all day today running around town for supplies." He looked at Jess, and at last, his eyes were clear, focused. "My family's in trouble," he said quietly. "We could use the money."

Jess gnawed on the edge of her tongue. They'd had a bad season, it was true. She could barely cover rent and food with what she'd been getting lately. John looked apologetic every time he cut her a check. Diane had a good job, though. Everyone assumed she carried her husband through years like this, though no one would ever say so out loud.

"Okay," Jess said, because she could think of nothing else to say.

Had she not been so worried about John, she might've marveled at how automatic it felt that night, running the boat by herself. She'd never gone out without him before, but she'd watched him so closely for so many years that it was instinct to her. She even managed to get a haul in, though it didn't yield much.

Every twenty minutes, she checked in with John over the VHF radio. He sounded bemused, back to his old self, his nerves from the dock dissipated. As the moon rose high in the sky and he got farther away, his voice became more static than anything else. She could still make out his words, though: "All good," or "Yep, still at it," or "You run my boat aground yet?"

And then. Just when she'd convinced herself he was right, that everything was fine. She'd composed an explanation to give to Diane when she got back, with an estimated date for John's return. Over the radio: "Fuck."

"John?" She fumbled for the receiver.

Silence for a moment, then, "Things sorta going to shit here."

Her knees buckled beneath her, whether from fear or the violent sway of the boat she couldn't tell. The receiver crackled. She bent closer, as if that would make it easier to hear. "John? Dammit, hello?"

"Got a fire."

She fell to the deck. Her hands shook.

"Look, J." He sounded so calm. How could he sound so calm? "My family. If I don't make it, tell them I—"

The pause was unbearable. Jess could not bear it.

"Tell them I tried."

Reading Group Guide

1. From the first page, you learn that the residents of Devil's Purse consider loss to be a way of life. How does this belief manifest itself in the story and the characters?

2. The novel seems first to be focused on the loss of John Staybrook but transitions quickly to its deeper interest—Lacey and the community that surrounds her. Why might the author have chosen to frame Lacey's story in the loss of John?

3. The community of Devil's Purse and John's disappearance is set against the seaside landscape: the rocky shores, thick mists, and rolling waves. How does this story reflect that of the town's?

4. What was the secret that surprised you the most in the book, and how did it change the way you viewed the townspeople of Devil's Purse?

5. Can you describe your feelings toward Matt? Would you be able to characterize him as a good or bad person, and why?

6. Maureen seems far more invested in finding her daughter's birth parents than Lacey herself. Why might this be the case for Maureen?

7. Annie and Lacey have a very complex bond. Do you understand Annie's choices, both while pregnant with Lacey and while counseling her? Do you think the secrets Annie kept justify Lacey's anger, and why? How do you think their relationship will continue?

8. What do you think is the significance of ending the book with John's death? If you could end it in a different place, where would you?

A Conversation
with the Author

You have personal experience with the fishing community. Where does that shine through in this novel?

I do! I've worked for and with fishermen since 2013. Over the years, I've learned that fishermen really are made of tougher stuff; the things they need to do on a day-to-day basis require bravery that most of us couldn't imagine. And their families are equally tough. Everyone who's married or related to a fisherman knows just how risky the job can be, and they have to live with that knowledge every single day. I'm hoping that grit and strength comes through in these characters.

Your previous book, *The Fifteen Wonders of Daniel Green*, is set in Vermont. *Lost at Sea* takes place in Massachusetts. What about the rural Northeast communities is compelling to you as a writer?

Well, they say "write what you know," right? I've grown up and worked in these communities my whole life, and it's such a huge part of my identity that it tends to bleed into my writing as well. I think it would be hard for me to do justice to the nuances in the fabric of communities in other parts of the country. So, I tend to stick with small-town New England.

All of the women in *Lost at Sea* are unique in their strength and perseverance. Is there any one character you see yourself in the most?

I see myself in Diane the most, even though it's probably not the most flattering thing to say! She's sort of prickly and knows that she is, but she's fiercely loyal to her family. She works hard, and the thing she craves the most is to be really and truly understood.

If you could meet one character from this book and share some advice, who would you choose, and what would you tell them?

Honestly, all of these women are wise in their own ways, and I'm not really sure I could "teach" them anything that they wouldn't eventually learn on their own. One lesson that they all struggle with at certain points along the way, though, is that family is really what you make of it and can be found in the most unexpected places.

If you had to choose a theme song for *Lost at Sea*, what would that song be? On the subject of music, what did you listen to as you wrote this book?

Is it too literal if I say "Not an Addict" by K's Choice? It's such a beautiful, heartbreaking song, and I think the message goes beyond the substance addictions that Annie and Lacey are dealing with. Almost every character is addicted to something—approval, independence, friendship, whatever—and a good deal of the book is about them learning to accept that about themselves and achieve balance, rather than endlessly seeking that thing out. Also (and here's where my music nerdery comes out), I really like the fact that much of the song is in a minor key, but it ends in a major key. It makes you feel like there's some hope in there for the future, even when things are feeling pretty bleak, and that's definitely something that I wanted to convey in the book.

As for what I listened to, I wish I had a cool answer for this, but the truth is I can't have music playing while I'm writing. I'm way too likely to get caught up in singing along and not get very much writing done! However, I'll admit I listened to a lot of '90s music in between writing sessions and was super excited to sneak a bit of that into Annie's chapters. Third Eye Blind, Goo Goo Dolls, No Doubt, Alanis Morissette, Foo Fighters, and especially Matchbox Twenty (my eternal favorite). What can I say? I'm a true "early millennial," and I've got some serious nostalgia for that music!

If you could live in one fictional world, which would you choose?

Harry Potter's, without question. I mean, right? I'm pretty sure almost anyone who grew up in the late '90s would say the same thing!

What is one thing that surprised you about becoming a published author?

Actually seeing my book on the shelves in bookstores has been amazing and surprising! I knew, logically, that they'd be sold *somewhere*, but seeing my name in those stores that I've loved my whole life has been pretty surreal.

SPOILER:

The novel closes with the radio call between Jess and John right before his death. Why did you choose to end the novel in such a sudden moment? What do you hope your readers will feel when they turn the final page?

Much of the book moves around these concentric circles of knowledge: who knows what about whom and how that all comes to light after John's disappearance. Jess knows the most about what happened to John, but not the why. I wanted to end with the simplicity and clarity of that moment, once all the messy, tangled family stuff had already been revealed. Also, I think it's pretty clear by that point that this isn't the sort of book where John is miraculously found alive, but I wanted to eliminate any doubt before the last page was turned! I hope readers come away with a sense of inevitability—as in, of course that's how it had to end—and a better understanding of who John was.

Acknowledgments

First of all, my heartfelt thanks to the fishermen and fishing families of the Cape. I learned so much from you in my time at the Alliance, and I hope my deep respect and admiration for you all comes through in these pages. And don't worry: none of the characters in the book is based on any of you!

Thank you always to my family for your support and tireless cheerleading. The next book will have a happy ending, I promise…

Thank you to Eric Smith, who gives the best pep talks of all and talked me down from many a ledge in the process of making this book. #TeamRocks forever.

To Grace Menary-Winefield, MJ Johnston, Kirsten Wenum, Kaitlyn Kennedy, Margaret Coffee, Michael Leali, and the entire Sourcebooks team: all of you turned me from a writer into an author. Words can never describe how grateful I am for that—and I really, really love words!

Thank you to the Dana Kaye team, who were instrumental in walking me through the process of getting this book out there and finding my readers.

Thank you to Mark Oshiro, Paul Parker, and Josh Boyce, all of whom helped me make sure I was getting it as close to "right" as possible.

Many thanks to my writing community, which has coached me through writer's blocks and steered me toward a better plot: Karisa Langlo, Allia Benner, and the Critical Mass crew at Writers' Loft.

And thank you, thank you, thank you to Chris. This life has taken us through some serious twists and surprising turns (and is about to get even more chaotic!). There is no one else I would rather build it with than you.

About the Author

Erica Boyce is a native New Englander, a graduate of Dartmouth College and Harvard Law School, and associate fiction editor at *Pangyrus*. By day, she works with fishermen and community organizers across the country to help keep small-boat fishing fleets in business. By night, she writes. She lives outside Boston with her husband and dog, a corgi named Finn. *Lost at Sea* is her second novel. She enjoys speaking to book clubs, and you can find her online at ericaboyce.com or @boycebabbles on Instagram, Facebook, and Goodreads.